A REALLY BAD HAIR DAY

Rob Preece

BooksForABuck.com

2008

A Really Bad Hair Day
Rob Preece

Published by **BooksForABuck.com**

ISBN: 978-1-60215-069-0

Chapter 1

My head was splitting in two, but I forced myself to take a sip of water before standing and approaching the witness.

He smirked at me, another overconfident soon-to-be ex-husband, thinking he was going to put his wife through the divorce wringer.

Inhale, Erin. Put on your game face. Intimidate this sucker. Let him know not all women cave.

I stepped up to the witness, got in his face.

"Mr. Hannah, isn't it true that you have repeatedly smoked marijuana in the presence of your child, Benjamin?"

He stared at me, his eyes bugging out, as if I'd transformed into something out of a cheap horror flick.

I'm Erin Tsong, twenty-eight, slender. In real life, I was okay to look at, but I'd trained myself to be scary in court. I was a divorce attorney so I liked that kind of reaction.

"You have snakes in your hair," Hannah blurted.

That took care of any misplaced sympathy on my part. I was proud of my cornrow braids and decorated them with little jewels. In the right light, they might look a little snakelike. But bug-eyes and facial perspiration was an over-reaction. It looked like Hannah's drug problems went a lot deeper than an occasional toke.

"Please answer the question, Mr. Hannah. Did you smoke marijuana in the presence of your son?"

"Jesus! Your honor, she's threatening me with those snakes. Get them away from me. What kind of a trial is this, anyway?"

"We're not talking about my braids, Mr. Hannah. We're talking about your drug abuse problem and how—"

"Snakes! Argh!"

Judge Harry Eagle banged his gavel. I expected him to throw the book at Hannah. Didn't happen.

"This court is in recess until tomorrow morning at ten. And Ms. Tsong, do something about your hair. I don't find your display particularly amusing or suitable for a court of law."

"Yes, your honor." I'd worn my hair in braids since college and Eagle had seen me that way twenty times at least, but in the courtroom, the judge is King, no question.

My client scooted out the door before I could talk to her—and everyone else cleared away in a hurry.

Okay, I was abandoned. Still, I figured Hannah had made my case and Franky Jamison, his low-rent lawyer was probably telling him that. Nobody was going to believe *anything* he said about drugs. Not after he'd wigged out on the witness stand.

I gathered up my papers, stuffed them in my laptop bag, then phoned the office.

I got Amelia DeRuby, the admin who keeps the entire office going. "Let me talk to the boss-man."

A few seconds later, Hale's gravelly voice came over my cell. "Get that divorce taken care of, Erin?"

"Sorry, Mr. Hale. The Judge continued the case until tomorrow. But here's the good news. I was probing Hannah about his drug use and he completely flipped out. He said he saw snakes in my hair. In response to a question about drug abuse. Is that too perfect?"

Hale laughed. "What a gift. Ole Jamison must have been shitting bricks. No wonder he asked for a continuance."

My silly grin faded. "That's the weird thing. Judge Eagle just announced it. Jamison didn't even ask."

"You must have missed it. Eagle is cleaning out his docket. He's getting ready for a fishing trip."

I didn't think so, but Hale was the boss. "Might be. Anyway, I'll be back on the case tomorrow and I'll finish nailing Hannah to the courtroom wall."

"You do that, Erin. I have to tell you that when we hired you, I wasn't so sure about your killer instincts. But you've got the right stuff."

In lawyer-speak, that constituted high praise, and I lapped it up. "Thanks, Boss. I'll see you in a few."

I headed out the mile or so to my car.

The security guard at the courthouse has a crush on me so I wasn't too surprised when he stared but couldn't get up the nerve to say hello. *Just another day*, I told myself. But maybe it was time to comb out the braids and chop off my hair into something that fit the lawyer image.

When I got to my Honda Civic I glanced at the mirror.

I'm not a vain type and don't spend hours staring at myself in the mirror, but movement caught my attention and held me riveted.

I froze for a moment, not wanting to believe what I saw. Not so easy. I'm a lawyer. I'm trained to lie only after I figured out what the truth was.

And no lie, something was moving in my hair. It definitely wasn't just my braids.

Hannah had been right. I did have snakes in my hair.

* * * *

I must have teleported out of my car. One second I was sitting in the driver's seat. The next, I was on the sidewalk, slapping at my hair and shaking my braids at the same time.

If someone saw me, they probably figured I was doing a crazy-dance routine. If it was another lawyer, they'd have figured I'd lost it—it's a dirty secret of our business that it happens. But I was past caring. I had snakes in my hair. Little black snakes that wiggled.

I had to get them out.

It took about twenty seconds before realized that I was slapping myself hard enough to leave bruises, but no snakes were falling to the ground.

Which meant I really had gone crazy. I'd been psyched by my client's soon-to-be ex-husband.

Not just him, of course. My Irish grandmother used to tell me I'd get worms in my hair if I didn't wash it every day. Which was impossible if you had long hair that you wore in braids. Probably Hannah had tripped some sort of guilt thing. I'd sassed back to my grandmother. But could she have been right?

"I'm just tired." I don't normally talk to myself. Santa Cruz already has plenty of people wandering around talking to themselves. But I'd cut myself some slack now. Besides, I wasn't really talking. I was more bargaining, working out my case like I would a lawsuit. "If I'd had snakes in my hair, they would have fallen out by now. So, my eyes must have been fooling me."

I'd heard poppy-seed bagels can make you fail a drug test. Given the casual and friendly doping atmosphere of Santa Cruz, it wouldn't be a total shock if I'd been given a little something extra in my lunchtime sandwich.

Yeah, that had to be it.

I took a slow deep breath before I collapsed from hyperventilation, then walked back toward my car.

"Hey, cool hair." The college-aged girl who addressed me had pointy ears. She was probably on the way to some sort of Science Fiction Con and thought I was going to the same place.

I gulped. "Thanks. Uh, what does it look like to you?"

"You've got the Medusa thing down perfect. The brilliant thing is, those snakes look completely real. Electronic, right? I didn't know better, I'd say they were alive."

She roller-bladed off.

Oh-shit, oh-shit, oh-shit. The poppy-seed bagel theory wasn't going to fly.

But hey, I reminded myself, I was talking to a girl in elf-ears. Not exactly a reliable witness.

I had to do what any lawyer would do, confront the evidence calmly and then decide how to deal with it.

I stepped back to my car, tilted back the Toyota's side view mirror and forced myself to look.

They were little guys, and their black color blended with the blue-black hair the Asian side of my ancestry had bequeathed me. But they were definitely snakes—and they were wiggling.

I screamed so hard my guts felt like they were coming up my throat.

My knees wobbled and I leaned against the side of my car to keep from sliding into the street.

I'd pulled over on one of the residential streets off of Ocean Street, about a mile from the courthouse. There were a few pedestrians around, but they quickly backed off when I started screaming. Nobody wants to get close to the crazy lady.

Like a dental patient playing with a sore tooth, I couldn't stop myself from looking again.

Still there.

One of the snakes spread its hood, or whatever those flaps on the side of snake faces are called, and hissed at me. Its open mouth showed sharp-looking fangs.

I wobbled again, smacking my forehead into the passenger-side window.

I jerked back. No telling what would have happened if I mashed the snakes. The one with the sharp fangs was probably just waiting for an excuse to bite me.

Okay, I reasoned. Maybe things like this happen all the time and people just don't talk about it. Sort of like when babies are born with an extra toe. The paramedics would know what to do. And I paid my taxes. I was entitled to emergency fire and rescue.

I pulled out my phone and dialed 9-1-1.

The number rang twice, then picked up. I started right away. "Hello. I have a problem."

Instead of a helpful police dispatcher, I was talking to an 'all of our operators are busy' message.

Not possible.

I dialed it again thinking my fingers were shaking so badly I might have pushed the wrong buttons. I got the same recording.

The good news was, my HMO answered when I called. The bad news was, they couldn't give me an appointment for three weeks. Three weeks wandering around with snakes in my hair, hoping none of them decided it was time to have Erin for lunch? I didn't think so.

Unfortunately, this was pretty much typical for my HMO. They manage costs by hoping things will go away, or patients will die before they show up for their appointments.

"There is special shampoo for head-lice," the HMO scheduler told me. "Perhaps you should try that."

I'd told her I had pests in my hair, not going into the specifics because the HMO reports back all medical problems to my boss—and who would want the partnership committee looking at a report of snakes? Even admitting generic pests was bad.

"I'll see what I can do," I promised.

"So you don't want the appointment in three weeks."

"I want it."

"You'll have to make the co-pay even if you cancel."

I wasn't earning the pay lawyers make in Manhattan or San Francisco, but I wasn't worried about the thirty-dollar co-pay. I *was* worried about snakes in my hair.

"Fine."

"I've got you scheduled then." She hung up on me.

I didn't think a head-lice shampoo would do the job, but the scheduler had been right about taking care of things myself. *Shaking* them out hadn't worked but there was a lot more that I could try.

First, I needed some equipment. I wasn't about to touch those things with my bare hands.

I phoned Amelia at the office, told her I was feeling a little under the weather so I wouldn't be coming back to the office that afternoon.

Life wasn't all bad. Sure, I had snakes in my hair, but at least I got to go shopping.

Chapter 2

Santa Cruz had gentrified from when I was a kid, but you could still find normal stuff there. On an ordinary day, I would have walked the mile or so to the Longs Drug Store; given the circumstances, driving was the socially conscious choice.

My nephew had left a towel in the back seat when I'd taken him to the beach a couple of weeks earlier. I wrapped it loosely around my head, stuffing my long braids up under the towel and trying not to think about what the snakes might do if they felt cramped. Snakes like the dark, right? They're always hiding under rocks and things. Maybe they'd just go to sleep and be easy to pull out.

Inside the drug store, I selected a hair pick, a couple of cans of cat food, and a pair of heavy-duty gardening gloves.

The high-school age checker gave me a suspicious look. "Some sort of big costume party going on?"

"Why?"

"Your head is wiggling under your towel. Like you've got some sort of mechanical device there. Very *Star Trek*. I've seen other sci-fi types today. You know, elves and vampires. Like, some completely radical makeup."

What a break for me. I couldn't go back to court without doing something about my problem, but in laid-back Santa Cruz, people were prepared to think you were a fan or an eccentric.

"One of the best Cons is in town," I lied. "You a fan?"

"A little. I love *Star Wars*."

Loving *Star Wars* is about as exceptional as loving chocolate. But I smiled like he'd said something wonderful.

"That'll be twenty dollars and eighty-seven cents."

I handed over a twenty and a one and headed out without collecting my change.

The little stream running through town is grandly called the San Lorenzo River. From the drug store, I walked to San Lorenzo Park, which I figured would be a good place for my snake-buddies to hang out once they came out of my hair. There were rocks and trees to hide in, and the stream had water if they got thirsty.

I'd pretty much persuaded myself the snakes weren't poisonous because I'd been carrying them around for at least half an hour and they hadn't bitten me yet, not even when I covered them with a slightly sandy towel. The fangs had to be my imagination, right?

So I didn't feel any guilt about leaving them near people.

Well, maybe a *little* bit guilty. I may have a killer instinct, but I like animals. So sue me. It didn't keep me from being a damn good lawyer.

Still, I felt bad for the snakes. It would probably hurt their feelings when I yanked them out of my hair.

Be tough, Erin, I told myself. *Not enough room on this head for all of us.*

I took off the towel and let my braids hang down.

"Here's the thing," I told my tenants. "I don't have anything against snakes, but everyone has to have their place. You'd be happier somewhere else. Someplace where you could roam around and seek your natural prey. This park should be perfect. You'll be able to hide under rocks and eat rats and things. To make the transition easy, and give you a healthy start, I'm putting some cat food out here. You'll have something to eat right away and won't have to worry about hunting on an empty stomach."

They didn't answer, but that wasn't a surprise. I mean, outside of the Bible, who's ever heard of talking snakes?

So I opened the cans, spilled the assortment of mixed grill, sea captain's choice, and beef and liver on some rocks. Then I got down on my hands and knees.

"There's your din-din," I told them, fighting my own gag reflex. Blech—cat food. "Yum-yum. Smell that powerful scent. Makes you want to just slither over and get some, doesn't it?"

I felt a little movement in my hair and took that as a helpful sign.

"I'll come back every few days and leave some more food," I promised. More bargains. "Especially in the winter when the rodents are hibernating."

"Whatcha doing?"

I looked up to see a kid, maybe five, staring at me.

"You like snakes?"

He shrugged. "I've got a doggy."

"Yeah? Well, I've got snakes. I came out here to feed them, but they don't come out if anyone is around. So back off."

"Nicholas. Get over here right now!" The woman, probably his mother, sounded frantic.

"Gotta go."

"Yeah. See you round, Nicholas."

He took a step backwards, then stopped. "They're wiggling, but they aren't coming out, you know. I think they're stuck to your head."

Oh, gag. "They aren't either stuck."

He looked doubtful. "I think they are."

Attached or not, none of the snakes had gone for the cat food. If I'd been in my office, I could have Googled *snake food* and found out if they only eat their prey live. I didn't mind bringing cat-food, but no way was I going to bring them live mice. The moral distinction between buying canned cat food and live mice may be flimsy, but hey, lawyers make their livings by creating flimsy moral distinctions.

I took a deep breath, sucking it up.

I'd hoped to lure the snakes out of my hair, but all along, I'd feared it wouldn't be that easy.

Nicholas evaded his mother and watched to see what came next. I was probably the next best thing to whatever cartoons his mom had dragged him away from.

"You'd better leave before your mom gets up the nerve to come close and grab you," I warned him.

"If one comes out, could I have him?"

"No. Besides, I think they're girls, not boys."

"Oh. Gross. I wouldn't want girls near me." To my relief, he turned around and ran back to his mother.

I slipped on the gloves.

"This might startle you," I told the snakes, "but I'm going to tug you out of my braids. Once you're out, I'll put you with the cat food."

"You are one sick woman." Nicholas's mom stood maybe twenty feet away, hollering at me like I was on the other side of town. "What are you doing bringing snakes to a public park?"

"You don't think there are already snakes here?"

"I'm going to report you to the police."

"Good idea. Dial 9-1-1, why don't you."

That sounded like a win-win. If she got the recording, she'd shut up. If she got an answer, I'd have the paramedics do the pulling.

She got the recording.

She didn't shut up.

Finally I got up and walked over to her. "Look, lady. I'm trying to accomplish something here. You want to help, take these gloves and pull snakes from my hair. Or you can have little Nicky do it."

"Nicholas."

"I don't mind if *she* calls me Nicky. I think she's cool." Nicholas had escaped his mom's again and wandered back toward me and the snakes.

"That does it, buster. When your father gets home, I'm letting him know everything."

"Aw, mom."

I held out the gloves. "Come on, mom. How about giving the snakes a tug."

"That is so sick." She grabbed little Nicky by the arm and ran out of the park.

I went back to where I'd left the cat food, got back down on my knees, and took a deep breath.

"Okay, buddies. Here goes. Out you come. As soon as you're untangled, I'll let you free. Right?"

They didn't talk, but I did hear a couple of soft hisses.

"That's agreement, right?"

I was procrastinating. I so didn't want to put my hands on the snakes, heavy gloves or not. Even if they weren't poisonous, they had teeth. Sharp teeth.

The snakes didn't answer.

I reached through my thick hair, feeling for things even thicker and more solid than braids, and found something that wiggled when my gloved fingers touched it.

Eeew. Snake.

I swallowed hard, then wrapped my hands around the snake. It felt warm and dry through the gloves. Not at all slimy or cold. Still, it was a snake and it was in my hair. It had to go.

The skinny girl hissed at me when I tightened my grip. But she didn't try anything nasty.

"Here goes, buddy."

I gave her a good hard yank.

Snakes stretch when you pull on them—who knew. But I knew snakes can't actually hold on. I mean, no arms, no legs, right? If I got a grip on one, out it would come. If I lost a little hair in the bargain, well, one advantage of my Eurasian genes was, I would grow more.

The snake should have come out like toothpaste squeezed from a tube.

It stretched, then just stopped coming.

For a second, as my headache multiplied into something that nearly knocked me on my butt. I thought I must have grabbed one of my braids along with the snake and was trying to pull it out by the roots. Until I checked.

No such luck. It was all snake. It wiggled, then swung down from my gloved hands and looked me right in the face, then stretched out its long forked tongue and licked me in the nose.

I fainted.

Chapter 3

I woke up, sprawled over the concrete. The sun hadn't moved, so not much time had passed. I looked around to make sure I hadn't gotten spotted and pushed myself up.

I'd brought my towel with me, which was lucky because my face had fallen directly into one of the mounds of cat food. I wiped stinky meat by-products off and stumbled down to the river.

A fallen coastal redwood created a still pond. I wiped the scum off the top, waited for the ripples to clear, then took a good look at myself.

I still had my snakes. It was hard to tell colors in the dark waters of the pond, but they looked like they blended in with my blue-brown braids.

I rested on my stomach and brought my face within a couple of inches of the water and saw what I'd been afraid of.

The snakes weren't *in* my hair. They were *part* of my hair. They were growing right out of my head.

I'd turned into a Gorgon.

At least I hadn't transformed anyone to stone.

I couldn't put the towel back on my head since it was rank with cat food. Instead, I found a piece of newspaper. As kids, my sister and I made pirate hats out of folded paper. After a couple of wrong twists, the knack came back and I created one of those hats. It was dorky beyond belief, but it covered my head would let the snakes breathe. Living snakes growing out of my head was serious. Suffocated dead snakes sounded worse.

I got a couple of strange looks from other drivers as I made my way home, but this was Santa Cruz. Nobody got too wigged out by the weird and unusual.

When I got home, I called my best friend, Becky Thorton.

"I'm busy working on a story."

"I'm in trouble. Real trouble."

A big sigh. "Give me half an hour. And you're buying the pizza."

Half an hour was perfect. I went into the bathroom, turned on all the lights, then flipped my makeup mirror to the magnifying side to check things out.

I counted: there were about twenty of the things, each about six inches long. They nestled there among the braids, black against the dark blue-brown of my hair.

The mirror fascinated a couple. They wiggled, hissed, spread their hoods and, I swear, even preened themselves when they realized they were looking at their own images.

"Don't even try to be cute," I warned them. "It won't work. You're out of here first chance I get."

I'd never heard that snakes could understand English, but they looked sad, like I'd hurt their feelings.

"I'll make sure you find good homes, though."

That didn't perk them up.

What did was the knock on the door. All of a sudden, all twenty snakes were leaning in one direction, wanting to find who'd made that interesting noise.

"It's my friend Becky," I explained. "I'm going to put a hat on so she doesn't get too scared. Don't let it worry you."

"I'm feeling sick," Becky said when she walked into my apartment, shoved a stack of papers off my couch, and plopped down.

Becky was always coming down with something. During the years I'd known her, she'd convinced herself she was suffering from smallpox, bubonic plague, Rocky Mountain spotted fever, botulism, anthrax, and athlete's foot. Her job at the newspaper means she always gets to research the disease of the day.

"Want a cup of tea?"

She sighed. "That might help. I don't know how you stay healthy all the time. You don't even take vitamins."

For Becky, not taking vitamins was right up there with farting in church.

"Just lucky, I guess."

"Some people are. Uh, you did say you were ordering pizza, didn't you?"

"You hungry already?" Stupid question. Becky was always hungry.

"Well, yeah."

I had to adjust my hat to use my phone and all of a sudden, Becky was on top of me, hitting me with a rolled up copy of a *Cosmo Magazine*.

"You have something alive on your head!" She repeated that about six times, screaming at the top of her lungs and smacking at my head the whole time.

It hurt.

It hurt more than I thought it would. It was just a magazine, after all. I'd have thought my skull could handle that.

I waited for her backswing, stepped in, and grabbed the magazine from her.

"Stop it, you're hurting me," I told the screaming woman.

"Snakes. You've got snakes in your hair." She was panting like she'd just finished an Iron Man Triathlon.

"I know that. But beating me to death isn't going to help."

"You're right." She ran into my kitchen, returning a few moments later with my garden shears.

She shoved them across the table I kept between us.

"What am I supposed to do with these?"

"Cut off the snakes. What else?"

"Me?"

She shuddered. "You don't expect me to do it, do you?"

"I can't cut them off."

"Erin, you can't be soft-hearted about snakes! I mean, they're not puppies or kittens."

My Pomeranian had died a few months earlier and I still wasn't over losing my dependable friend, so I could understand where Becky was coming from. But that didn't mean I could reach into my hair, grab a cute little animal, and snip them in half. I felt bad enough wanting to deny them the home they'd picked. And considering how bad it had hurt when I'd tried yanking them out, I wasn't sure chopping at them was a good idea, anyway.

Becky had knocked off my hat at the beginning of her attack. While she'd been hitting me, the snakes had wiggled around and done their hissing thing. Now that things had calmed down, they twined themselves around my head like a wreath.

"I'm not cutting them off. For one thing, I don't kill animals larger than cockroaches. For another, did you notice they're attached? If I cut one off, I might bleed to death."

"Better dead than snakes in your hair," she muttered.

I'd had the snakes for about three hours now. That I knew about, anyway. In that time they hadn't bitten anyone, made any little messes in my hair, or done anything that would have got them sent to the principal's office in school. Capital punishment sounded harsh.

"No killing. Of me or the snakes."

"But—"

"Let's come up with another plan. Come on, Becky. I'm just a lawyer. Everybody knows we don't have any imagination. You're a writer. It's your job coming up with good ideas."

"I'm a reporter, not a fiction writer. I have no idea what to do about snakes growing out of someone's head. And I'd better be hearing that pizza delivery soon because I'm getting grumpier by the minute."

When I'd tried to call for pizza, she'd attacked me. I reminded her of that. This time, the call was problem free.

"You think we're going to get that dweeb, Bobby, delivering again?" she asked. "How come they never have hotties delivering pizza like in the movies?"

"Because that's the movies," I reminded her. "Hotties get jobs modeling or acting. And Bobby is nice. He's just waiting for his growth spurt."

"He's been waiting a long time."

"Guys take longer." I knew this because I'd taken off when I'd been eleven, growing eight inches in one year.

"Too bad they can't take longer when it comes to sex."

I giggled. "Can you imagine what a guy would do if we were doing it and my snakes started crawling on him?"

I thought it was funny. Becky turned green and dashed toward the bathroom.

* * * *

My best friend still looked pale when she emerged from my bathroom about five minutes later.

She perked up when she heard footsteps outside my door, followed by a hammering so hard it shook ceiling fluff down.

"Coming," I stuck my hat back on my head.

"You're paying, right?" Becky asked.

"Are you sure you can eat?" I opened the door but was looking at my friend.

"Ohmigod, look at that," she said.

I turned. The pizza delivery guy was huge. I'm five foot nine. I'm used to looking guys in the eyes, or at least in the chin.

This guy had to be close to a foot taller than me. From side to side, he made five of me.

"I don't want any trouble," I said. I tried to remember where I'd left my Mace.

"I thought you ordered a pizza."

"Oh. Pizza delivery. I was expecting someone else. Twelve ninety-seven like always?"

"Right."

His voice was familiar, if I mentally toned it up from a deep bass to a high-pitched squeak.

He handed over the pizza and I noticed his toes and heels hung over his sandals, his shorts were so tight they were cutting off the circulation in his legs, and his t-shirt ripped at his biceps.

"You must be new around here." Becky's voice had gone vamp mode.

"Come on, Becky. It's Bobby."

"Bobby is a midget."

"I sort of had a growth spurt," he rumbled.

"Told you he would," I reminded her.

"A foot in a week? That's not a growth spurt, it's a disease."

"I have to buy new clothes," Bobby admitted. "And I'm hungry all the time. If you don't pay me for your pizza right away, I'm going to take it back to the truck and eat it myself."

Now that I thought about it, Becky had a point. When I'd been growing my fastest, it was more like an inch a month or so, never a foot in a week. Then again, I'd had mine spurt early. Maybe Bobby had been suppressing his. Okay, I was in denial. I didn't want to admit something was going around.

"Think about it this way," I said as I paid Bobby, including a couple of bucks for a tip. "You might have an NBA career ahead of you. Or professional football. Big as you are, you won't be stuck delivering pizza. Uh, not that there's anything wrong with pizza delivery."

His eyes lit up. "Man, I never thought of that. I was just thinking how I couldn't afford to eat enough to keep up all this weight I've gained. But, yeah. I almost made the varsity football team my senior year. With the added size, I should kick butt. Cool, Erin. You're all right."

"You're welcome, Bobby. Thanks for the pizza."

He hustled down the stairs to my apartment at twice the speed he usually managed. Of course, if you're that big, you only need to use every third stair or so.

I watched him go.

One day he'd been in a dead-end job, sharing a house with eight other guys. A week later, Bobby had a shot at the American dream.

I still had snakes in my hair, but I also had pizza. Not a bad deal.

Becky wouldn't sit with me. She ate in the living room, watching me. I think she was making sure I didn't slide any mice onto the pizza.

After we'd each eaten three slices, she found my wineglasses and poured both of us a healthy slug of Merlot.

"I'm not sure—"

"You're not pregnant. And even if you were, how would you even if snakes had birth defects? It's not like you can count their little toes. Maybe alcohol would make them more normal."

"Snakes *are* normal."

"Not when they're growing out of your head."

"Good point." I took the wineglass.

"If you won't cut them off, what are you going to do? You can't go to work and let your snakes bite people."

"They don't bite."

"Are you sure? Maybe they do tricks, too."

"If they were going to bite, they would have bitten me by now. I've had them for hours, tried to yank one out by the roots, and best friend whacked them with a magazine."

"Maybe they like you but don't like other people."

"Snakes don't have that kind of feeling."

"And you know this, how?"

Another good point.

"We'll shop for hats tomorrow," she said.

I never turn down shopping opportunities. "I'm calling in sick anyway," I admitted. "I need to figure out what to do."

She shrugged. "Cutting them off is the easiest thing."

The snakes tightened their coil around my head, almost as if they understood Becky's horrible suggestion.

"You aren't helping."

Chapter 4

It took me forever to fall asleep.

Lying on my back crushed the snakes—and made my headache worse. Lying on my side was even more painful. Lying face down was happy days for the snakes but threatened to suffocate *me*. The suckers had noses, but if they were sharing their air, I couldn't tell it.

It took hours before I figured out how to construct a sort of hammock for my face that let me breathe without crushing my symbiotes.

As a result, I was in a lousy mood when someone pounded on my door.

I rolled over and felt a jolt of pain from the snakes, reminding me of everything. Nope, not a nightmare. Not a bad hair day that would just go away.

This was my life, with snakes.

I padded toward the front door, putting a yellow plastic grocery bag over my head before I opened it. I didn't want to give heart attacks to any of my aging, but still drug-abusing, neighbors.

"I thought we were going shopping." Becky was dolled up and anxious. "And what is that on your head? Did you decide to suffocate the snakes?"

I snatched the bag off my head. "Ohmigod. I didn't even think about that. Do they look all right?"

"You are so gross. And yes, they're still writhing. Looks like they've even grown. You should cut them off before they take over completely."

I rubbed my eyes. "Not going to happen. I need coffee. What time is it?"

"Time to be up and shopping."

I looked into the kitchen, squinting my eyes to read the clock on the stove. "Hey, it isn't even seven."

She laughed. "If I'd waited until later, you'd go to the office. You're so compulsive."

Busted. "What about you? Don't *you* have work to do?"

She shrugged. "I'm working crime beat this week. We can swing by the police station and the sheriff while we're out. Take me two minutes to write up the latest 'man gets drunk and picks a fight story. No problem."

"Good with me." Becky made coffee while I left messages for Hale,

Amelia, and my paralegal, Kay Davis, letting them know I was sick and asking them to beg Judge Eagle for a break. Calling in sick wouldn't help me make partner. Compared to going to work wearing undisguised snakes, it was career-success genius.

I dug up some granola I'd bought at the Whole Foods store in Watsonville, and Becky and I ate it with soymilk. A couple of cups of coffee and I felt fully human again. Well, fully demi-human. The snake half of me felt, uh, fully snaked, I guess.

I dug up a floppy black felt hat that a nearly forgotten romance had left behind when he'd snuck out in the morning. It wasn't great, but it was better than a yellow plastic bag.

The hat didn't cover the snakes, but it kept them shaded. Someone would really have to be looking to see them, and even then, they might mistake them for my braids.

"Where first?" Becky reapplied her lipstick. "Want to head over the mountain to San Jose? I haven't been to one of the really big malls for months."

If Becky vanished into a mall, I wouldn't see her again for hours. "Let's stay around here."

She pouted. "Oh, all right. I'm so ready to blow out your credit cards. This is going to be a blast."

Becky took my credit card and bopped into one of the thrift shops on Mission. An hour later, I had three hats she swore would make me look sophisticated, cultured, and snake-free.

I wasn't so sure, especially of the one with cherries and fake bananas. "This will make me look like Carmen Miranda."

"Don't be negative. It's perfect for after-work and stuff. I wasn't thinking you'd wear the fruit-bowl into court."

One of the snakes *was* interested in the fruit. It extended from my head and ran its little forked tongue over the terra cotta texture of the miniature banana.

"I think I have a vegetarian snake." I don't know why I whispered, but I did.

"They're getting bigger." Becky's voice pitched higher and higher as she spoke until she ended up squeaking. If she'd talked much longer, she would have been talking to the neighborhood dogs, not the humans.

"They aren't going to hurt you. Now get in and shut up."

She did, and came up with an idea. "Let's go up to the University."

"What for?"

Santa Cruz is a university town, but the school is a few miles away on the top of a mountain. As a result, we townies often forget about it, except when we want students to spend their money on our services, or are looking for cheap, well-educated labor.

"Who knows all about snakes? Scientists, right? So, we go up there, find some snakologist, and ask him what's going on. Maybe other people have snakes in their hair too. And a snake scientist would know that. Maybe they can deal with snakes in hair. It's science, babe. They work miracles all the time."

She was right. So, why hadn't I thought of it? Maybe because Becky often used college professors as sources for her articles. I saw them more as divorce clients—or opponents.

The university is in the middle of a redwood forest and is divided into multiple campuses (it's sort of based on the Oxford model of colleges within a larger University—except instead of being named after religious things like Trinity College or Mary Magdalene in Oxford, they're named after famous capitalists like Merrill Lynch and Crown Zellerbach). We eventually tracked down Dr. Sabrina Boxter, Ph.D., Full Professor and, according to the department secretary, the state's number one snakologist.

"Office hours are posted." The professor didn't look up from her computer when we knocked on the glass-fronted door to her office.

I pushed open the door and went in anyway.

The professor was about forty, but she looked to be in great shape. I guessed she spent a lot of her life clambering around rocks looking for snakes, rather than sitting on her rear in front of a computer. She wore a pair of jeans and a khaki workshirt that would have fit right in on one of those TV animal shows. She looked about as welcoming as the snakes in terrariums around her office.

Boy did those snakes take notice when I walked in. All of a sudden, her office sounded like a leaky teapot. Hisses mixed with the clunk of little snake bodies against the glass walls of their prisons.

"I'm Erin Tsong, and I'm not a student." I wondered whether I should arrange a mass jailbreak for imprisoned snakes.

The professor blinked up at me, then reached for a pair of glasses. "If you aren't students, what are you doing here?"

"We've got a snake problem."

A big sigh. "It isn't April Fools Day. If it's a guy/snake, call the police. If talking about reptiles, call animal control. Either way, leave me alone."

I took off my hat. "I was hoping you could help with the girls. They're sort of attached to me, but..."

"Jesus. Are those things real?" She reached for a pair of gloves and lunged for me at the same time. "These are beautiful specimens. And that's a—a Libyan blacksnake. Those are nearly extinct! And you're treating them like hair ornaments!"

She kept looking for the *Surprise, you're on Candid Camera* cameraman until Becky closed her office door.

"They are snakes, but they also seem to be a part of her," Becky said. "They're growing out of her head. It's weird."

Boxter squinted behind her oversized glasses. "Weird isn't the word. There are no snakes capable of living in symbiosis with humans. And these are definitely vipers."

I got a really bad feeling. "Vipers. That's a ... special kind of snake?"

"Yes, poisonous." She sounded completely calm. Well, why not—she didn't have snakes in her hair.

I managed to collapse into one of Boxter's chairs. I never fainted, and now it seemed like I was doing it all the time.

"Shit," I said. "They aren't biting me so I figured they didn't bite."

Boxter brushed a gloved finger against one of my snakes' neck. "They appear remarkably healthy. And quite calm considering the circumstances."

"Don't you think this is weird? I mean, I've got snakes in my hair."

The Professor was treating this like it was some sort of science experiment rather than real snakes in a real woman's hair. Of course, maybe she knew I was a lawyer. I could imagine all sorts of lawyer jokes getting started about this.

"Of course it's weird. It's unprecedented. I'd say it's impossible but I'm a scientist. I don't deny reality."

"Not *completely* unprecedented," my friend said. "The Gorgons of Greek mythology had snakes for hair."

Boxter sighed. "You haven't been listening to Professor King, have you? He believes in all those myths. I think he has the hots for Aphrodite. Sort of like that Pygmalion guy."

"I'm just saying—"

"I don't believe in pre-literate myths and I've been hearing way too many of them over the past couple of days. It's like the entire scientific community has gone nuts."

I couldn't let that one pass. "Oh, no. The Mycenaean Greeks weren't pre-literate. They had a complex alphabet called Linear B. It just happens that this alphabet was lost during the dark years during which Mycenaean civilization—"

"And how many scientific accounts of Gorgons come up in your personal analysis of Linear B?"

"Uh, well, I haven't exactly—"

"Then don't bother me with it."

Boxter took a firm grip on one of the girls and tugged.

"Ouch," I said.

"They're not just attached to the outer scalp. They're solidly a part of you. Down to the bone."

"I can feel it when you squeeze them."

Boxter wrinkled her forehead. "That hardly seems possible. Close your eyes."

That sounded risky. On the other hand, the professor was the expert. It wouldn't have made much sense to go to her if I wasn't prepared to do what she said.

"Ouch. Hot." Something burned the back of my head.

"Humm." She paused. Then, "how about now?"

"Cold. Real cold."

"Enough. Open your eyes."

She tossed an ice cube into a coffee cup on her desk and sat down. "Right. They aren't snakes."

"But you said—"

"So I was wrong. Snakes eat, excrete, and reproduce. Your specimens don't do any of those things. What you have are snake analogues. They're a part of you."

"Does that mean they aren't poisonous after all?"

"I can check that." She grabbed one of the snakes, shoved its face against a little glass tube, then squeezed it until a few drops of a clear liquid trickled down into the tube.

The pressure of her gloved hand around the snake's throat wasn't exactly comfortable, but it didn't seem to be choking the snake, or me, either.

Once she'd gotten enough of the liquid, Boxter opened a cabinet on the wall, took out an eyedropper and added a different liquid to the tube.

The mixture turned a bright blue.

"It's poisonous. Don't go biting anybody."

"I'll make a note not to. So, what does it mean that I've got poisonous snake analogues in my hair?"

"It means I can't help you. Get out of here."

"But—"

"Look, snake-girl. The entire scientific community is going nuts lately. There's something going on that doesn't make any sense at all. I'm sorry that you have problems, but you're not a student, you're not a professor, and you're not a grant administrator. Which means you're not on my priority list. Now get out of here and let me get back to work."

She physically shoved us out of her office.

A male student walked by, checked out my body, raised his gaze to my face, then screamed and ran out of the building.

"That was a big success," I grumbled.

Becky looked at me. "Let's get something to eat. It's been hours since breakfast."

Chapter 5

"You've got wings on your back."

We'd found a vegan place down the hill from the university and settled into comfortable chairs on their outdoor patio—until a waitress flitted up to us. Literally flitted.

"It's weird, isn't it?" the waitress said. "I tried to call my doctor, but —"

"Let me guess. They told you there was a three-week wait."

"They told me six weeks."

Three weeks was a long time, but six weeks was impossible. Especially if you had weird growths.

"Can I ask you a personal question?"

She shrugged. "Fair warning, though. I'm straight. And no, I'm not interested in experimenting."

"Nothing like that. About your wings. Are they attached to your body, really part of you?"

"My boyfriend tried to pull them off and it hurt like the devil. And they seem linked into muscles I never noticed before."

She flitted away and I confronted Becky.

"There's something going on."

She got it at the same time as me. "No kidding. This is a mega-story."

"If you listen to Boxter, it's scientifically impossible, but it seems everywhere. I've got snakes in my hair. The waitress there, Lisa, has wings. Bobby grew a foot in a week and turned into a giant. I saw a girl on rollerblades with elf-ears. The checker at the drug store said there were other costume-types around."

"And Boxter said there was some kind of science crisis." Becky got her notebook out and was scribbling.

When my fruit plate and Becky's veggieburger arrived, we took a quick break from conversation.

I felt a tugging at my hat—one of the girls was straining.

Well, duh. She'd been interested in the Carmen Miranda hat. Of course she'd be interested in the guava. I cut off a piece and fed it to her, then gave a bite each to the other guys too.

"That is so gross."

"Want to hear something really gross? I can sort of taste the guava at the back of my throat. And I haven't eaten any myself. Just the girls."

Becky covered her ears. "Way too much information."

"Sort of like hearing our waitress talking about sex with bat-wings, huh?"

"Worse."

I waited until Becky's most serious hunger pangs had been sated and she seemed to be slowing down a bit."

"The thing that doesn't make sense is, how can we change? I mean, I've heard of birth defects where kids have a tail or something, but not once they're grown."

Becky scratched her head. "You remember that story I wrote a few months ago, about DNA research."

She was always doing science stories. I couldn't remember this one but it didn't matter because she was on a roll.

"You know that only like two percent of your DNA is actually chromosomes, right? The rest is two things, switches and junk. Junk DNA is interesting because a lot of times it's got copies of active chromosomes, but they're turned off and not accessible. Who knows, if you turn them on, with the right switches, maybe they create mythological creatures."

"We go three thousand years without any and all of a sudden we're overrun with monsters? I don't think so."

"I've got to make some calls, do some research, but tell me this. Have you been feeling okay lately?"

"I had a monster headache yesterday."

"Could be a virus, then. A virus is a little package of genetic information. Scientists think a lot of evolution is caused by viruses snipping around in the cell nucleus."

Becky snapped a few pictures of the waitress, and some of me, concentrating on our weirdnesses.

I made her promise not to identify me.

"Deal. It's not like I'd have to disguise you much. You're not the only Asian in the bay area."

"Half Asian. I'm an outcast from both worlds."

"What you are is paranoid." She snapped a couple more pictures, then waited for me to pay the check.

I left a big tip for the waitress.

"Know what I think?"

"What?"

"I'm going to win a Pulitzer with this article. Gotta go."

* * * *

I was in a lousy mood when somebody pounded on my door the next morning.

Two mornings in a row was a bit much. Especially since it was before six this time.

I grabbed my cell, mashed 9-1-1, and put my thumb on the send button before looking out the peephole.

Dressed in a tweed jacket with leather elbow patches and a pair of jeans, the man could only be a college professor.

"It's not even six in the morning," I shouted through the door. "You'd better be here to tell me my building is on fire."

"Ms. Erin Tsong?"

"Is my building on fire, or isn't it?"

"I need to talk to you. It's important."

Important to him didn't mean important to me. If he hadn't been halfway cute, I would have told him that. But what can I say? I'd always been just a little superficial. Besides, I was awake.

"Give me five minutes."

I padded back to my room, threw on jeans and a baggy sweater, then wrapped a towel around my hair.

Maybe I'd look like I just got out of the shower rather than like I was covering up my snakes.

The hunky guy was still outside my door. Not exactly waiting. His nose was buried in a book. *THE GREEK MYTHS, Volume II*, by Robert Graves. I'd missed that one in school.

Still, there's something about a man who reads.

Not enough to make me absolutely crazy, though. I put my cell in my pocket and picked up my mace. Just in case.

"I'm Erin Tsong." I let him into my apartment and pointed toward a low chair that has a nasty habit of grabbing whoever sits in it, making it tough for them to move quickly.

"I'm Callum King, assistant professor at U.C. Santa Cruz."

Why did his name ring a bell? "How lucky for you." I pointed the mace at him. "Getting to assist those real professors must be fun. You said it was important."

"An assistant professor doesn't... oh, never mind. I brought coffee."

Coffee isn't that big a deal, right? They make coffeemakers so smart you just have to give them water and they'll grind the coffee, brew up a pot, and have it nice and hot exactly when you need it in the morning. All it takes is a memory and the slightest bit of mechanical know-how.

Unfortunately, I never remembered to put in water the night before. And mechanical know-how without caffeine first was a challenge.

So, a free cup of coffee was tempting. And I did have my mace if Dr. College Professor tried something funny.

"Coffee buys you two minutes. Starting now."

He looked slightly flustered. I guess professors aren't used to having time limits. Which explained some of the really dreadful lectures I'd sat through in college and Law School.

"I'm at Merrill College. With Dr. Boxter? At a faculty meeting last night, she mentioned you. She thought I'd be interested."

"Are you a herpetologist?" I'd learned the right name for snakologists.

He got a confused expression. "I'm Assistant Professor of Literature and the Classics." He inhaled, struck a pose, and let loose with what I guessed was his standard justification. "You've got to understand that just because it was written by dead white men doesn't mean ancient literature is irrelevant to our current society. I mean, when you consider all of the—"

"I'm not arguing," I said. "But you're down to one minute."

"I'm an expert on the Gorgons."

Chapter 6

An expert on Gorgons? Hearing myself labeled a modern Medusa wasn't comfortable.

"When Dr. Boxter ran into me," he said, "she mentioned your name. There aren't that many Erin Tsongs in Santa Cruz."

Yeah, Tibetan-Irish mixes aren't exactly common. "You can help with my snakes?"

That was my goal, right. To get rid of the snakes in a way that wouldn't actually kill them. But I'd grown attached to them. I'd miss the little buggers but I couldn't keep them. Even my braids got questioning looks at a law firm where long hair was dangerously frivolous, and where being frivolous was close to a mortal sin.

"I don't know about helping you. But you can help *me*." He grinned at me, as if inviting me to celebrate.

Wonderful. I had snakes in my hair and I was supposed to help him. "I'll bite."

He pushed away, his face a picture of distress.

"I wasn't talking literally about biting. What kind of help do you need? And why should I care?"

"Professor Boxter said the snakes were really a part of you. They're not just glued on, not even parasitical. According to her, they're sharing nourishment and sensation with the human aspects of your body."

"Boring. Twenty seconds."

"Uh, for her, that indicates a closer level of symbiosis than is normally observed. For me, it represented everything I've been working for, ever since I was a little kid and heard the Greek Myths for the first time. Your manifestation of Gorgon attributes will revolutionize our understanding of Greek mythology."

"Five seconds. And this is a good thing because?"

He was on a roll, though, and nothing I said was going to stop him. "Everyone assumes the Medusa story is metaphorical. Freud weighed in with the whole castration thing and nobody's taken mythology seriously since. I mean, snakes near your face is about oral sex, right?"

He didn't even catch my glare before he went on. "Stupid, I know, but that's what people want to believe. If the Medusa syndrome is real, it transforms our whole world."

I didn't see how this helped me. "How lucky for you. Too bad you're out of time."

I admit he had sort of a sexy grin. He showed it to me.

"Work on the Gorgon hypothesis might mean tenure. Classics programs are always under threat. People don't understand how important great literature is to a full comprehension of the world."

"I imagine there are a lot of people out there who just think that the myths are fun stories that you read to your nieces and nephews when you're tired of dinosaur stories." Just about everyone, for example.

"That's it exactly," he said.

He started to surge forward in is chair, so I pointed the mace at him. "Sit still there and talk. You're over two minutes so you're into grace time."

"No problem." He took another sip of his coffee. "If Gorgons are real, what about the traditional deities? Gorgons were gods, after all. This offers a research track orthogonal to anything done in generations. Heck, it won't be one article, it'll be a career. I'll be able to attract graduate students. Tenure is just the start. Maybe I'll end up with an endowed professorship. It'll be wonderful."

Four years of college and another three in Law School meant I was used to listening to professor-speak. That didn't mean I liked it. But I didn't mind being called wonderful and I hadn't finished the coffee he'd brought.

"I'm happy for you and your career. But guess what? I've got a career too. I need to get to work or else I won't have one for very long."

He paused and stared at me. "A head full of poisonous snakes would be a disadvantage for most jobs. What do you do?"

"I'm a lawyer."

He considered. "I take it back then. Should be an asset."

He almost got a faceful of mace for that. But I caught just the tiniest hint of his grin. He'd made a joke. I'd always been a sucker for a man with a sense of humor. Maybe because I was humor challenged myself.

"I'll wear a hat."

"Oh. Right." He looked dubious, but what did he know? He was a college professor—talk about your basic disconnect from the real world.

He jabbed a finger in the direction of my head. "Uh, would it be all right if I looked at them now?"

I glanced at my watch. I had time and didn't really have an excuse not to.

I took the towel off my head.

He simultaneously surged forward and withdrew, so that his body made a wave motion.

"Wow. They're the exact shade of your hair. With your striking facial characteristics, you will stand out in a crowd."

Striking facial characteristics? That sounded good.

"Thanks. I guess."

"I mean it. You do know how Medusa became a Gorgon, don't you?"

"If you say it's because she liked playing with men's penises, I'm going to mace you."

He sighed. "No, no. That's the Freudian crap I've fought against my whole career. Completely misses the point. According to Greek myth, Medusa was a woman so beautiful the Goddess Athena feared the competition."

"So she made her ugly by giving her snakes."

He shrugged. "That's the Greek myth. Of course, in mythology, actions often backfire. Snakes don't make you ugly."

King stood and headed for the door while I tried to figure out what he was saying. Had he really said I was attractive because I had snakes in my hair?

"That's it? You're going to get famous because you took one look at me, Professor King."

"It's Callum." His smile was just a bit shy. "You can call me Cal."

That was a mark in his favor. Most professors I knew gloried in having their titles rattled back to them. "You can call me Erin, then."

"Thanks. And no, I have a lot more questions to ask you. But you said I only had two minutes. And you keep pointing that mace at me like you mean it."

I'd given him eight minutes, not two. And he was running away just when he'd gotten started saying nice things about me.

"I can give you a couple more minutes. I thought at first that you might be a flake."

"I've been called worse." He looked around, found a stool for the low Japanese tea table I used as my dining room set, and straddled it. "Can I ask you a couple of questions, then?"

"Why not?"

Cal took a ballpoint and a tiny pad from his jacket pocket. "Right. Have you ever had anything to do with snakes before? Have you dreamed about snakes? Why do you think you, of all people, became a Gorgon?"

Good thing I was a lawyer. I'd learned how to keep track of questions. "No, no, and who knows?"

He sipped from his own cup of coffee while he considered my answer. "No dreams at all."

"I dream about being Perry Mason."

"Really? That's odd. I've always dreamed about flying."

"I think that's supposed to mean—"

"Have I mentioned how much I dislike naive Freudian analysis?"

"Got it." And what had I been thinking. Was I actually flirting with this guy? It had been a while since I'd dated, but surely I wasn't so desperate I'd take advantage of a guy who was only talking to me because he thought I could make his career.

"Let me try something. He gargled something. "Did that mean anything to you?"

"I think it means, 'Sing, goddess, the wrath of Achilles, Peleus' son, the ruinous wrath that brought on the Achaeans woes innumerable, and hurled—'"

His eyes got big. "That's amazing. You translated it almost perfectly, although some might question the over-ornate English." He was a good looking enough guy, given the Professor costume, and his excitement gave a glow to his cheeks. "That was archaic Greek. The opening to *The Iliad* by Homer. That you understand it can only mean—"

"It means I went to college. I had a professor who used to shout out the opening lines of the Iliad. Would you like to hear the start to Beowulf? I can do that too. Being a lawyer doesn't mean I'm an idiot. I don't blame you for the confusion, though. Some lawyers I know aren't the brightest bulbs."

"Oh." He settled back down in the chair. "You didn't learn Archaic Greek from the onset of the Gorgon effect?"

"No."

He gargled something else, but I just shook my head.

"Guess I missed that class. So this spoils your whole premise, right?"

"Well—"

I looked at my watch and was surprised to see I really was running late. It hadn't seemed like I'd spent that much time with Cal. From past experience, I knew this was a bad sign. Men are distractions. And I had enough distractions. I had to make partner. I had student loans coming out my ears and was sick of being broke. A few years at partnership salary and maybe I'd make time to think about men.

"Look, it's getting late and I've got to run. Since we've pretty well disproved the theory that I'm the original Medusa come back to life, maybe you can get on with your day and let me get ready for mine."

"That was the closest I can come to ancient Libyan, but it wasn't very good. Nobody exactly knows how they talked."

"Libyan? I'm supposed to speak some Arab language?"

"Not Arabic. Arabs conquered North Africa in the seventh and eighth centuries. The historical Medusa would have been Neolithic or early Bronze Age. According to the legend, Medusa lived in Libya, in North Africa. Your family isn't from North Africa, is it? You have an exotic look that could be from anywhere."

"With a name like Erin Tsong? I don't think so."

He made a dramatic forehead-slapping gesture. "Sometimes I get so excited about my ideas, I forget about common sense. But you said you were Irish-Tibetan, didn't you? Celts have an interesting background, with a definite Libyan slant. And there is at least one legend about the mountains and the distant east." He rushed on as if afraid he wouldn't be able to get the words out unless he managed it in one breath. "How about I take you to dinner tonight. Who cares whether you speak Greek or not? What matters is that you're a real Gorgon. You prove that myths have a foundation beyond the metaphorical crap. I can see publications out the wazoo."

Did I want to listen to this guy go on about the seventh and eighth centuries B.C. and A.D.? I wasn't sure. Ancient history wasn't really my strong point. On the other hand, Cal was cute, smart, paid for coffee, and said I was pretty. My mother, my sister, and Becky would never forgive me if I turned down a date just because Cal went on about his favorite subjects. If I could put up with legal-speak I could put up with anything.

"Call me later and we'll talk about it." He did look like he had a pretty good body beneath his professorial tweed.

I handed him my card, shoved him out the door, and got ready for a day at the office.

It would have been better if I'd called in sick again.

Chapter 7

"Nice hat, Erin."

Julian Hale, Managing Partner in the firm of Hale, Storm, and Stunk (really), met me as I slipped in the back entrance to the firm's three-story office building.

"Thanks, Mr. Hale. You know how it is. Some days you can't do anything with your hair."

I thought I was being funny, but then, I'm humor challenged. Hale didn't think I was funny at all.

"I hope you're feeling better after being sick yesterday. Judge Eagle wasn't happy about delaying the Hannah v. Hanna divorce case. I told you he was trying to clear his docket."

"I feel much better, thanks. Guess it was one of those twenty-four hour bugs."

He peered at me. If I'd been short, or Hale tall, this wouldn't be a problem, but I was an inch or so taller than he. He didn't look down at my hat, he looked up from under it.

Be still. I didn't know if my snakes were telepathic, but it couldn't hurt to hope.

"I understand you ran into a little trouble during your cross-examination in the Hannah v. Hannah case."

"Trouble? I covered this on the phone, sir. I was crossing Mr. Hannah on his drug use, per your instructions on the case, when he flipped out. He made my case. I'll nail him today."

Hale shook his head slowly. "I don't think so, Erin. Mrs. Hannah asked to be assigned a different attorney. Apparently she was disturbed by the direction your questions took. I gave Joe Slocum the case."

"I see." This was *not* the type of client reaction that lifts an associate to the hallowed realm of partner status. "I thought that Mrs. Hannah and I had established a rapport."

"*And* Judge Eagle requested that we bar you from his court."

My stomach lurched. Eagle presided over more than two thirds of the contested divorces in Santa Cruz County.

"Did Judge Eagle give you any justification?" Not that he had to. Judges could do what they wanted.

"He said you showed his court disrespect. According to what he told me, it was only as a favor to *me* that he didn't hold you in contempt. I don't want to use up any favors the judge might owe me on things like that."

Oh, shit.

"I don't understand how that could have happened, sir. I have nothing but respect for Judge Eagle. I believe that my cross-examination style, while confrontational, was fully in accord with Judge Eagle's instructions. And with your own tactical advice, sir." I was trying to establish shared interests here. I was also laying the 'sirs' on thick since Hale loved it when women sucked up to him.

"There was some discussion of snakes."

"Snakes, sir?" I'm afraid I squeaked a little.

"Snakes in your hair."

"Why would I have snakes in my hair?"

I was hoping for a laugh, a slap on the back, and agreement that those other people must have been having a bad day. Instead Hale knotted his forehead tighter than anything I'd tied since I'd been a Brownie. "That's the question. Why do you have snakes in your hair, Ms. Tsong?"

"Pardon?"

Playing for time was a mistake. "You were in the top ten percent of your law school class at Stanford, Tsong. And I spoke plain English. Don't play stupid with me."

"Right sir. The answer is, I don't know why I have snakes in my hair. I went to the UCSC yesterday to talk to a snake professor there. She didn't know."

"Did she tell you how to get rid of them?"

"No, sir. Nobody seems to know how to do that."

Hale rubbed his eyes. "What a goddamned mess."

"I could wear a hat. With the snakes covered, no one would know."

He shook his head. "Won't work."

Oh, shit. "I bought a variety of hats, sir. I'm sure one of them will do the job."

"We can't have snake-haired lawyers representing clients. Every time you lost a case, the firm would get sued. Wouldn't matter if it was your fault or not. Any jury in the country would award damages."

This was worse than I'd thought. "That's ridiculous, sir."

He puffed up. "Don't tell me what's ridiculous. Lawyers don't have a lot of built-up good will. That's why we have lawyer jokes." He took a deep breath. "I've got to take your cases from you, Erin. I'll keep you on the payroll, but doing research for the other lawyers. I can't afford to have you in front of the judges."

"But—"

"Look, Tsong, my mind is made up."

Without cases, I was a glorified paralegal. Without cases, I was more likely to win the state lottery than make partner. Still, I *did* have snakes in my hair, which put me in an awkward bargaining position. I also owed more than a hundred thousand dollars in student loans. I decided to grovel.

"There's something going around," I pleaded. "I've seen elf-ears and wings and a troll. My Gorgon-hair is part of this pattern." That was when I had a brainstorm. "Whatever's happened must be covered by the Americans with Disabilities Act. Reasonable accommodation would be asking me to wear a hat. Restricting me from litigation would be unlawfully harsh. Surely you want to protect our firm from ADA complaints."

My brainstorm was a really bad idea. I'd forgotten to grovel and gotten on my lawyerly high horse. Hale didn't react well to threats.

He grabbed the lapel of my blazer and twisted. "Listen, missy. I hired you because you convinced me that you had the balls to play with the big boys. But maybe I was wrong. If you're going to get girly and whine about the ADA, then—"

I'll never know what Hale's 'then' would have been.

I got madder and madder as he twisted my jacket's fabric. That suit was still on my Visa card—and it wouldn't ever be the same after he'd twisted the life out of it. The snakes picked up on the mad. I knew how to bottle up *my* anger. The snakes, not so much.

My hat went flying when one of the girls pushed her way free and threw herself at my tormentor.

Hale reeled away, his face turning a pale putty shade highlighted by dark purple cheeks. Not a good look.

A good lawyer learns to tolerate cognitive dissonance. Which means, she can believe two things at once. Apparently Hale had managed that. He both believed in my snakes and he didn't.

The snake's lunge for his throat made a complete believer out of him. "You—"

I retrieved my hat and shoved the snakes back under it. I was so mad, I didn't even worry that Dr. Boxter had told me the girls were poisonous.

"Mr. Hale, you assaulted me. That was completely inappropriate."

"*I assaulted you?*" He shook his head in dismissal. "No, I don't think so. I don't think you'd find a jury in the state who'd believe you. I tried to help you, let you keep your job. I believed your snakes would be safe in a restricted work environment. But I'm big enough to admit when I'm wrong. And boy was I wrong.

"But…"

He held out a hand in the 'stop' gesture. "I'll accept your resignation, delivered to my desk in the next hour. If I don't see it by then, I'll fire your butt and blackball you with every firm in Northern California."

Crying would just prove I didn't belong in the rough and tough world of law, so I gritted my teeth and swallowed.

"I'll clean out my desk and leave a resignation letter with your admin," I promised.

My hat wobbled a little. The girls were still mad.

"Uh, no hard feelings. Right, Tsong?"

I didn't even pretend to answer that. Of course I had hard feelings. I needed this job. And finding another one with a bad reference and with snakes in my hair didn't figure to be easy.

Chapter 8

Kay Davis and Amelia DeRuby were the only people with the guts to stop by while I threw my stuff into boxes and typed up a resignation letter. And *they* sort of snuck in.

Kay was a paralegal in her early thirties. Amelia was a legal secretary in her late thirties. No matter what Hale might think about his own ability, it was Amelia who kept the office running. The three of us had bonded from the day I'd joined the firm a year earlier, the two slightly older women took me under their wings and let me know which of the males could be trusted and which was engaged in sabotage. The funny thing was, Hale had been one of the trustables. Not so much when it came to reasonable accommodation with snakes.

They helped me pack, but they didn't get close to my bad hair day.

"When I heard about you and the snakes, I thought it might be part of the disease going around," Kay said.

"Is there a disease?" Maybe it was too late for Becky's story.

"One of my daughter's friends grew a tail. She can hardly walk, but boy can she swim."

I'd tried the ADA angle on Hale, but seemed that the news was ignoring it. With what was going on, why wasn't Santa Cruz headline central?

"Has this been on television?"

"That's funny, isn't it? It's like, business as usual. But some of the reporters and anchors just aren't there any more. Out in the blogosphere, people are talking. I've heard a lot of theories."

Kay spent her days on the computer, digging up financial information for our cases—mostly spouses hiding money in community-property California. Sometimes she wandered into the world of conspiracy theory.

"You hear of any other snake-haired women? Maybe we could unionize and hire out as rat-catchers."

Kay wrinkled her forehead, then abruptly straightened it out. She violated California convention by caking make-up on like a televangelist's wife and didn't want to leave cracks. "Not Gorgons. But you wouldn't believe what I have heard of."

I picked the least likely possibility. "Vampires?"

She was on a roll and wasn't going to let my guesses disrupt her. "Vampires, sure. Also trolls, fairies, shape-shifters, werewolves, even leprechauns."

I needed to see if Becky had learned anything else. I couldn't believe Kay's laundry list of monsters.

I pulled my Law School Diploma and my State Bar certificate off the wall and tossed them into a box. "Leprechauns, huh? I wonder if Hale would have let me stay on if I'd turned into one of the little people instead of a Gorgon."

"Or if you didn't send your snakes to attack him," Amelia reminded me. "Most leprechauns aren't equipped with deadly weapons."

Kay giggled. "On the flipside, Hale has the hots for you, Erin. He might grab you and demanded the pot of gold."

"That is so gross," Amelia said.

"Would one of you mind returning these to the library?" I shoved a stack of books to the side of what had been my desk. I'm out of here."

"We're still going to do our Wednesday night out, right?" Kay demanded. "We girls have got to stick together." She looked at me. "But not *too close* to the attack-snakes."

I felt that lump in the throat thing and I swallowed to get rid of it. Despite the snakes, despite getting fired, despite everything, these women were my friends.

"I won't be able to do anything expensive until I get another job," I said. Thanks to bankruptcy so-called reform, the banks were going after slow-payers without mercy.

"We can do cheap," Amelia promised. She liked trying out the fancy new restaurants and clubs that opened in the Santa Cruz or San Jose areas, so this was a big sacrifice for her. I let her know I appreciated it.

"Hey. All for one and one for all," Amelia reminded me. "Besides, some day you're going to be super-successful and then you can hire us for gobs of money."

"Tell you what? Either of you two gets married, I'll do your divorce for free."

"You're all heart, Erin." Kay giggled, though.

With their help, the packing went quickly. I didn't have a lot to show for the job I'd given three years of my life to.

* * * *

At ten in the morning, I should have been in court. Instead, I had a car full of cardboard cartons and nothing to do.

Shopping counted as self-destructive behavior, but I didn't want to go home to my empty apartment. I compromised by heading for Pacific Street, Santa Cruz's Disneyesque version of an old downtown main street.

The street normally bustled with kids who should have been up the hill attending classes, aging souls who looked like they'd gotten lost during the *summer of love* and hadn't been found since, and moms driving Volvos.

Shops sold surfing gear, the latest CDs, fine art, and fancy sandwiches. A mix of talented and completely talentless musicians set up their instruments on shady patches on the sidewalk and, depending on their skill level, entertained or horrified the crowd.

A 'closed' sign in front of the New Age shop that dominated a block of the street surprised me. With all the weird things going on, they should be doing big business.

The street's energy seemed off.

Unlike Los Angeles or San Jose, where everyone is in a hurry, everyone thinks they're important, and almost everyone seems to believe that a smile might break their faces off, people in Santa Cruse usually smile when they pass each other.

Thousands of adolescent students exploring their sexual energy combine with the hundreds of surfers and beach-bunnies from the nearby beaches to give the city on the bay a sizzle. People on the street are always aware, checking out the competition, assessing the possibilities.

Today, a current of fear overlaid the usually friendly sexual beat.

My phone rang and several people gave me dirty looks as I dug into my purse and yanked it out.

As if talking on the phone while walking wasn't Santa Cruz's favorite sport.

"What's up, Becky?"

"Got more on my story. I got a strange answer when I called your office. What's going on?"

"I got fired. Justin Hale doesn't like the girls."

"Doesn't like girls? I heard he's straight as a board. He was trying to pick up on me at the firm's Christmas party, and I was there as *your* date."

"I'm not talking about women. You know, *my* girls? The no-legged ones."

"Oh. I guess the hats we bought didn't do the trick?"

"Not so you'd notice. Tell me about your story."

"I'm down at the jail."

"You need me to bail you out?" My mother had been an accountant, which meant she'd made sure I had a rainy-day fund stashed away. Things were going to be tight with no income. Still, I couldn't leave my best friend rotting in jail.

Becky sighed. "I'm not *in* jail, I'm *at* the jail. Working."

"Oh. And?"

"This vampire dude got arrested. They say he attacked a UCSC student and tried to suck her blood."

"Where did it happen?"

My question must have caught her by surprise because I almost heard the sound of her brain reshuffling answers.

"Near the museum."

"The one just off Pacific?"

"Right."

That explained why people were looking at each other with as much fear as sexual appetite. Santa Cruz is a good-sized town, but its rumor grapevine would make the smallest village proud.

"You think I should know this because—?" Surely Becky didn't think I'd drop everything and ride to the rescue of some creep who thought that long teeth gave him the right to attack women. I'd be more likely to join the crowd putting a stake through his heart.

"Guys are phoning in wanting to volunteer to suppress what they're calling 'the beasts,' asking for arms and ammunition. They want to slaughter the 'beasts' before they go wild."

It sounded like something out of a cheap Hollywood western.

"*Before* they hurt anyone or commit any crime at all?" I didn't have to graduate in the top ten percent of my law school class to know *that* was wrong.

"Thought that would get you. By the way, it's not just vampires. They want to go after everyone who's been changed. The sheriff is meeting with the D.A.'s office trying to come up with something based on the terrorism laws about holding people who've been transformed indefinitely as material witnesses."

My knees buckled. "You mean?"

"I mean, people are going crazy. Until things calm down, you'll want to keep your hat on and lay low. You might even talk to Hale about reassigning some of your cases, stick with research for a few weeks."

"Didn't you hear what I said? I got fired."

"You said that but you can't mean it. You're their future star."

"Hale fired me. One of my snakes got a little ... over-excited."

"Oh. Ah, is he all right?"

I almost hung up on her. I'd told her I was out on the street, unemployed and broke, and she worried about the jerk who'd fired me.

I pretended to misunderstand her question. "Fortunately, she didn't actually reach Hale so he couldn't actually hurt my poor little snake."

"That is so gross."

"If you say so." I was getting used to the idea of having snakes—and more than a little defensive about them. I didn't like it when people insulted them.

"I have a question for you," I said. "You know we saw some strange things when we were out yesterday. And today, we've got this vampire attack thing. So, how come the networks haven't picked up on this? I'd think every reporter in the country would head for Santa Cruz. If this isn't big news, what would be?"

The silence on the line was deafening.

"Becky."

"You can't tell anyone I told you."

"Tell anyone what?"

"I'm not supposed to know this. Nobody is supposed to know. But I was getting coffee this morning at just the wrong time. The Department of Homeland Security is telling every newspaper, television station, and radio station in the country to chill on reporting this stuff until they figure out what to do. They've threatened to arrest anyone who prints anything that isn't vetted by the government first."

"Prior censorship is clearly a violation of—"

Becky got mad. "I'm telling you what's going on. If you want to live in your lawyer-world, that isn't my problem."

"This isn't just around here, is it?"

"Why would it just be Santa Cruz, Erin? It's everywhere in the country. Maybe around the globe. I got to some people before they stopped talking, though. Turns out that just the right virus could unlock some old fragments of DNA—and change some of the switches that decide whether we're normal or not. And, get this, they could change grownups, not just embryos. I'm onto something. But be careful if you want to stay alive long enough to read it."

I crammed my hat down hard. The girls caught my nervousness and wiggled.

This was so not the time to be calling attention to myself.

The wiggle wasn't much, but all of a sudden, I was hyper-aware of the people around me.

These weren't ordinary laid-back California types. You don't make it to Santa Cruz unless you're *fully laid-back*.

But nobody smiled, nobody flirted, nobody snuck sexy hidden looks at each other. Suspicion hung as heavy in the air as the morning fogs that often blanket the city.

That *this* group could be nervous and worried said two things. First, the vampire attack had hit some emotional core. And second, the rest of the country was probably worse. Which meant things were really screwed.

* * * *

Most Santa Cruz restaurants boast vegetarian menus. Not so the Courthouse Café across the street from the jail.

The Courthouse Café appealed to cops, lawyers, and cop-wanna-be's. It served food heavy in meats and fats. Green was not a food group here, it was a St. Patrick's Day beer color.

I ordered a grilled cheese sandwich while Becky got a corned beef monstrosity.

"I'm sorry about your job," she said when I joined her in a booth at the front, where we could watch the action.

A half a dozen or so of Santa Cruz's finest sat around the café drinking coffee and flirting with the waitresses. Flirting with bus-boys in the case of the female cops since the Courthouse Café's staff was sex-role stereotyped.

Nobody looked worried about incipient mob violence. But I didn't miss their air of suspicion. They weren't obvious about it, but they checked out everyone who entered, their hands close to their weapons. Their talk was a little too loud, their animation slightly forced.

"Yeah the job. Well, it was fun while it lasted." I took a sip of my raspberry-peach iced tea. Pretty good for a cop hangout.

Becky was drinking Diet Coke. "Have you thought that this is the universe telling you something?"

"Like, you didn't wash your hair as much as your grandmother told you, so *die*? Next time the universe wants to tell me something, have it send an e-mail."

Becky froze.

"What?"

"One of them is moving toward me. Make it stop."

I'd been waving my sandwich to emphasize whatever point I'd been trying to make, so naturally one of the girls came to investigate.

"She isn't going to hurt you, Becky. She's just interested in the food."

My friend shook her head dramatically. "This place is full of cops. You've got to keep those things under control."

"Is there a law against having a bad hair day?" I kept my head facing Becky and sprained my eyeballs checking out the cops.

Which was when I first noticed I could see behind me. Not real clearly, and with color overlays that seemed related to heat instead of visual cues. But when it comes to seeing out of the back of your head,

42

being less than 20-20 isn't a shock.

"No joke. Things are getting dangerous, Erin. Besides, those snakes creep me out. And I'm your friend. Think what they'd do to strangers."

I was thinking about what they could do for me. If I could see through their eyes, that meant they really were a part of me, like Boxter had said, not something that just got stuck on when I wasn't looking. In that case, having them removed would combine attributes of murder with self-abuse.

I waited until the cops got distracted by a particularly disgusting joke and then broke off a tiny bit of the sandwich.

I held it to my slithery buddy, felt the flick of her tongue against my fingers as she grasped the bit of sandwich, then gently put her back in under the hat.

Becky looked green. "I'm not hungry."

"You're always hungry."

"Not after that."

It took her a good forty-five seconds before she started eating again. That was half a minute longer than I had guessed.

I waited until she'd taken a big mouthful of her sandwich before I spoke. "What sort of message do you think the universe is sending me?"

Wanting to talk and not being able to had to be Becky's worst nightmare. She glared at me as she chewed.

A forced swallow. "There's a vampire in jail. There's a lynch mob outside. It's like *To Kill a Mockingbird*."

Oops. From watching *All the President's Men* on late night TV Becky had decided to become a crusading journalist. Bringing up *Mockingbird* meant she was on a roll. "Let me guess. You're Scout."

"I'll be Scout if you'll be Gregory Peck." She sighed dramatically. "God was he sexy in that movie."

I shook my head. "Do you seriously think I'd defend some rapist?"

"Innocent until proven guilty."

"He deserves a lawyer who wants to defend him, not a lawyer who wants to put a stake through his heart."

I could tell Becky was pissed when she actually put down her sandwich and wiped her fingers with a napkin.

"People who ignore the universe's messages *always* regret it. Besides, you haven't heard his side of the story. And the rumors are getting worse. It's gone from one guy attacking one woman to a plague of vampires and other magical creatures attacking all the normal folks, trying to wipe us out."

I weakened. "He probably already has a lawyer. And I'm not an ambulance chaser. Oh, and I'm busy."

"Like you have so much to do now that you're unemployed."

"If I want sarcasm and lectures on how to lead my life, I'll go to dinner with my father. At least he pays when we go."

"Sorry." She took my hand across the table and gave it a squeeze, then withdrew quickly.

I noticed she kept her eyes on my hat, watching for any unexplained movements. "You know I worry about this kind of thing," she said.

And Becky really believed the universe sent messages. I figured the universe had more important things on its mind than worrying about how I paid the rent, but being raised by a bad-tempered mostly-Buddhist father and a devoutly Catholic mother might have made me skeptical.

"If you get court-appointed, you'd make some money at least," she reminded me.

There was that.

Chapter 9

The second I pushed the phone's *On* button, he started talking. "There are a lot of mythical creatures coming to life all of a sudden?"

It took me a second to recognize the deep voice. "Professor King?"

"Cal. And I need some time with you."

After having lunch with Becky, I'd carted boxes into my second bedroom, which I'd always meant to set up as an office anyway, then printed out a bunch of cards with my name, cell number, and home phone number on them. I was in business.

If Cal had called an hour earlier, I could have put him to work with the heavy lifting. Typically, that hadn't happened.

"There are vampires and trolls and leprechauns running around," I reminded him. "I just have snakes in my hair. What makes me so special?"

I could hear his smile over the phone. "That's one thing I'd like to find out. So far as I've learned, you're the only reported Gorgon. That makes you somewhat special, don't you think?"

"Not really. I hear nobody is reporting anything."

"I've gotten dozens of e-mails. They're reporting different magical species, but none has said anything about any actual gods showing up."

"It makes me just weird. Besides, I'm not a god. And I thought Athena turned a mortal woman into Medusa because she was too beautiful or something."

His chuckle was sexy even over the tiny speaker in my phone. "That's the standard cleaned-up-for-schoolchildren classical Greek version. There are Gorgon legends. One thing for sure. Even in the classical Greek version, Medusa isn't the only Gorgon. And the other Gorgons *were* immortals. The children of Phorcys and Ceto. And Phorcys and Ceto were gods, of a sort. Although they weren't officially part of the Olympic pantheon."

"Newsflash, Cal. I'm not a god."

He ignored that comment. "So, why don't we have dinner tonight? That seafood place out near the yacht harbor is supposed to be nice."

"I've had a bad day, Cal. I wouldn't be good company."

"Tomorrow? I can pick you up at seven."

I sighed. A good-looking guy wanted to take me out to dinner, I could use the free food, and I was still hesitating. Considering how almost everyone else, including my best friends, had reacted to my snakes, I should jump up and down in celebration that a smart and good-looking guy, was even talking to me. Then again, I'd be happier if Cal had wanted to take me out because I was me, not because he thought I was a reborn goddess who was going to make his career.

"Call me then and we'll set up the details. But, yeah, I'm free."

"I don't normally generate this level of enthusiasm with my dates. I guess I'd better sign off before my phone gets overheated and explodes."

Okay, I deserved that.

Amelia called almost as soon as Cal hung up. She'd gone to bat for me and Hale, Storm and Stunk would cut me a five-week severance check, which was more than they normally do for someone who resigned. She also told me she'd e-mailed me the information I needed to file for unemployment but that, since I'd quit, it would take a while before I'd get any money.

I went on line to check my Visa balance. Shopping was a bad idea. If it was offering jobs, it was time to listen to the universe.

Lots of counties let judges pick the court-appointed attorneys who serve in their courts. This creates an inbred system where lawyers help judges get re-elected and judges make sure the lawyers make a living. To prevent this, Santa Cruz County has a public defender's office with full-time public defenders.

Which means that there aren't as many opportunities for unemployed attorneys. But the public defenders are notoriously under-manned and outgunned. In high profile cases, they sometimes hire outside talent.

I called the Public Defender's office.

After five minutes of pressing numbers at the beeps, I ended up talking to Mona, whom I'd met at the 'young lawyers social' after the County Bar Association meeting a few months earlier. Mona was only a couple of years older than me, but she was already director of the Public Defender's office. Which says something for the pay scale they were able to offer and something more about what a go-getter Mona was.

When I explained my goal, she had only one question. "You actually want to represent Vic, the Vampire, Ventoro?"

"You're kidding. That's really his name? The poor guy."

"Well his name is Victor Ventoro," Mona admitted. "People are calling him Vic the Vampire."

"Talk about pre-judging a case."

She paused, then went for the kill. "He also calls *himself* Vic the Vampire. But from the way you're talking, you really *do* want to get involved."

I waffled. "I'd think lawyers would be lining up from everywhere. It's high profile. You could probably get attorneys looking for the *pro bono.*"

I hoped I was also making it clear to her that I wasn't willing to go the free route.

"No publicity. Zero. Judge Hilz has imposed a gag order. No one is allowed to discuss anything, not even the theory that Vic is a vampire."

"A gag order will have to come off when the trial starts," I said. "Free and public trials, remember. I did pass Constitutional Law."

"Don't count on it, Erin. These people are making up the rules as they go along."

Making it up when it came to basic legal procedures? "They can't just make up rules. We have laws. This stuff has been litigated."

"Don't try to convince me. I'm a lawyer too," Mona said. "But they're claiming unusual circumstances and public danger."

"It's an assault case. How many rules would you need?"

"Nothing about this is simple." She paused. "Would you be willing to sit second chair?"

"Are you first?" Mona had been two years ahead of me at Stanford. She'd been a decent student, but nothing brilliant, finishing somewhere low in the top half of the class.

On the other hand, she had more energy than any ten people and, working for the Public Defender's Office, had handled dozens and dozens of cases. In contrast, I had practically no experience in criminal work. While Mona had climbed to the top of the Public Defender's office, I'd struggled to bill hours as a divorce attorney. I could learn a lot working with her.

"Nobody in the office will touch this thing. When that happens, I get stuck. Besides, given the possible sexual angle on this thing, female attorneys would be a positive."

I thought about it—for all of two seconds. "Pay me and I'm in."

"Deal. Why don't you come by now? We can do the paperwork and I'll get Judge Hilz to sign off on your expenses.

* * * *

I didn't get over to the public defender's office until after six, but Mona was still there, shouting into the phone and banging on her computer keyboard.

Mona was a big girl. About thirty, about my height, she outweighed me by a good fifty pounds. Her dirty-blonde hair didn't look like it had seen a stylist or even a comb lately, so I guessed the color was her own rather than out of a box. She wore a blue work-shirt over a pair of khaki pants that made her hips look twice as big as they needed to. The woman could be attractive with a little work. Hell, with her curves, she could be a knockout in a Marilyn Monroe sort of way. Instead she looked like someone the mob would send to break your kneecaps.

"Want a piece of pizza?" She gestured toward a box that looked like it had been there for a long while, grease leaking through to soak the legal papers beneath it.

My stomach grumbled and the girls wiggled. But a second look at the pizza box didn't make it look safer. I wasn't hungry enough to risk food poisoning. Besides, I caught the odor of pepperoni. It'd never been *proved* that pizza pepperoni had animal meat in it, but I wasn't going to take the chance. "No thanks."

She put her hand over the phone's transmit. "Have a seat, Erin. Five minutes, max, and I'll be done."

I didn't know who she was talking to, but whoever it was got a serious attitude adjustment.

In exactly four minutes and fifty-three seconds, timed by my PDA, Mona hung up her cell.

"You didn't tell me you had snakes in your hair."

That did it. I was going to retire this hat. I was zero for fooling about a million people.

"When I took my oath as an attorney, I didn't see anything where I promising to stay snake-free."

She looked worried, but I caught a hint of a grin, too. In her job, she had to like fighting lost battles. Because, despite some big-publicity mistakes, cops usually do arrest the right guys. Mona probably lost ninety percent of everything that dropped into her lap.

"Okay," she said. "Still, we're going to have a tough time with Vic the Vampire. The question isn't whether it's legal. The question is, do we really want to wave snakes in the jury's face?"

"I think the question is, do we believe people can be denied their basic legal rights just because they happen to have been transformed by whatever disease is going around?"

Mona had opened her mouth to interrupt about halfway through my statement. When I finished, she snapped it shut and nodded. "Let's get your paperwork filled out and then we'll go visit Vic the Vampire. Uh, alleged vampire."

* * * *

Just like that, I was employed and on a case. I might earn a third of what I'd made working for Hale, Storm, and Stunk, but I could stretch out my student loan payments and get by. There was a lot to be said for not losing my apartment.

"Want me to drive?" I asked. Mona had an ancient SUV that got such bad mileage she'd have to pay someone to take it from her. With gas prices as high as they were, even keeping my hybrid pumped up was expensive.

"We can walk. I probably didn't need that tenth piece of pizza, anyway."

Fortunately, Mona's office was only a couple of blocks from the County Jail. Even more luckily, I'd known Mona was a casual sort and hadn't gone into full job-interview mode. Which meant I wasn't wearing heels.

"Visiting hours are over, ladies," the Sheriff's Deputy told us.

"We're here to confer with our client, Victor Ventoro." Mona went from friendly to no-nonsense quicker than my snakes could strike.

"I'm not sure—"

"*I am sure.* Mr. Ventoro has a right to representation. We need to speak to him and we mean to do it now."

"Maybe." The Deputy stared at Mona for a moment, then identified me as the soft touch. "It's like this. Vic the Vampire is already in a meeting."

Speaking to me didn't work. Mona lit into him. "Damn it, Deputy. Calling Mr. Ventoro 'Vic the Vampire' prejudices the case. My client will not be questioned without legal council. And don't pretend that you don't know that rule."

"Ole Vic is meeting with an egghead, not with cops," the Deputy assured us. "He agreed to the meeting with no coercion."

"I don't care if he's meeting with the Pope. He's not talking if he doesn't have a lawyer present. Now take me to him before I get mad and make things happen."

I gave him my impression of a steel-eyed glare. I wasn't sure what Mona hoped to accomplish by pissing off the staff, but I wasn't going to undermine her. Hell, I was taking notes.

"I'll take you right there."

He buzzed for relief. When another Deputy came out from a back room brushing powdered sugar from his uniform, the first guard led us back into the jail.

I'd spent a summer working for the Santa Clara County D.A.'s office while I'd been in law school, so I wasn't completely unfamiliar with the modern jail. Still, the stench hit me like a jackhammer.

The girls shriveled up under my hat. The smell of ammonia, urine, feces, old sweat, and cheap fried food assaulted their scent glands. Which made it worse for me.

A Plexiglas wall separated us from the prisoner area, but it barely muffled the sound of televisions and the murmur of male conversations.

I fought my gag reflex. "About enough to make you give up on the male species, isn't it?"

From the look Mona gave me, I realized I should have saved my *bon mot* for Becky or the girls at the office. Unless I missed my bet, Mona *had* given up on the male species. Whether because of her experience with prisoners or simply because that wasn't her inclination in the first place, I wasn't going to guess.

The Deputy opened the Plexiglas door to a meeting room and ushered us in.

I recognized him at once.

Not Vic, 'the Vampire' Ventoro. My new client was a complete stranger to me. I recognized 'the egghead.' Cal King sat across the table from the vampire, chatting as if they were old friends.

Oddly, I felt hurt. Which didn't make any sense at all. Had I really wanted my disease to be so rare that Cal would obsess on me and be unable to talk to anyone else?

"Erin." Cal got to his feet, stepped over, and pumped my hand. He held on for just a second too long and I felt that boy-girl chemistry churning so I yanked my hand away.

"I didn't know you knew Vic," Cal continued as if I hadn't just snubbed him. "He's having a tough time. Six prisoners jumped him when they found out he was a vampire. He was just telling me about how he evaded their attack."

I couldn't leave him dangling. "Cal, this is Mona Hapsburg. She's the lead attorney in Mr. Ventoro's case."

Cal shot Mona one a million dollar grins. "Nice to meet you, Mona. I'm glad Vic is getting some help. I'm convinced the cops are railroading him."

Mona ignored both Cal's words and his outstretched hand. "Mr. Ventoro. You agreed that you would not talk to anyone without me or another authorized attorney at your side. Yet when I walk in here, you're chatting up a storm. Are you *trying* to sabotage your case, or are you just naturally self-destructive?"

Mona's method of client management wouldn't pass the sniff test back at Hale, Storm, and Stunk, but following their rules had gotten me fired. Time I learned something new.

Vic shriveled a little under her glare. "Sorry, Mona."

"Were you always so tall?" Cal fumbled for his notebook, his eyes fixed on Mona. "I've heard accounts of giants, but I haven't actually seen any. Vampires are a dime a dozen, though. Vic is just the one the cops chose to make an example of."

Maybe because Vic was the one who'd decided to get it on with an unwilling female? Since Vic was my client, I didn't say it out loud.

Mona kept glaring. "I am not a giant. I'm simply a woman somewhat above average in size. I have been taller than average since I was born. In fact, though, I'm no taller than Ms. Tsong who, I note, you didn't say anything about."

Mona's response dropped the temperature in the conference room to the artic range.

The chill didn't slow Cal, though. "Tough break for the two of us, huh? A few of us are stuck being normal even when the lucky guys are turning into myths. Don't feel bad about it."

"I *don't* feel bad about it, Mr. King."

Cal flinched a little. He probably hadn't been called 'mister' since he'd been in grad school. He might not mind informality, but if he were going to get formal, he would have wanted the 'Professor.'

"I'll come back when the lawyers give you the go-ahead, Vic. And I'm looking forward to our date tomorrow night, Erin." He took a breath. "Nice to meet you, Mona. Maybe I'll see you around."

"Not if I see you first."

That finally pushed him over the line. "Wow, that was so clever. Do they teach clichéd repartee in law school?"

"Get out of here, Cal," I said. "You aren't being helpful."

"Right. I'm gone." He gave Vic a male-bonding shoulder punch, Mona a wave, and me a wink. "See you tomorrow, babe."

Babe? Where had that come from?

Mona acted like Cal had never been there, for which I was grateful. I couldn't explain the apparent coincidence of Cal being with my new client. But Mona was more interested in her client than in the love life, or lack of love life, of her new associate.

"Mr. Ventoro, this is Erin Tsong. She's the number two attorney on your team. I'd like you to tell her what happened this morning."

Vic sulked. "I already told you."

"Now you get to tell it again. Isn't that lovely?"

Vic didn't look like he thought it was lovely.

I sat in the chair Cal had abandoned and tried to break the ice. "How'd you get that scratch on your face, Mr. Ventoro? Or would you prefer that I call you Vic?"

"Everyone calls me Vic the Vampire." He seemed proud of a name that would probably convict him.

"I'll call you Vic, then."

When he said nothing, I asked again about the scratch. "Does it relate to the attack Professor King mentioned?"

"Nah. I mean, yeah, a couple of prisoners jumped me. I think the guards set me up. But they couldn't catch me." He pointed to his scratch. "This happened when that bunch of vigilantes mobbed me."

"I'll talk to the guards after this interview," Mona promised. "Their job is to protect you, not encourage other prisoners to terrorize you."

"I took care of them myself. Broke a couple of ribs, knocked out some teeth, and they backed right up. The guards put me in solitary, which is okay."

Vic was slender and he looked quick, but he didn't look capable of handling several men. Especially not the kind of men who spend time in prison. Either he was lying or something strange was going on. I didn't think he was lying—not about this, anyway.

I leaned forward. "How many men jumped you, Vic?"

He shrugged. "Maybe five. They moved *slow*. I had all day to figure out what to do."

Although Becky and I would sometimes watch uplifting movies like *To Kill a Mockingbird*, we really loved horror movies. So I had a working knowledge of the vampire legends, as interpreted by Hollywood. And Hollywood insisted that vampires could move fast. Fast enough to disable or kill multiple opponents.

I studied our client. According to Mona, Vic was thirty-one. The man in front of me could have been any age. He didn't have wrinkles and his hair was jet-black, but his eyes spoke to more years than I could count. A black widow's peak descended deep into his forehead, and his skin was deathly pale.

"Do we have a photo of what Vic looked like before his transformation?"

Mona grunted.

"Let's get one."

"How is that going to help the case?"

It was a fair question. I didn't have a clue whether it would help Vic or not. I just wanted to see the changes. It would help me understand what was going on. One thing for sure, if we didn't look into it, the prosecution would. No lawyer likes being blind-sided.

Vic grinned, showing his canines. They extended a good inch over his lip, which had to make it hard for him to close his mouth with them inside.

"Take me through what happened," I said. "From when you first saw the woman until the police brought you here. And don't bother making yourself be the hero. We need the truth if we're going to defend you."

* * * *

The case would be tricky.

Vic's story was that the alleged victim, Leone Cornelison, had taken one look at his ultra-Goth vampire look and begged him to bite her. He'd wanted to try out his new teeth, so he and Leone had snuck away from the club where they'd been dancing, found a quiet place where they thought they could be undisturbed, then all Hell broke loose.

According to Vic, a group of men had followed the pair from the bar, attacked him before he'd had a chance to try out his vampire fangs, and beaten him as well as the girl.

The story was too convenient. Innocent man led on by a female and then falsely accused. "She didn't ask you to break up her chiferobe, did she?"

"Huh?"

Mona and Vic missed my *To Kill A Mockingbird* reference but that didn't mean anything. Just about every male accused of rape or attempted rape will claim that the woman was willing.

"Did you bite her?"

He sulked. "I didn't get the chance."

"Did you rape her?"

"Rape her? Are you kidding? If I'd done her, which I didn't, it wouldn't have been rape. Not in a million years."

"Is that a no?"

"Definitely a no. For all I knew, she was loaded with diseases and I didn't have a condom."

"And her blood wouldn't have been."

Vic looked at his feet. "Hey, you're not so dumb after all. I didn't think of that."

I wasn't sure what Vic *had* thought of. Turning into a vampire might make you fast and take care of receding hairlines. Apparently it didn't make you smart.

I'd been taking notes while Vic talked. Now I turned to Mona. "We need to talk to the alleged victim and the vigilantes. And we need to find out what really happened in Vic's alleged assault in jail."

Something wasn't adding up, and I was afraid it was Vic's story. He didn't look like a guy who'd been attacked by two groups of men, he looked more like a guy who'd been scratched by a woman who didn't know how to defend herself.

"I'll take the men," Mona said. "You see if you can get through to the woman. Tomorrow."

53

"What about getting bail for Vic?"

Mona shook her head. "Judge Hilz says that Vic is a flight risk. Something about turning into a bat and flitting away." Her laugh wouldn't have convinced the most gullible jury.

"*Can* you turn into a bat?" I asked our client.

He shrugged. "Not that I know of. But I can drink your blood. It's supposed to be super-erotic for the female. No offense, but you look like you haven't gotten any lately."

Chapter 10

To my surprise, supposed victim Leone Cornelison confirmed Vic's story when I visited her the next day.

Leone was a professional student. In her ninth year at U.C. Santa Cruz, she was on her twelfth major and worked part time at a minimart to pay for partying and extras, while relying on her parents for tuition and dorm fees.

I'd enjoyed college, but my father had made it clear that tuition was between my bank and me. The bank drew the line after law school.

Leone offered me a cup of tea and, when I refused, futzed around with making herself one.

"Anyway," she explained once she'd sucked down half a cup, "we were just starting to make out when a bunch of losers started hitting Vic. Not for long, though, because Vic was quick.

"Did you tell the police what happened?" I couldn't believe they would hold Vic with this weak a case.

"Why would I want him in jail? He can't bite me from there."

"You still want him to bite you?"

Leone was a year or two younger than me and hadn't lost her freshman fifteen pounds. The extra weight looked good, all soft curves.

"Everyone knows that a vampire bite gives you a huge sexual charge. Darned right I want him to bite me."

"Since there weren't any vampires until a couple of days ago, how can anyone know that their bites are erotic?"

She rolled her eyes. "Don't you read anything? Anne Rice, Charlaine Harris, Laurell K. Hamilton? They may not agree on much, but they all come down on the sexual side of things. It's in all of the classics."

"But that's fiction."

"So's having snakes in your hair. But I notice you manage that. How come I didn't get turned into something cool? I mean, I could use snakes in *my* hair."

It was a good question.

After covering a few more of the bases, I got Leone to sign a brief statement confirming Vic's claims, and collected her promise to appear as a witness on Vic's behalf.

* * * *

I'd arranged to have lunch with Amelia and Kay and went there next. Despite the town's growth, traffic is still a bit of an alien concept in

Santa Cruz. I stuck the parking ticket, donated by an overly aggressive University cop, in my glove compartment, wound my way down the hill, and bee-lined for the pancake place.

My former co-workers were already waiting.

I slipped past the door guard and made my way back to the booth they'd claimed.

Amelia got up and slid in next to Kay, letting me have one side to myself. Well, myself and the girls.

I felt hurt that neither wanted to sit next to me, but realized I was being silly. Who would choose to sit next to someone with poisonous snakes coming out of her head?

"Are you sure you don't need a paralegal for the Vic the Vampire case?" Kay demanded before I could put my rear in my side of the booth.

"News travels fast. But no need," I said. "The alleged victim is going to testify that she was a willing participant."

"So?"

"What do you mean, so? She's over eighteen. With the victim testifying on his behalf, you couldn't convict Satan himself of attempted rape. If the D.A. doesn't no-bill the case, the judge will toss it. And if the judge doesn't toss it, the jury won't even bother sequestering."

"You're the lawyer, hon, not me. But can you just agree to have someone bite you and suck your blood? Wasn't there that case years ago about some German guy who agreed to be killed and eaten? Just because you agree doesn't make it legal."

"Completely different," I argued. But my stomach tightened a couple of notches. Kay was right. Assault is a crime even if the victim is willing. Could you be guilty of attempted assault if you'd agreed to participate in kinky sex? If the D.A. wanted to make the case, he could.

"Let's eat," Amelia said. "In the two days since you quit, Mr. Hale has been running around the office like a nut job. If we don't get back in exactly one hour, his blood pressure might burst something."

For once, the girls were well behaved. The waitress didn't even give me a second look as she served my friends, took my order for pecan pancakes, and got us all glasses of Diet Coke.

Amelia took a sip. "Let's start with the man."

"Vic? He seems like a normal guy. Works as a mechanic during the day. Parties at night. Not your type."

Amelia shook her head. "Not your client, the other one. The possible romantic interest."

My stomach churned. We were romance junkies. I'd dished plenty of advice when Kay or Amelia had been interested in guys. But this was the first time they'd turned the spotlight onto me. "I have absolutely no idea what you're talking about."

Kay giggled. "Then you don't know that a certain tall dark and handsome Professor Callum King stopped by the office yesterday afternoon. He seemed interested." She made a Groucho Marx waggle with her eyebrows. "I mean, *real* interested."

"And he's completely dreamy," Amelia added.

"He thinks I'm going to make him a star since I'm the only Gorgon he's heard of."

"He might be interested in your snakes," Kay admitted. "But he asked questions that had nothing to do with reptiles."

I faked a calm I didn't feel. "What sort of questions?"

Kay looked smug. "Whether you had a boyfriend. What sort of places you liked; what kind of foods you prefer. Stuff a guy might want to know if wanted to impress a girl."

My heart did a sort of flutter-flutter, then the girls did a little bit of a wiggle and I remembered something. I had snakes in my hair. If I was going to get back into the dating world, I needed to set my sights on someone like Vic the Vampire or Bobby the pizza-delivering Troll. Unfortunately, Bobby was too young and Vic, despite being innocent of the charges against him, was too gross. They may call snakes slimy, but a picture of Vic should sit in the dictionary next to the definition.

"Where's he taking you?" Amelia wanted to know.

"Jeez, you guys. I'm working on the biggest case in my life and you want to know where some guy is taking me to dinner."

Kay nodded. "Cases come and go."

"Guys come and go, too."

"I'm more interested in the coming part." Kay blushed at her own *bon mot.*

"And you haven't had many guys around," Amelia added. Amelia had been married twice and wasn't in a hurry to tie the knot a third time. But she thought women should give the institution a try.

Kay ripped a piece of bacon apart, separating the more meaty part out from the fat. My snakes got interested, one of them reaching forward.

"Don't be gross," Amelia said.

I shoved my girl back under the hat. *I'll give you something to eat later,* I promised, mentally. I had an irrational craving for meat. Considering that I'd become a vegetarian at the age of thirteen, this was a bit strange. Maybe Becky was right and the girls weren't vegetarian.

Kay popped the shredded bacon in her mouth, chewed, and swallowed. "A legal case can't keep you warm and it can't give you the lay of your life. I want to know where he's taking you, too."

"I can't tell you because I don't know," I said. It wasn't a lie, completely. He'd said something about seafood at the harbor, but he hadn't actually named a place. The last thing I wanted was for my girlfriends to show up to inspect my date.

"You know more than you're letting on. What are you afraid of?"

I sighed. "Do we have to talk about me? What about you, Kay? Wasn't that guy from UPS sort of interested?"

By the time Kay and Amelia had to get back to work, we'd dissected their relationships, the two of them had let me know where I'd gone wrong with the last three guys I'd dated (not enough sex, too much sex, and not enough sex in that order. Good news for Cal, I guessed. It was time for too much sex again). We'd also agreed to meet again in a week.

My girlie side wanted to hurry home and get ready for my date with Cal. My lawyer side said I needed to bring Mona up to speed on my interview with Leone.

My father's Buddhist principles gave me the strength to keep the girlie side down.

As victories went, this one felt rotten.

* * * *

An hour after I'd drifted into the office, Mona told me I was worthless and shoved me out the door. "Have fun on the date. But please don't give me any details afterwards. I know the mechanics already."

One of my serpentine associates wanted to take issue with the shove, but I transmitted calming thoughts to it. For a miracle, my mental commands worked.

When I got home, my phone was ringing.

Not mother. I willed it so hard that one of the snakes stuck straight out in front of my head like a guy with a boner.

"Law Offices of Erin Tsong." I'd decided to sound professional, especially since my friends all called me on my cell. Who knew? Maybe it was a prospective client.

"Erin? Are you all right?"

And I'd had such hopes for my psychic abilities. "Hi, mother. Why shouldn't I be all right?"

"You need to spend more time watching the news."

"Why should I watch the news when I have a perfectly good mother to keep me up to date?"

"You know, darling. You're not very funny. Don't try."

"I'm listening, Mother. What news did I miss?"

"The Surgeon General says America is suffering from a plague. People are turning into monsters and assaulting normal people. You should come home where your father and I can watch you."

Growing up, home had been Santa Cruz. When I'd left for college, my parents had moved to Florida to take care of her mother's aging parents.

"Are you okay, Mother?" My mental image of my parents was eternally youthful, as they'd been when I'd been a child, but they were in their fifties now, still active, but no longer really young. "Are you safe?"

"Of course we're safe. We have your uncles and cousins to take care of us. Thank goodness none of *them* became monsters. The Surgeon General he speculated that some flaw in the DNA of those affected by this monster plague makes them susceptible."

"Uh, Mother, I've got bad news."

She gasped. "Don't tell me that your friend Becky is a monster. Her parents were wild when they were young, but Becky always seemed completely sensible to me."

"Not my friend. Me."

Silence stretched out like an open freeway. I imagined my mother processing what she'd heard, going through the grief stages, with an emphasis on denial because denial was what my family specialized in.

"That's impossible. You sound just like yourself."

"I am myself, but I have snakes growing out of my head."

Another pause and a quick shift to blame. "I should never have married your father. Since the days of Saint Patrick, there hasn't been a single snake in Ireland."

"You love Dad. I just won't go to Ireland."

"Of course I love him. He's your father." My mother paused for a moment, caught her breath, then moved quickly into the 'rationalizing' stage. "Having snakes doesn't make you a monster. The Surgeon General listed werewolves, vampires, elves, trolls, brownies, and giants. He didn't mention Gorgons. It's just coincidence that you developed snakes at the same time that other people became affected by this disease."

I had to give her credit, I don't think anyone could have come up with a dopier explanation. "I don't think so. I'm pretty sure I've got it."

"Even more reason for you to come home. You can't just wander around suffering from a plague. Someone has to take care of you."

Her argument would have been more persuasive if she hadn't been making it a long time before I'd become a Gorgon.

"I've got a job, Mother." (Sort of. But she didn't have to know all those details.) "And bills to pay. You'll be happy to hear I've moved into criminal law. No more divorce cases."

"Thank goodness. According to Father Phillip, divorce will keep more people from heaven than any other sin in America. I cringe when I tell my friends what you do for a living."

I decided not to tell Mother my first client happened to be a vampire. Divorce law might sound more appealing.

Mother had an uncanny nose for evasion, though.

"So, tell me about your clients? You need to be certain that none of them are guilty before you represent them. Like in that nice Matlock show we watched when you were a little girl. Once you're certain that they're innocent, and can pay their bills, it wouldn't hurt to look at the men. A woman who spends her life without children is an unfulfilled woman. And I'm still young enough to enjoy being a grandmother. It isn't just your sister's responsibility."

Only my mother would think defending criminals would be a good place to meet men.

"You've spent too much time with your sisters-in-law," I said. "Because that isn't you talking. You found much more fulfillment from your art than from children."

I heard a long exhale over the phone. "I wasn't the mother I should have been for you and your sister, dear. But I'm trying to do better. I want you to be happy. And *you* don't have art to fall back on. No, dear, you need a man. Besides, being a grandparent is easier than being a parent."

This was supposed to make me want children? And it wasn't as if art was such a lucrative career to fall back on.

I should keep my mouth shut, but I took the easy way out. "I do have a date tonight. A college professor."

"High time you come out of your shell, darling. But remember this: academics don't make much money. Are you absolutely certain he isn't a fortune hunter? Everyone knows lawyers are well paid. He might never want you to stay home with the children."

"I said a date, mother. Nobody is talking about children. And would you want grandchildren with snakes in their hair?"

"This is my fault, isn't it? I should have drawn the line when you wanted to wear those long braids. Mom always said it was only a matter of time before vermin took up residence in them."

Thanks for that. "I've got to go, Mother."

"Well for goodness sake, wear something sexy. You can't expect to catch a man if you wear baggy sweaters and pants all the time."

I looked at the baggy sweater and jeans I was wearing. However frustrating my mother could be, she knew her daughter.

"Some men like women who dress for comfort."

"The technical term for those men is blind, Erin. You've got a wonderful body. Would it hurt to show it off?"

"Two minutes ago, you said the college professor was a loser. Why do you care if I impress him?"

"To get a real boyfriend you need a placeholder boyfriend. Men are competitive. They want to steal you. Start where you can and trade your way up."

My mother might be right in her cynical reading of the opposite sex. I still didn't want to hear it. "I've got to go."

"I love you, darling."

"I love you too."

"Oh, one more thing, Erin. You don't really have snakes in your hair, do you? I know you love to jerk my chain."

"They're really there."

"Oh." Denial was starting to run thin. "I was afraid of that. I love you anyway. Talk to you soon."

* * * *

I flipped to a news channel and looked in my closet. My mother was right. Baggy sweaters, t-shirts, and conservative business suits vied for space. Flirty date clothes were not in evidence.

"More on the breaking news of this horrible plague." The television newscaster used that grim tone they use to announce the death of celebrities. "According to sources in the Federal Bureau of Investigation, a number of the new monsters have been arrested. John Angels, the FBI spokesman, states that whatever is changing their outward appearance is changing their behavior as well. And not for the better." He looked up into the camera. "Are the monsters trying to live up to their horrid appearance? Or are the changes that transform their outward forms perverting their very souls? With me in the studio the Reverend Jim Sutters with his considered opinion of this question."

The Reverend Sutters's opinion, considered or not, was that the disease was the mark of Cain. "You see one of the monsters," he said, "turn your back on him. Don't talk to hem, don't buy from them, don't let them shop in your store. The Bible says we're not supposed to reward them for their sins."

I usually manage to last longer than three minutes when I watch TV. Not this time. I turned off the set and focused on my closet.

Focus didn't help.

It was too late to shop, even if I wasn't concerned about running up the credit card. I decided to try something I'd seen in a magazine Kay carted into the office.

At the back of the closet I found a black suit I rarely wore because the skirt was too short for business attire. When I did wear it, I wore a beige silk tank under the jacket. To prove my mother wrong, I dispensed with the tank.

The higher of the jacket's two buttons connected directly under my breasts. The second button was a couple of inches lower. Since I don't have a lot in the chest department, I didn't think anyone was going to get bent out of shape by the cleavage. Showing my navel was different. It hadn't been out in public since I'd graduated from college and retired my bikinis to the back of the closet.

I'd decided to change back into a baggy sweater when I heard the knock on my front door.

Just like a man to be on time. And I didn't have roommates to keep him entertained while I changed.

He's interested in me for his research. I kept reminding myself of that, but my stomach was still clenched and the girls wove themselves into braids from the shared anxiety. I plopped a black beret on my head and made my way to the front door.

Cal looked good.

He'd replaced the professorial tweed with a leather jacket and a pair of jeans that clung to his legs and made me glad that the styles had changed from baggy to tight.

I almost slammed the door in his face. "I'm overdressed. Sorry."

"You look incredible. Uh, what did you do to your hair?"

I would have settled for the first sentence. The hat was supposed to cover things. Apparently it didn't.

"I wear it this way a lot. Is that a problem for you?"

"No problem. I just wondered if they get enough air."

Right. Cal wasn't there for my scintillating company. Take away the snakes and Cal would be gone so fast he'd leave sonic booms behind.

"Can I see them?"

My first date in high school had asked the same question, but he hadn't been talking about snakes.

Unlike then, I didn't say no. I took off the black beret that I'd hoped pulled the outfit together, making me look Parisian rather than slutty.

Cal studied me and I waited for condemnation and fear to creep into his eyes. I didn't see it. Of course, he was a professor—which had to be the next best thing to an actor.

"They're amazing, you know." He bent a little closer. "I think they have different personalities. This one is shy, the one in front is preening."

"Wouldn't that be snakealities?"

He considered, then shook his head. "No, I don't think so. The word personalities in that context would refer to the personification of—"

Silly me. I was talking to a college professor. "Never mind. Can I put my hat back on?"

"Just a second. I can't believe this."

One of my snakes was centered with my nose and just above my hairline. She preened for Cal, stretching, expanding her hood.

"Amazing. A perfect representation of the ancient symbol of Egyptian royalty. I defy the so-called experts to deny this."

He pulled a palmtop computer from his back pocket and scribbled something with the stylus. "As you know, Erin, Gorgons were traditionally viewed as being from Libya, in North Africa. Now Africa is a huge continent, but could it be coincidence that a serpent in the center of the upper forehead became a symbol of Egyptian royalty? Instead, consider a link from the ancient Libyan creator goddess, through the Egyptian Pharaoh culture, to Greek mythology. Add some historical research and a comparative shot of your snake and the traditional Egyptian crest and I've got a paper that five journals will fight to publish. And I owe it all to you."

For a second, I thought he was going to kiss me.

I backed away. I've kissed my share of near-strangers, but I hadn't kissed anyone who was more interested in my pets than he was in me.

The snakes sent a quick mental remonstration about my use of the word pet. They were, they reminded me, as much a part of me as my breasts or vagina. And several of the guys I'd kissed were a lot more interested in body parts than in anything else I had going on. Come to think of it, maybe *most* of the guys I'd kissed were into body parts rather than the whole woman.

My mistake, I signaled, wondering when I'd gone into dialogue mode with the girls. *But now you need to go undercover.* With the Surgeon General's irresponsible talk, I wasn't ready to go any more public with the girls than I had to. I wouldn't deny them, but I wasn't going stick them in other people's faces either. A lawyer learns to pick her battles.

"Are you okay with seafood?" Cal asked. "I mentioned that place near the yacht harbor but I'm open."

"Well—"

"On the other hand, I've been looking for an excuse to try it since I moved to Santa Cruz."

"I'm a vegetarian." When he'd asked about my dining habits, my girlfriends had neglected to tell him.

His face fell. "Oh. Well look, if you—"

"But I'm sure they'll have something I can eat. This is Santa Cruz. A restaurant wouldn't stay in business for long if they didn't give options."

He perked up.

I don't know why people get bent out of shape about vegetarians. I don't try to force my eating habits on other people. Why should other people feel offended by mine? Especially since mine were healthier and more ethically sound than animal-eating?

The girls wiggled some more beneath the beret. They didn't agree with my feelings about animal eating, even if they were willing to eat fruit when I fed it to them.

Cal grinned. "I made reservations for seven-forty-five so we should get a move on it if we don't want to be late."

* * * *

Given his jacket, I was halfway expecting a motorcycle. Which would so not have worked. My skirt was so short and tight that I would have showed off my butt to get on the back of a bike. Cal might get to see my butt eventually, but it wasn't going to happen tonight, and it wasn't going to be a cheap thrill either. Nor would the girls be happy under a helmet.

Instead, Cal drove a classic convertible Mustang.

"Wow! Nice car."

"It was pretty much a heap of rust when I found it but I put it back together in my spare time. I like to use my hands."

The girls wiggled. They liked the idea of his using his hands. I got a little tingly myself, but I just nodded.

He opened the door for me, let me in, then walked around to the driver's side.

He took his time checking out my legs as I got in, and just happened to glance down my cleavage. Cal was interested in my snakes, but he was male and he was going to look if he had the chance. If he'd been obvious, I would have had to slap him down. Since he stayed subtle, I savored the flattery.

Chapter 11

I hopped out of the car while Cal reluctantly handed his keys to a valet who didn't look old enough to drive. During casual chitchat while Cal drove the few miles between my apartment and the restaurant, we'd discovered shared interests in running and in spelunking. But I still felt uncomfortable about my outfit and didn't want to run the risk of flashing him while getting out of the car.

Cal ushered me into the restaurant, gave his name to a hostess, and confirmed that he had reservations.

Two steps in and I realized I was missing something by sticking with vegetarian restaurants. The place was beautiful.

Huge aquariums lined the walls and formed the dividers between sections of the restaurant. Brilliantly colored fish glistened as they swum patterns through the water.

The tinkle of sterling silver on fine china and the gurgle of hundred-dollar bottles of wine being poured mingled with expensive-sounding conversations about stock portfolios, trust funds, and million-dollar outsourcing deals.

If I'd made partner at Hale, Storm, and Stunk, I might have dined in places like this all the time. As it was, I needed to appreciate it while I could. A dinner here cost a week of what the county would pay me to defend Vic the Vampire.

The hostess decided we were a first-date couple and stuck us in a relatively secluded corner. "Can I get you a cocktail before you start?" She brushed her tits over Cal's arm.

"Just the wine list," Cal said.

A point against him. My mother can't stand it, but I prefer to make my own choices, in restaurants and in life. When men assume they make all the choices, I don't like it.

"Unless you'd like something." I'm not sure if Cal caught an escaping glare was just finishing an extended thought. Anyway, it was a quick recovery. Full points after all.

"A glass of wine with dinner will be fine."

Wuss. After the past couple of days, I could have used something strong enough to take the paint off.

On the other hand, Cal was paying and professors didn't have expense accounts. I would have been rotten to run up the bill.

Cal considered me seriously. "I'm dying to know this. How'd an

Irish-Tibetan mix come about?"

"True love. My father was a T.A. in my mother's physics class. His English was so bad she couldn't understand anything he said, but she pretended to be dumb so he would help her. The way he tells it, nobody was more surprised than he when she aced the class. It took another couple of years before she admitted she hadn't really needed all that tutoring. Just the tutor."

"So your dad is a professor?"

"Scientist. After he got his Ph.D., he worked for Intel and some of the other big semiconductor places. Now he's semi-retired. Consults when people have problems with nano-scale chipmaking." Which was probably more about me than Cal wanted to know. "What about you? Professor Boxter implied that your obsession with the Greek myths is a joke around the University. Why choose something that makes you an outcast?"

His smile would have charmed the panties off a tougher woman than me. Which reminded me, we hadn't even talked about the 'W' word. As in, did he have a *wife* back home somewhere?

"People thought Schliemann was crazy before he the factual basis for the legends of Troy. If archeology proves many myths, why not assume some truth behind others?"

I stretched my mind for something I could say that would sound intelligent, yet head the conversation in a different direction. Think, Erin. What to say?

"Are you married?" *That wasn't it. If he didn't already think he was going to score tonight, you just as good as told him. Why else would a woman want to know if a guy was married?*

"Huh?"

Unfortunately, there was no way to unblurt. "I can't answer your question about myths until you answer my question. Are you married?"

"My question was really intended as rhetorical. I sometimes get defensive about my fields of interest."

And he wasn't answering my question. Time to call a taxi.

I gathered up my purse.

"But no, I'm not married."

I settled back down. The conversation got a lot more interesting. "Instead of assuming that all of the myths were bogus, you decided they were all real?"

"Pretty much."

We ordered, then Cal back to me.

"Myths that had been believed by millions of people over hundreds of years must have *some* basis in fact. I started with the theory that the Greek Gods came from the oral traditions handed down by the Mycenaean civilization wiped out in the Greek Dark Ages. Just like the legends of Troy. But the more I researched, the more I saw commonality that could not be explained by a known common source. I mean, it's easy to look at Indo-European gods like Zeus, Thor and Indra as descending from a proto-Zeus worshiped when the proto-Indo-Europeans wandered the steps of Russia. But when sub-Saharan, Semitic, Han, and proto-Austronesian peoples share gods, monsters, and other myths, you have to wonder what else is going on."

"Sorry I asked."

"Did I get carried away?" He ran his fingers through his dark hair leaving it at least as tousled as when he'd started. "I sometimes forget I don't have to lecture all the time."

"No, that's okay. That proto-Austronesian threw me off." His intensity, his energy and interest were purely sexy, though. It's a girlie fantasy to imagine that a guy might turn that intensity and energy into pleasing his woman, but being a brass-balls lawyer didn't make me immune to girlie fantasies.

I held up a hand when Cal inhaled, clearly prepared to tell me exactly what made a population proto-Austronesian versus proto-whatever-else.

"From the way you're pursuing me," I said, "you think there's a connection between the plague the Surgeon General says is sweeping the country and your old myths."

"Except it isn't a plague, exactly."

"No?"

"If something made you smarter, faster, or let you recover faster from injuries, would you call that a disease?"

I shook my head.

"We're seeing is what those ancient Greeks saw back when. I think we're *recovering* from a disease rather than getting one." His eyes got a far-away look. Then he came down to earth in a hurry. "So, you're defending Vic the Vampire. He's accused of assaulting one of my students."

Alarm bells went off in my head. Even though Cal had contacted me before the alleged assault, he could be trying to influence the case. Damn. Every time I persuaded myself to start thinking about Cal in my bed, I walked into another ambush.

"I'm a lawyer. I defend people charged with crimes. I didn't realize there was a connection with your students."

"Wouldn't it be interesting if his blood turned out to be amber in color, like that of the gods outside Troy."

"I'm not bleeding my client for you."

Cal looked puzzled, as if he couldn't understand my reluctance. Well, that figured. He probably thought that the world shared his obsession with ancient myths and their modern manifestations.

"No problem. I bet the County has already done blood testing. Anyway, things are looking up for me. I've gone from being an embarrassment to the department to becoming an expert on the transformation. Thanks largely to the preliminary notice I put out after I contacted you, I got two separate calls from the government with offers of research grants. I owe you a lot already. And if the whole Gorgon thing is as special as I think it is, I'll owe you a lot more."

The arrival of our dinners broke off our discussion before I could get him to explain why he thought Gorgons were more special than, say, vampires. I liked the snakes, but there were people walking around with cloven hooves, wings, and super-sizing. Compared to those, snakes seemed small potatoes.

Speaking of potatoes, the girls were urging me to take a closer look at the food. Sensations from the snakes' highly developed sense of smell transmitted themselves into my brain making me more aware of taste and texture than I normally was.

Which was too bad in a way. I couldn't afford chef-prepared food every day. Before the snakes had arrived, that hadn't mattered: my tastes weren't sophisticated and I didn't miss it. Now, it was a minor tragedy. At least, that was what the snakes told me. *Their* scent and taste organs were fully operational.

Cal had ordered something with shells. I'd gotten a Portobello mushroom stuffed with artichokes. Both smelled delicious.

A bottle of wine Cal selected arrived with the food. After he went through the cork-sniffing and wine-tasting ritual and approved his selection, the wine steward poured. I took a sip.

Yum. Northern Californians are fussy about their wines. It's a privilege of living in one of the world's great wine centers. Even by California standards, this was really nice. Again my snake-senses enriched my taste-buds.

Little tingles of pleasure surged through my body as I savored the wine. My first bite of the mushroom burst onto my taste-buds like a surprise attack.

Wow! If eating a mushroom was this good, I was going to have to be very careful not to confuse the way my snakes deepened my senses for sensuous feelings toward Cal. Because the longer I sat in the restaurant across the table from him, the more those sensations felt like sexual desire and the more I wanted to drag him home. The guy was seriously cute and I had been too long without a man in my bed.

Shallow? Sure. But lawyers are supposed to be shallow.

Another small bite of my mushroom, this one equipped with a bit of the sauce and a tiny hunk of artichoke, sent me back into taste-bud ecstasy. Yummy.

My nose savored the tangy scent of mushroom, herbs, and artichoke, but the girls were sending their own signals—they thought I'd made a mistake not getting whatever fishy thing Cal had picked.

That was when I blew it. I closed my eyes to savor the subtle flavors of mushroom, fresh herbs, and tangy artichoke and forgot where I was— or the consequences of failing to pay attention.

I blissed out, chewing the best food I'd eaten in years. For just a couple seconds too long, I ignored the writhing under my beret.

With the rest of me distracted, the snakes poked their little heads out and strained toward Cal's plate.

"I can order a second entrée if your, uh, alternate selves are interested."

I snapped my eyes open and commanded the snakes to come back immediately. "I—"

Whatever I was going to say, apology, denial, excuse, got interrupted by a very large male dressed in a black tux that showed bulging lumps of oversized muscles in his arms and chest. The black bowtie was handy to let us know where his neck was situated. Otherwise he had the shoulders-merging-into-head look.

"I'm afraid there's been a terrible mistake, ma'am, sir. I'm going to have to ask you to leave. Now."

"What?" Cal objected. "I've only had two bites."

"We'll be happy to package up the remainder of your meal. But you are no longer welcome in this establishment. Please do not attempt to return."

I don't know if they call them bouncers when the prices were this high, but that's what this guy was. He pissed me off.

"We're going to sit here and finish our dinner." I wasn't going to let some over-muscled jerk push me around. "So back off."

I forgot to warn the girls to back off, and two of them reared up, knocking the beret to my lap.

Mr. No-Neck did back off. But not for long. He called for reinforcements—a bevy of sou-chefs, equipped with long knives and meat tenderizers.

"We are a first-class restaurant," the bouncer announced. "We cannot subject our diners to eat with the medically infected."

Medically infected? That damned Surgeon General. From what Becky had learned from newspaper sources, and from what Cal had learned from his funding, nobody knew whether the transformation could be transmitted. Since I was the only known Gorgon, the chances that someone could just catch it from me seemed slim.

"If I can survive middle-aged men with their bimbo arm-candy, they can put up with me. We came here to enjoy a meal, made proper reservations, were seated by an employee. We're going to eat our goddamned food."

"Erin." Cal sounded ready to cave. "You don't have to prove anything here. We can—"

"Oh, no. You've wanted to eat here for years and that's what we'll do. We'll sit and enjoy the view of the yacht harbor and those pretty fishes swimming around the aquariums. We'll leave when we're good and ready. Maybe we'll stay for coffee and dessert, my treat. We haven't done anything wrong. We were minding our own business when No-Neck here decided to interfere."

People of mixed race like me lean in one of two directions. There are mild and self-effacing types who go along with whoever squawks the loudest. Then there are us who fight back when we get pushed. If you're in the first group, you might as well forget about ever becoming a lawyer. Lawyers might be mostly creeps, but we are fighters.

"This isn't a fight we can—"

"Are you saying that you won't leave?" The bouncer seemed to be having problems comprehending simple English.

"Fuck off." He couldn't misunderstand that.

* * * *

I'd put the beret back on and managed to swallow another couple of bites of the mushroom. Cal didn't even bother trying to eat. He kept on looking at the line of tough guys that the bouncer had lined up, keeping a solid wall of humanity between ourselves and the rest of the diners.

They didn't make any moves, though, so I judged I'd won our little confrontation. Eating while surrounded by ten burly guys from the kitchen staff wasn't my fantasy of a perfect date, but it was better than caving in. Right?

Wrong.

The police must have been close. At least six of them arrived within two minutes.

They stormed into the restaurant, followed the directions of the greeter who'd seated us, and barreled to our table.

A forty-something cop with streaks of silver in his hair got in my face. "Lady, you are under arrest for trespassing and creating a public nuisance. Put your hands on the table where we can see them."

"You're arresting *me*? This is absurd."

I'm a fighter, but every fighter learns when to quit. I quit when one of the cops pulled his pistol and pointed it at me.

"We'll be happy to add resisting arrest to the list."

"We'll go peacefully," Cal said. "Come on, Erin. You've made your point."

I hadn't made much of a point at all. But the cop with the gun didn't look much older than the parking valet. And he looked scared. A frightened man is a dangerous man.

I might make a political point if he shot me, but I didn't count points when guys pointed guns. I wanted to stay alive.

"I'm coming with you." I put my hands on the table. Of course, my mouth still couldn't stop from running. "But you're violating Santa Cruz County Code by enforcing unlawful behavior here."

"Tell it to the judge." The older cop slipped handcuffs over my wrists while another cop dumped a blanket over my head, covering the girls in the same way they might cover a streaker at a ballgame.

"This is a complete overreaction," Cal argued.

"Can it, unless you want us to haul you in as well."

"I'll be fine, Cal. I'll have to catch up with you later if you need anything more from me."

"I'll get you out," Cal promised.

I hadn't done much criminal law, but I knew that wasn't going to happen at this hour of the night.

* * * *

Santa Cruz has a reputation for coddling its criminals. If that's true, I'd hate to see the jails that don't. The Santa Cruz County jail was no summer camp.

I was thrown into a holding tank with half a dozen other women: one accused prostitute, three who'd been running an alleged methamphetamine lab, and two who appeared to be in for the same reason I was there—a nervous overreaction to the Surgeon General's paranoia about the transformation.

"I know you," the fairy said.

The troll just stared at me.

I looked back at the fairy. Memory is important for a lawyer. You never know when something witness three says on day four of a trial just might contradict what witness twenty-seven says on day eight. "You're that waitress, right? Your boyfriend threatened to dump you when you grew wings."

"Who wouldn't?" one of the meth manufacturers demanded. "Wings on your back and you expect people to treat you like you're human or somep'in?"

The little waitress wasn't holding up well. She had an ugly bruise over one eye and one of her wings drooped. She cowered away from the meth junkie. I had to believe at least some of her abrasions came from the non-transformed losers in the holding tank with us.

"I'm Erin Tsong. Do you need a lawyer?"

The waitress glared like her problems were my fault. "I haven't done anything wrong. Why would I need a lawyer?"

"It's great you haven't done anything wrong. But once the police pick you up, you need a lawyer. Period. The police want to prove you guilty, not to discover the truth."

Not that lawyers are much help to a lot of the people railroaded into prison for crimes they hadn't committed. Still, we're the only hope a lot of innocent people have.

The waitress moved a little closer, but only a bit. She had to choose between a methamphetamine dealer who'd already been violent to her and a friendly lawyer. Clearly she found that a tough choice.

"You're a lawyer? You picked a funny way to troll for customers."

"Who you calling a troll?" The other transformed person, a woman who'd gone almost as wide as she was tall, was in the waitress's face.

I got between them. "She means trolling like fishing. And you're only a troll if you believe it."

"Yeah? Well, I used to be a babe. So what, do I get wings or cute pointy ears? Oh, no. I get something special. Now I'm half human and half muscle-bound gorilla. So spare me your pious proclamations."

"Half gorilla? That's a laugh. From what I can see, you'd be all gorilla except gorillas are supposed to be smart." The methamphetamine abuser wasn't short, but she was giving up a good fifty pounds on the troll, and her heft included a lot of fat. From where I stood, it looked like the dealer was the one who'd come up short on the intelligence department. Of course, meth rots out brains.

"Back off," I told her.

"Or what? You'll flash your boobs at me, pretty girl? Didn't your mother teach you how to dress?"

I'd kept the beret while my head had been buried under a blanket and a bunch of cops ran their hands over my body searching, they claimed, for hidden weapons.

I pulled it off now, though, and told the snakes to put on an angry show. It wasn't hard. The restaurant staff and the cops had gotten me mad and this meth chick had pushed me over the edge. If the cops didn't have cameras in the holding tank, I would have *really* let them go.

The meth chick's eyes didn't focus at first. She grabbed my suit jacket lapel and got into my face.

Since I wasn't wearing a blouse under the jacket, her dirty fingernails rasped against my unprotected skin, which made me even madder, even as it scared me.

The girls caught my mood swing and thrashed. Then the snake in the center of my upper forehead lunged for her.

The meth chick's eyes crossed, her knees wobbled, and she let go in a hurry, sliding to the floor in front of me. "Jesus. You've got snakes growing out of your head."

"No shit, Sherlock. Now back off. Leave my friends alone."

She pulled back a couple of feet, just out of range, and studied me. "Those things poisonous?"

"That's what I hear. Want to find out for sure?"

Muscles twitched in her wrists as she tightened her fists. She was going to attack. She was, anyway, until one of the snakes reared its hood and spit at her.

She tumbled to the floor to avoid getting hit with snake-spit, then backed away. "You've got to be insane."

"That's weird," the troll said. "I could tear those drug chicks apart, but they didn't back away from me."

"She's a meth addict. She's more afraid of creepy things that ordinary violence. To her, my snakes are creepy."

They didn't seem so creepy to me any more. For one thing, they'd just saved my life. I was surprised how quickly I'd gotten not used to them, but to actually like them.

"No kidding." Troll-girl stretched out a hand. "I guess you're all right."

I shook it. "Thanks."

The non-altered criminals huddled on their side of an invisible line running down the middle of the cell. I introduced myself to the fairy, whose name was Lisa Hall, and the troll, whose name was, unfortunately, Itsy Swift.

Unlike the non-altered, my fellow transformed were held on bogus charges. Itsy had accidentally put her hand through the sheet-metal skin of a parked car when she'd been jostled from behind. Lisa had gone into her own apartment after her boyfriend kicked her out. She had a key and she'd been attempting to retrieve her property, but he'd caught her at it, held her at gunpoint with what was almost certainly an unregistered handgun, and called the police.

According to her, she'd been listed on the lease, which would make her entry completely legal. But the police had it in for the transformed, and were inclined to believe the normal no matter how unlikely their stories were. Naturally the apartment manager refused to go to bat for Lisa.

Unfortunately for them and for me, neither of my new friends had the money to pay for a private attorney.

"You have a right to court-appointed attorneys," I explained. "You don't have to pick me. If you don't pick me, the court will select someone for you. It might be better for you if you hire a normal lawyer. Meaning someone who hasn't been transformed."

"Can you get us out?" Itsy wasn't making commitments.

"I think so. For now, anyway. They can't arrest all the transformed without a massive jail construction project."

"Get me out and we'll talk about your lawyer skills."

"I don't know if I even want to get out." Big ball-tears stood out from Lisa's eyes like silver bubbles in a bottle of cheap champagne, ran down her cheeks and dripped off her pointed chin. "Where would I go? My boyfriend took the apartment and my money. I just have one day's tips, and that won't last long. And my boss has a thing about criminals. I know he'll fire me."

I thought about the nice office I'd just set up in my second bedroom. Then I looked at Lisa.

"You can share my place until you find your feet. But first we need to get out of here."

Which was easier said than done.

Growing up, I'd watched reruns of *Night Court*. There, no matter what the time of day, a magistrate was available to set your bond or simply to tell the police to let you out. Santa Cruz hadn't had the level of crime to keep a night court busy. So, we spent the night in the County lock-up while we waited for daytime and a magistrate to set bond for us.

Since we were just being held, not yet formally charged with crimes and certainly not convicted of them, we weren't entitled to special amenities, like mattresses, pillows, and blankets.

I nearly froze every time I even leaned against the wall. When I sat, I spotted the monitoring videocamera swiveling in its cradle, moving for the angle shot that would let some perverted guard look up my skirt.

I stood back up. Then I let the girls hiss at the camera for a minute or so before sticking the beret back on my head.

An audible sigh came from the non-altered side of our jail cell when I covered the girls.

I just had to hope that the judge wouldn't believe they were a danger.

Chapter 12

The judge let us all go on our own recognizance.

As I'd suspected, the jails were filling up. And it wasn't just the transformed getting thrown behind bars. Whatever was going around had kicked off a crime wave. Assault, rape and murder cases took precedence over penny-ante accusations of trespassing or damage to property, or even drug production.

"This doesn't mean that you are not guilty of serious crimes," the judge explained as he let us all go. "You must remain available to the police. At any time, you may be remanded back to the county jail."

A Sheriff's deputy led the three of us transformed women out to the courthouse steps. "If you leave the County, nobody will go looking for you. We've got plenty of your diseased types without having to bring more in. You know what I mean?"

I knew what he meant—I didn't like it.

Being out of jail let me feel vaguely victorious, like we'd won a battle. Itsy didn't look like she shared the sentiment. She was itching for a fight with the jerks who had shoved her or with the cops who had arrested her.

"Lay low," I urged her. "With this arrest in the books, they'll be watching you. Next fight you're in, it won't matter who starts it, you'll be the one who gets in trouble."

"Then it might as well be me who starts it," Itsy reasoned. "'Cause I sure didn't do anything last time and they still took it out on me."

I couldn't argue with her logic so I made sure she had my phone number for when she next needed a lawyer.

Lisa stuck close to me. She was probably afraid I'd come to my senses and change my mind about her staying with me.

"You'd think the cops could at least drive us back to our cars," Itsy said.

I handed her a couple of dollars for bus fare. So far, this ambulance-chasing lawyering was costing me more than it was bringing me in business.

The troll took the money. Instead of waiting for the bus, she headed for a coffee shop. Well, that had been a great investment.

Lisa and I got into the bus stop line, along with the meth addicts who'd shared our cell.

They pretended they didn't see us at first, and we returned the favor.

Spending the night together hadn't made us pals. I did make sure the beret was loose.

Then the troublesome meth-girl elbowed me in the side.

I took issue. "You messing with—"

"Chill. I think that hottie's waving at you."

I'd gotten so wrapped up in the bus schedule I hadn't bothered watching the traffic. Sure enough, Cal was signaling to me from his convertible Mustang.

The morning fog hadn't completely burned off, but he still had the top down.

He steered into the bus lane. "I was still pulling strings with the County Board when I got the word you were out. Sorry you had to spend the night."

Okay, the guy got points for following through on his promise, even if he hadn't sprung me.

"No problem. I made some friends."

"I ditched my classes so I can buy you breakfast to make up for the dinner we didn't get to finish." He paused, then leaned forward. "Uh, are those wings on your friend's back?"

"Genuine fairy wings," I said.

"Cool. According to most legends, several of the immortals had wings. But they're typically depicted as birdlike rather than batlike. In Christian art the angels follow that tradition."

"If you say so, Cal. This is my new roommate, Lisa Hall."

"Nice to meet you, Lisa. You're welcome to join us for breakfast."

A little blue car pulled in front of Cal's Mustang. The hybrid engine whined as Kay jammed on the brakes.

"Here's the cavalry," Amelia shouted from the passenger side. "Hop in. The bus is almost here and it'll run right over Kay's car."

I glanced at Cal, then at Kay and Amelia. I hadn't slept all night. I had morning breath, a scrape on my butt from where the cops had dragged me across the restaurant carpet, and I was grumpy. If I went with Cal, I'd have to watch what I said and I'd probably scare him with the morning breath. With the girls, I wouldn't have to worry about how I looked or what I smelled like. Part of me still wanted to go with him.

"Tell you what, Cal. Give me a call later today. I still need to recuperate from last night."

He looked at me, then nodded. "If that's what you need." He shifted his Mustang into gear, but paused before jamming the accelerator. "I've never had a date quite like last night."

"Me either. With a lot of luck, neither of us will again."

He laughed, so I guessed I'd taken the right tone. "Later."

Sure enough, a bus was heading in, and the driver didn't look like he was going to let a tiny blue car keep him from getting to his destination. Lisa and I piled into Kay's car.

"We're supposed to be delivering some papers to the court," Kay explained as she wove through traffic.

"Turn in here." We were at a strip shopping center. The center wasn't much, but it did have a donut shop.

As soon as Kay braked, I ran inside and bought four coffees and two-dozen donuts.

* * * *

Half an hour later, Kay had filed her legal papers and the four of us had achieved sugar-and-caffeine highs.

Kay and Amelia had to get back to the office, so Kay dropped us at my apartment and took off.

I tried to figure out what I'd do with Lisa.

"*All* your stuff is in your boyfriend's apartment?"

"It was my apartment too."

I opened my own apartment door. "We should be able to get a court order allowing you to pick up your stuff, but you'll probably have to enumerate it."

"Enumerate?"

"List."

She giggled. "Do I have to list all of it? There's some stuff I wouldn't want a stranger to read."

Way too much information. "I've got a better idea. Leave that for your ex-boyfriend."

Lisa made a sour face. "I paid for them and I don't want him using them with some other chick."

"He's a loser, remember."

My new roommate sighed. "But he can be—"

"What he can be is history. He turned you in to the cops, right? For trying to get your stuff back?"

She stiffened her spine—a pretty good trick considering the muscles that let her flap her wings. "Right. He's history."

About time.

I kept my apartment in minimalist décor. Partly because I spent my paychecks on school loans, but mostly in reaction to my mother's overflowing neo-Victorian style. I did have a futon, though, which would work as a bed for Lisa until we came up with something better.

She helped me lift the futon into my office, then I got her a couple of towels and a washcloth, shared one of my pillows with her, and we were good to go. Or so I thought.

"I don't have anything to wear."

I looked at her. Lisa *might* reach five feet, compared to my five nine. Since I mostly wear pants, we weren't going to be doing a lot of wardrobe sharing.

"We can go out shopping later. In the meantime, I've got a pair of running shorts and a t-shirt you can have. Why don't you go ahead and shower first? And then call your boss and see if you still have a job."

Lisa nodded and headed into my one bathroom. I'd had roommates when I'd been in law school. I hadn't liked it much then, I'd only gotten crankier in the years since.

After our showers, Lisa discovered that she was indeed fired. We agreed that naps were a higher priority than shopping—which said something about how tired we were.

I turned off my phone, put on a nightshirt, adjusted my pillows for the girls' comfort, and was out like a lightbulb.

A sharp rap on my front door pulled me from a kinky dream that involved Cal, his Mustang, and my snakes doing very nasty things to his body.

I pulled a bathrobe over my nightshirt, padded through the living room and looked out the peephole.

It might have been my dream, but I really expected to see Cal.

No such luck.

I threw the door open.

An attractive woman, tall with long legs, dark hair, pale skin, and blue eyes that just might have x-ray properties stood with her hands on her hips. A silk top showed off nice curves. Her sandals were more stylish than anything I could afford.

"Mother? What are you doing here?"

"Where did you expect me to be when I hear my daughter is in trouble?"

She stepped back and checked me out. "You really are in trouble, aren't you? I hoped you were kidding about those snakes."

"You flew across the country because you were worried about me?" I knew she'd taken care of me when I'd been a baby because I'd survived, but that was about all I could say for her mothering. On the flip-side, she made a heck of a shopping partner.

"I flew across the country because I knew you wouldn't take care of this for yourself. I spoke to several doctors. Only one of them is willing to have anything to do with you transformed people. But fortunately, that one is a surgeon."

She studied the girls critically. "He can cut those suckers off and sew you right back up. Fortunately your hair is thick enough to cover the scars. The government hasn't gotten around to registering monsters yet. So, if we can get you fixed, you'll pass as normal. Nobody will ever know. Isn't *that* wonderful."

The girls curled on my head, shrinking away from those hateful thoughts.

"I would know."

"You're making a big legal productions out of this. It would be a straightforward operation. Like removing a wart. No big deal."

I sighed. It was a big deal and it wasn't going to happen. The snakes might not be smart, but they had feelings. It would have been one thing if they could have lived on their own. But they couldn't. They were part of me and they depended on me. I wasn't going to let them down. No slicing and dicing for my girls no matter what.

Unfortunately, leaving mom on the doorstep wasn't an option.

"Come on in, Mother. Would you like a cup of green tea?"

She wrinkled her nose. "Are you still drinking that?"

"You taught me to drink it. Antioxidants and all, right?"

"It's passé. People are drinking red wine again."

"Green tea, Mother? Or nothing?"

She sighed. "Oh, all right."

I left my mother in the living room, filled the electric kettle with water and flipped the switch—just in time to hear a scream.

Lisa, wearing nothing but thong panties and a sports bra, stood over my mother, who had collapsed in the middle of my living room floor.

"I swear I didn't touch her."

I crouched down to feel her pulse and make sure my mother was all right. "I know you didn't. She's my mother."

"Did she know about your snakes? When *my* mother finds out about my wings, she sure won't be visiting."

Mom was breathing normally and her eyes fluttered open so I figured she was fine.

"She's found a doctor who'll cut off the girls."

Lisa's hands went back to her wings in a protective gesture that sent my heart out to her. "But they're a part of you. How could you cut them off?"

My mother struggled to a seated position and pointed at Lisa. "You have a demon in your home, Erin. A sex demon, a succubus, sent by Satan to steal away your man."

"I don't have a man, mother. And Lisa isn't a succubus. She's a fairy. You know, like a fairy godmother. She does good."

At least I hoped Lisa did good. When she opened her mouth, I wasn't so sure.

"What about the hottie at the bus stop? If he wasn't a boyfriend, he sure wants to be."

I went back into the kitchen to turn off the water and to think how to deal with that. After all, I had told my mother I had a date.

I decided on honesty. "That was Cal. He wants to research me."

"I'd let a guy like that research me if he wanted," Lisa said. "Often as he wanted, too."

"I told you." My mother got off the floor and straightened her slacks. "Father O'Brian says we're in the last days, with a plague of demons. You've got to pick sides, Erin. Snakes and the bat-wings say you're heading in the wrong direction."

Growing up, we'd gone to church on Sundays, but our Catholicism didn't extend past that. Since my father remained Buddhist, the rest of the family practiced a moderate and accepting version of Christianity. After my parents had moved to Florida, though, my mother's social life had centered on her church. At the time, I'd been happy for her. But if her priest was going to diss me and my friends for something we had no control over, I was changing my opinion.

"I'm not going to have my snakes cut off. Lisa isn't going to have her wings cut off, either, but she's still not a succubus. Since we're all just different humans and the end times aren't happening right this minute, let's get acquainted. Mother, this is Lisa Hall. Lisa, my mother, Mary Tsong."

Training and good manners won out over fear. "Nice to meet you, Lisa. I'm afraid that I may have over-responded to your informal attire and your, uh, wings."

Lisa looked down at herself. "Ohmygosh. No wonder. You mentioned lending me some t-shirts, Lisa, but I wanted to make sure that you don't mind if I cut the back out of them. It hurts to wear clothes over the wings."

I had a wealth of t-shirts from the 10-k's I ran on weekends so I fished her out a couple.

My mother found a pair of scissors and helped Lisa cut a hole in the back of the ones she liked. "So Lisa. How long have you and Erin been friends?"

I tried to catch Lisa's attention but I was too late to head off the answer.

"Just since last night when I ran into her in jail."

"Oh." My mother's smile was practically frantic. "Erin is your lawyer?"

"You bet she is. When she faced down those meth-addicts in the holding tank with us, I figured, she might be a criminal, but I like her style."

"Criminal? My baby is a criminal?" My mother fluttered her hands over her chest and sighed dramatically. "Oh, Erin. Can't you see that Father O'Brian is right? You've got to have those snakes removed before they get you into even more trouble."

The funny thing was, she had a point. If Santa Cruz, one of the most open-minded counties in California, reacted this badly to the strange transformations that were going around, I hated to think how the rest of the country would deal with them. Having the snakes cut off would allow me to blend with the untransformed majority. To pass for normal.

Could I do it?

My father had often told me the story of his grandfather, who had fled Tibet with his family when the Chinese had invaded. "In every person's life, there's a time when they need to choose between doing nothing and taking action," he always concluded. "That was the time my father had to choose."

Well, this was the time I had to choose. I could accept the girls, recognize that they had changed me, that I was someone new, someone special, but also someone who would forever be on the outside of society looking in. Or I could reject them and seek the protective coloration of being normal.

I don't want to claim any particularly advanced morality. If it had just been pointy ear-tips or something, I might have made the other choice. But I couldn't give up this new aspect, these new parts of who I was. The girls enhanced my senses, gave me new emotions and abilities. I just wouldn't pretend they weren't part of me.

My next trick was explaining this to my mother. Tact was critical. "The snakes stay."

She sighed. "You've gotten causey again, haven't you?"

"Maybe. Can't help it."

My mother finished cutting holes in the back of my t-shirts, tossed the stack to Lisa, making sure she put one on, then opened my closet, tutting her teeth and shaking her head at the limited selection.

"You're absolutely certain you won't have this simple operation and make your life better? You could have your boobs done at the same time. You've always wanted to have some extra shape up front."

"I'm positive. And I've learned to live with being an A-cup, too."

"Then there's only one thing for it. We *need* to go shopping."

* * * *

Four hours later, all three of us had new outfits thanks to my mother's platinum credit card. We'd also found a Mexican restaurant that didn't discriminate against the transformed, sucked down a couple of margaritas each, and were feeling happy.

I pulled into my parking lot when I realized that my mother was still with me. "So, mother. Where are you staying?"

"I thought I would stay with you for a few weeks. Since both you and Lisa are unemployed, we'll have a lot of time to spend together."

Uh-oh. It sounded like I'd just gone from happily living by myself to having two roommates. Which was at least one too many in a small two-bedroom, one-bath apartment.

"Don't worry, I'll take the couch," she offered.

Too late. Lisa already had my futon.

She didn't really mean her offer, anyway. Good-old Catholic guilt would kill me if I make my mother sleep on the floor while I rested on my queen-sized bed.

"Mother, you know that isn't going to happen. I'll run out and buy a sleeping bag for myself. You can have my bedroom and Lisa will sleep on the futon in my office." I had a couple of sets of keys from when I'd thought a boyfriend and I were going to get serious and I handed one each to my mother and Lisa. "Back in a couple."

"We'll carry in the clothes," my mother said. "And I think that young man of yours will be very happy when he sees the party dress you bought. The jet-black beads bring out the rich color of your hair and the sn—" she coughed. "Uh, your sn—well, the girls."

I didn't bother reminding her that Cal wasn't my 'young man.' Instead, I maintained a straight face, trying not to react to the way my mother was willing herself to accept this new aspect to her daughter.

"You're still on Florida time, Mother. Don't stay up for me."

"All right. But I feel guilty about kicking you out of your own bed."

The game we played was, first she made me guilty and then I had to make her feel good about it. "Don't worry, Mother. The snakes are happier near the ground, anyway."

My mother bought that lie, which meant I could go to the camping store and buy a sleeping bag, then stop by the grocery store and buy some fancy coffee beans, fruit and cereal so we wouldn't be three hungry and grumpy women in the morning.

Chapter 13

A huge dog, his fur glistening silver in the moonlight, trotted by my car as I pulled into the sporting goods store.

"Hi pooch." I cautiously opened the car door.

The animal turned toward me, his teeth flashing.

Drool dripped from his mouth as he eyed me and his eyes held a red glow that seemed less reflection and more generated light.

That's when I noticed he wasn't wearing a collar. I considered slamming the door and running.

Dogs are most dangerous when they're defending their homes. When they're out in the world, they tend to be peaceful. But this guy didn't look peaceful. He didn't look friendly either. In fact, I wasn't completely sure he was a dog.

"Mistaken identity," I said. "My apologies. You're a werewolf, aren't you?"

He growled.

I could almost hear words in his growl. Almost, but not quite. The menace, though, came through perfectly.

Think fast, Erin.

"I'm happy to meet you. I'm Erin Tsong. I'm a lawyer defending those of us who are transformed into magical and formerly mythical beings. I'm a Gorgon myself."

I held out a business card, then realized he couldn't take it. Chatting with a werewolf in his wolf form was bad. Watching him convert into a naked man so I could hand him my card was a direction I didn't want to go. And from the equipment hanging between his hind legs, he was definitely a male.

"Feel free to call me if you get into any trouble," I babbled. "Unfortunately, the officials are cracking down on the transformed like us."

He growled again, but this time with a bit of question.

I blathered on like a complete idiot, hoping he'd decide I was harmless. "Transformation doesn't free you from your obligations to society. But neither does it free society from its obligations to you. You're still covered by constitutional requirements of equal protection under the law."

He shook his head slowly, mockingly, then barked a short laugh. After studying my business card for a few moments, he trotted off on his werewolf business.

I'd thought picking up a sleeping bag would be easy. I hadn't realized how many choices you had to make. I called over a salesman to help me.

Another mistake.

"Just about everyone is buying guns in addition to other survival equipment," the salesman said. "With vampires and werewolves, why not get a little insurance. I was listening to"—he named a radio commentator famous for his annoying whiney voice and his outrageous political views —"and he says this thing that's going around is God's punishment for America's sins. Makes sense to me. So, I say, what can it hurt to blow a couple away? Maybe they were trying to get you, but even if they weren't, you're just saving the next guy the trouble."

The snakes writhed under my beret but I radiated calm to them. Attacking this idiot would only confirm his strange beliefs.

I smiled and pretended to be blonde. "Is the disease limited to America?"

He shrugged. "Who cares about the rest of the world?"

"It wouldn't say much for God's aim if he wanted to punish America but managed to hit the entire world, would it? Sounds like your radio commentator is as idiotic about this as he is about everything else."

His face turned a purple shade completely wrong for the florescent lighting. "You one of those sick fucks who think it would be fun to have bestial sex with a wolf?"

Okay, then. Here was a sales guy who really knew how to put the customer first.

"Oooh. Not getting any? And with an attitude like yours, that's no surprise. Tell you what. Is there another salesman here? Because I'd hate for my commission to go to a bigoted, woman-hating egocentric."

He stormed off and I found a woman with a store badge on her vest.

"Are you trying to cause trouble?" she demanded. "He's calling the cops. The guy went crazy when his wife turned into a troll and hit him back when he tried to put her in her place. Crazy or not, the cops listen to him."

I wondered if the saleswoman might be passing.

I pulled my beret a few inches back from my forehead exposing one of the girls. Since they had different personalities, I decided to come up with names for them. The one in front was Jennifer.

"You really think I should let him walk over me, sister?"

She looked behind her as if expecting the walls to sprout ears like my head did snakes. "I don't know what you're talking about."

"Sure you don't." I checked her out more closely. Her thick black hair and long sleek torso reminded me ever so slightly of a seal. "I won't mention the word *silkie*."

"Jeez, not so loud. You are so very wrong."

"Sure I am. Done any good surfing lately?"

"How about I help you with your order and you get out of here. I need this job."

Before I'd gotten fired, I would have told her that it was illegal to dismiss employees just because they were transformed. Instead, I let her help me pick out a synthetic down sleeping bag guaranteed to be comfortable down to twenty degrees below zero and an air mattress she promised wouldn't leak during the night and leave my bony butt on the ground.

"I understand why you're in the closet," I whispered at the checkout. "But what you do for others will come back to you."

"I used to believe in all that new age magic stuff, but no more."

"You believed in magic when there was no evidence for it, but change your mind when there were werewolves and vampires, fairies and gorgons around. If that's not magic, what is?"

She swiped my credit card. "Okay, here's my attempt to get the universe on my side, so pay attention. Buy one of those guns Harvey was talking about. The normals are loading up with them. If our, I mean your, people can't fight, they'll get wiped out."

I thought about it. For maybe a quarter of a second. That's how long it took me to realize that if it did come to fighting, I'd be about as useful as a screen door on a submarine. A hundred and twenty pound chick should fight her battles in the courtroom rather than in the killing fields.

I passed another werewolf and an angry looking troll as I made my way home. I assumed at first that they were out for nefarious purposes. But then I wondered whether they might roam at night because they'd be hunted down during the day.

My mother and Lisa were both sleeping by the time I got home. Which meant I'd be stuck hyperventilating into my air mattress by myself.

I took a deep breath and started to blow.

After ten seconds, I was suspicious. After thirty seconds, I knew something funny was going on. A girl can't just exhale forever. I shouldn't be able to fill an entire air mattress on one breath.

Snakes don't giggle. At least mine don't, but they can radiate a happy sort of contentment, and they were. They were doing their part in blowing up the mattress and enjoying themselves at the same time. I'd been wrong when I thought they couldn't breathe for me.

Thanks, girls, I sent.

When I got the entire thing set up, I made extra-sure that the girls were comfortable before I let myself drift to sleep.

* * * *

I tucked myself deeper into the softness of the sleeping bag savoring the air conditioner breeze. Until I reached some magical self-aware moment.

My apartment was built before air conditioning arrived in Santa Cruz. One reason the rent was low enough for me to live there was they'd never retrofit it. No air conditioner, but an air conditioning blow. Something funny was going on.

I forced my eyes open.

Lisa balanced on the back of one of my tea table chairs. She leapt from the chair in a huge whirl of flapping wings—and fell to the ground. The wings didn't even slow her, let alone help her fly.

That explained the air conditioning blow. Lisa's wings might not give much lift, but they sure stirred up a breeze.

Lisa shook her head, then clambered back up the stool and repeated the process.

More wind. No more takeoff.

"When I was a kid, I used to swing as high as I could on a swing set," I said. "Then I'd jump off and try to fly. I really thought I could learn how if I practiced enough."

Lisa let out a little scream when I started talking. When she realized it was me, she thought about what I'd said.

"*That* was a normal childhood fantasy. Normal children don't have wings and their bones are too solid so of course they can't fly. I do have wings and I'm a fairy with light bones. *I* should be able to fly."

"I can't fly. I haven't seen anyone who can fly."

"You don't have wings."

"No, but I have snakes."

She sighed. " You have snakes and they're fully functional. I saw the way your snake spit at that drug addict in jail. But what are my wings? Decorations, that's all. I'm tired of being a decoration. I want to be powerful. I think I'm the only transformation that isn't improved at all."

Some people would argue that having snakes growing out of your head is no improvement. But since I'd been getting friendly with my new aspects, I wasn't one of them.

"What about elf-ears? How functional are they?"

"Long ears should let elves pick up lower wavelengths than normal humans can hear. It's basic antenna theory. Not to mention more space for earrings. Vampires have added speed. Werewolves can shift between two legs and four—perfect for times you need to cover ground. Vampires have alternate diets. And your snakes protect you."

That much was true. If anyone got close to me, the snakes were ready to strike—whether I wanted them to or not. And my experience blowing up my air mattress the previous evening said they might just have a nest of other capabilities.

Which gave me an idea.

"I had a cockatiel when I was a kid. We had cats too, so the bird couldn't fly around much. And after a while, he got so he couldn't fly at all because his muscles atrophied. But when I took him with me to college and left the cats behind, he didn't have to be locked up any more. A few weeks of practice and strengthening his wings and he could fly like nobody's business."

"Lisa isn't going to be able to fly." My mother emerged from my bedroom wearing one a brand new nightgowns I'd bought to impress a short-lived boyfriend with something slinky. The boyfriend had disappeared and the unworn nightgowns had been relegated to the bottom of one of my drawers. But then, my mother had never made any bones about searching through my stuff. Made me wish I had a few guilty secrets to startle her with.

"You don't know that," I said. "Lisa might just need practice."

"Unlike you, I took physics in college." She grasped the gossamer fabric of Lisa's wings. "Look at these suckers. They don't have the surface area to get her off the ground. Think about an eagle or a hang glider and imagine that wingspan in comparison to the weight of her body. She'd need wings at least twenty feet long."

"What about a hummingbird? They just beat their wings fast. Same with bats, right? Maybe that's why Lisa has bat wings. They're supposed to beat fast."

My mother shook her head, completely unconvinced. I wasn't very convinced either. Lisa's wings had beat plenty fast when she'd jumped from my chair. Even at his weakest, my cockatiel had slowed his fall when he'd flapped.

"I had another idea," I said. "Have you been to the Monterrey aquarium?"

Lisa shook her head.

"Well it's really cool. They have a parcel of penguins. Their wings are too small to fly in the air, but they fly just great in the water."

"I've never been a water person," Lisa said.

"You live in California," I reminded her. "Time to get over your fears."

I left Mona a message that I'd be late, and then found a bathing suit for Lisa. The girl definitely needed a pick-me-up.

Lisa might have been eight inches shorter than me, but she had a nice shape to her. She looked better in the ancient bikini I dug out of my college clothes collection than I ever had. Her pectoral muscles fused with new muscles lapping her shoulders and back and controlling her wings, all of which made her already curvy assets curvier.

My mother and I put on one-piece suits and the three of us went down to the apartment pool to check out my theory.

Ten minutes later, I headed up to my apartment for my stopwatch. For a girl who'd been afraid of the water, Lisa was a natural. We'd have to try her in an Olympic length pool, but she looked like a record-breaker to me. And I'd swum on the U.C. Santa Cruz Banana Slug team in college so I had some idea how fast a serious swimmer can be. Plenty of scholarship swimmers from other schools had breezed by me during my years on the team. Lisa didn't just breeze by, she flew by. Literally.

I hated to end the fun, but the apartment manager started toward the pool and I decided it would be better to avoid him. Not that we were doing anything wrong, it was just that since the transformation I didn't have to do anything wrong to get into trouble.

* * * *

I left my car keys with my mother and Lisa, taking the bus to Mona's office.

The lawyer looked up from her computer and her pizza boxes. I thought she was wearing the same jeans and t-shirt she'd had on when I'd seen her last. Only the pizza was new. Still, we'd have to talk styles and hygiene before I sat second seat with her.

She didn't waste any time. "I've got bad news."

Just what I needed. More bad news. "Sorry I didn't call yesterday. I was busy and we didn't have anything on the docket."

"No problem. That's not the news."

Had our case gone south? "Don't tell me they persuaded Leone Cornelison to change her story."

Rape and assault cases generally came down to a 'he said, she said' situation. The strength of our case was that both Leone and Vic were singing from the same hymnal. Santa Cruz had a long tradition of leaving people alone with their weirdness, as long as they didn't bother anyone else. I was counting on that to protect Vic.

"Not that either." Mona pulled a stack of papers off a chair and gestured for me to sit. "Judge Hilz's clerk called. He says you're currently charged with felony trespass so he revoked your court-appointed status. I can't pay you after all."

I didn't buy the Judge's excuse. He knew the trespassing thing was bogus. "Can he do that? I'd think it would be up to the state bar association."

"If he says you're not a court appointed, you don't get paid, end of story. Nobody is going to reverse him on that."

Court-appointed attorneys didn't make *much* money, but there was a huge difference between not much and none. Still, I felt obligated to see this thing through. "Can I still sit second? *Pro Bono* until we get Hilz to change his mind?"

Mona shrugged. "Disqualifying you would be a bit of a risk for him. The bar association might not like it, and that could hurt him in the next election. He'd rather you just go away."

Staying with the case was a no-brainer. There was no reason to believe that the transformations weren't permanent. And if they were, I was going to have to establish a name for myself with the transformed community. Defending the first major case involving an alleged transformed perp would contribute to my reputation, even if it left my pocketbook empty.

"I'm in. This'll be my *Pro Bono* work for the next century."

"You sure?" She took a sip from a coffee cup that I swear had been sitting in the same spot two days earlier. Mona definitely needed some help, and the fashion police weren't going to be enough. "Maybe you should spend your time looking for a paying job."

"I'll do that too. But Vic needs a real team and you need my help. Maybe I'm crazy but I think the exposure will do me good."

Mona sighed. I could tell she wanted to reassure me she'd find a way to pay me something—and couldn't.

"I'll try to change Judge Hilz's mind about the money. He's not usually unfair."

Maybe because he wasn't usually facing werewolves, vampires, or Gorgons. "In the meantime, let's see where we are with the Vic the Vampire case."

We were about where I'd expected in a case where one of his two attorneys had spent her time in jail, shopping, and trying to assuage the ego of a fairy-roommate. Mona had held down the fort, hitting up the D.A.'s office for paperwork and trooping over to the jail when the police had wanted to question Vic again, but she had other cases too. Vic needed more.

One advantage of being unemployed is having plenty of time.

I got on the phone with the assistant district attorney assigned the case, told him I'd take his offer of a plea bargain to Vic but would recommend against accepting it, and learned the names of the cops who'd been involved in the arrest. Cops are never in a hurry to return a defense attorney's phone calls, so I'd have to track them down and check out their stories against the written reports they'd filed.

To my surprise, I was having fun. The need to repay student loans had driven me to pursue income—to the extent that I'd forgotten why I'd gone to law school in the first place. Fighting to get an innocent man off an unfair rap was more satisfying than negotiating a divorce deal between two people who should never have married in the first place.

Equipped with names, I headed toward The Dubliners, a cop bar not too far from the city police station on Center Street.

It would be interesting to see how the cops reacted to the presence of a Gorgon in their community.

Chapter 14

I was *not* Ms. Popularity at The Dubliners.

I wore another of Becky's hats, this one a cute thing with a hint of veil around the edges. Hats like that had last been fashionable in the early fifties, which seemed retro enough for them to come back into style.

With my hat on, and a pair of tight jeans that showed off my long legs, the cops *started out* friendly enough.

Less than three minutes after I'd walked into the bar, though, the cops started ignoring me.

It wasn't my hair. It was my questions.

"I'm looking for Officer Billy Orlando." I'd mentioned that fact to three cops, each of whom had instantly tuned me out. After those snubs, the bartender seemed my best bet.

"Why should I help you?"

"I'm not trying to get him in trouble. I just want to ask him about an arrest he was made."

"You have complaints, the police got channels." He turned his attention an already clean beerglass.

"Who said anything about complaints? From everything I've heard, Officer Orlando made a good arrest."

"So you're looking to give him a reward? Maybe you baked him a cake or something. Why is it I'm having a hard time you?"

I smiled. "Perhaps your doubts spring from ignorance, because you rarely deal with an attorney of my charm and class."

That earned a laugh. "All these years I've thought it would be impossible to use the words 'attorney,' 'charm,' and 'class' all in one sentence."

I considered slipping him a fifty for his help. A good look around the bar spared me that expense. He stood to lose a lot more than fifty dollars if he chased away his primary customer base. Then there was the fact that fifty bucks loomed a bit larger in my world than it had a couple of hours before, back when I'd thought I had some sort of income.

What I needed was a plan.

I fished the fifty bucks out of a pocket anyway and put it on the bar where it stuck in a puddle of spilled beer.

My move got me a stare that said I'd read him right. He wasn't going to take a bribe. Not one I could afford, anyway.

"No bribe," I explained. "A bet. I'll bet my fifty bucks against you identifying Officer Orlando, that I can close both eyes and still tell you whether you're pouring the pale ale or the dark stout." I pointed to the eyes in question, the ones on my human face, so there would be no issue about me cheating.

The bartender shrugged. "I wouldn't sell out a cop for a hundred, which is basically what you're offering with a fifty-fifty shot. Besides, you could probably smell what I'm pouring. And you'd peek."

Well, of course I was going to peek. I was a lawyer, which meant I was the queen of loopholes.

"You drive a hard bargain. Well, if you really want to take advantage of me, I'll also identify whether it's a twelve, sixteen, or twenty-ounce mug. That would be one chance in six if it was just chance. Pretty good odds of you pocketing the fifty."

He looked at the fifty. Then he looked around the bar.

"Any of you guys put her up to this, I'm going to find out. Whoever it is, no credit from now on."

Nobody volunteered anything, which didn't surprise me since I didn't have a confederate. Not that wasn't attached, anyway.

The bartender sniffed my fifty, then pulled out one of the markers people use to find counterfeits. The bill passed.

He looked disappointed. "Your money is real. So it's a bet. But there's one more thing."

"What's that?" I hated surprise conditions.

"You lose, you leave. You're bothering my customers. People come here to drink, not to talk to nosy civilians."

Noon was way too early to be drinking, but I figured most of the cops here had come off shift. At least I hoped so. Orlando was supposed to be working night shift, which meant he would be tired and maybe drunk by now. It isn't a combination I look for in men, but Orlando and I weren't going to have magic moments, anyway.

"Deal."

We shook hands and he called one of the cops to come over and blindfold me.

"You said *one* more thing. This blindfold makes two."

"Tough."

"I said I'd close both eyes. Don't you trust me?"

"Trust a lawyer." He slapped his knee. "Girl, you got me twice in one day. You really are a crack-up, aren't you?"

Fortunately, I'd tucked the snakes up under the hat. As it was, a couple of them got a little squeezed when the cop tightened a bar towel around my eyes.

"Now pinch her nose."

"Nobody said anything about pinching—" The second half of my sentence got all nasal as the cop clamped his thumb and forefinger over my nose. His not-completely-clean thumb and finger. Yuck.

"I'm pouring now. You've got thirty seconds to identify the type and size. Twenty-nine. Twenty-eight."

I hadn't agreed to a time limit, either. I hate it when people change the rules.

I hadn't used my connection with the snakes in this way, but I had faith in the girls. I projected a signal. *Tell me what he's pouring.*

Fortunately, the beermugs were different shapes as well as sizes. Snake-brains don't do well with numbers or ounces. The twelve-ounce beer came in a standard mug shape. The sixteen was a vial, like an oversized test tube with a flat bottom. The twenty had a bulb at the bottom. Different shapes or not, the girls weren't used to picking out beer containers. And their sense of color was weird.

"Fifteen seconds."

Panic reared. I could ill-afford to blow fifty bucks, but the loss of control was what really scared me. Not only was I blindfolded, the cop behind me pressed his thigh against my butt, and grasping my arms, holding them close to my sides.

My blindfold was the bar towel the bartender had been using to wipe down his glasses. Although the cop held my nose, I picked up the stench of stale beer and detergent through my mouth—or through the girls.

"Five."

I can't exactly describe the picture that my boss snake, I named her Sharon, projected to me.

It wasn't anything like a television picture. The image came from a part of my brain that definitely wasn't my normal sight center with at least as much temperature as light in the scale visible to humans. But the shape. Was it—

"Two seconds."

"Twenty ounce. Guinness Stout." I shouted my answer in a hurry in order to beat his unfair deadline.

"Well darn. How'd she know that?"

* * * *

Orlando was the cop who'd held me. Which wasn't a big surprise. He'd probably signaled the bartender to agree to the deal.

With his slight frame, smooth cheeks, and the little bit of baby fat that clung to his face he looked about fifteen. Of course, as I climbed toward the big three-oh myself, soldiers and cops had started looking like

94

babies.

"Can I buy you a drink, Officer Orlando? And would you rather that I call you Officer Orlando, or may I call you Billy?"

"*You* can call me Officer Orlando. And I'll buy my own damn drink."

"I'd be happy to—"

"I don't let chicks buy me drinks. If I did let a chick buy me a drink, it wouldn't be one with snakes in her head."

Got it. This wasn't a friendly conversation.

"I already told the bartender, but I don't know if you heard me. I'm working for Vic Ventoro. We're ascertaining the facts of the case. I've read your report, but I want to get into details you may have left out."

Oops. He physically withdrew when I used the words 'left out.' Time to recover.

I went soothing. "I'm sure you included all of the *factual* points in your report, but you wouldn't have listed your opinions and feelings because you wouldn't want to prejudice the detectives working the case. Right now, I'm trying to get a feel the circumstances surrounding the incident. I need exactly the type of material a good officer wouldn't put in his report."

I smiled, hoping groveling would convince him I was on his side.

Orlando didn't look mollified. "Opinions don't have a lot to do with police work, ma'am. Fact is, the guy's a vampire. Another fact, we don't want his kind molesting our women."

Jeez. I never thought I'd hear that kind of talk in Santa Cruz. *Our women?*

"I'm glad you mentioned molestation," I said. "We're trying to understand the circumstances of the arrest and the prior activities of the civilians who called you in."

"What about it?" He was still defensive, but we were back to facts.

"I understand the civilians stopped Ventoro's behavior *before* you arrived on the scene. Did you see any physical evidence of molestation?"

"Hell, yeah. That slut's shirt was halfway off, her tits flopping around like nobody's business. What more do you need?"

Mr. Sensitive, Orlando wasn't.

"You assumed from Ms. Cornelison's dishabille that she'd been assaulted?"

"I don't know from dishabille. I know she was messed up and that vampire was looking to suck her blood. Can't arrest a guy for that, what can you arrest him for?"

Try a crime, I almost said. But I wasn't here to educate Orlando. I was here to put together the case for my client. If we needed to tear Orlando a new one, we would do it on the witness stand.

I forced a ditzy smile. "I was confused about one more thing. Your report does not name any of the civilians who, uh, *apprehended* Mr. Ventoro. Can you explain why not?"

"Didn't figure they needed to be involved."

"I see…" I let my voice trail off in question.

"Look, are we just about done? I put everything in my report. I was doing my normal beat on Pacific. I heard an altercation. I approached the scene, arrested that blood-sucking vampire, and sent the civilians on their way. The second officer on the scene made sure Ms. Cornelison was taken to the hospital for first aid and a rape test."

The rape test had come back negative. Leone hadn't engaged in sex, forcibly or otherwise, in the twenty-four hours leading up to the incident. There was more than one way to rape a woman, but from what Leone had told me, she hadn't gone through any of them.

"Just about done." I said that mostly because that's what lawyers say to keep the interview open. Like a telephone survey taker, I'd ask as long as Orlando kept answering. Especially if he kept giving me answers that helped Ventoro's case.

Orlando must have guessed he wasn't convincing me. "You're going to say it was voluntary, aren't you? That the slut asked for it. Typical lawyer. Blame the victim is what we call it. I had my way, they'd lock up you defense lawyers first 'cause you're worse than the criminals."

I hate rapists as the next girl. But a rape charge didn't fit these facts.

"If you'd seen the scratches on Vic the Vampire's face," Orlando continued in his attempt to persuade me, "you would have known he'd been in a fight."

"I'm waiting for the photos. Unfortunately, by the time I got to him, he'd been assaulted in prison."

Orlando chuckled. "Glad to hear it. Guy tries to suck the blood out of normal chicks has to expect blowback."

"Just a few more questions," I lied. "Did you question any of the civilians who apprehended Mr. Ventoro?"

"Sure. I had to find out what had happened."

"But you didn't write down their names?"

His grin looked as fake as it was. "I already told you this. Last thing they need is the newspapers dragging their names in the dirt. They're heroes, but you lawyers would make them out like the bad guys in the whole story."

"Still, your second-hand report is inadmissible. Without the witnesses to the alleged molestation, how do you intend to make a case?"

"Tell you what, snake girl. We'll put Vic the Vampire in front of a jury with his slimy look and his teeth hanging out. They'll see he's a blood-sucking, bat-loving, soulless vampire. After that, ask any questions you want. Won't matter a lick cause he's toast. Wanna know why? 'Cause our kind of folks, normal American kind of folks, don't want his kind sniffing after our women. Know what else? Some slutty foreign chick with long legs and snakes coming out of her head isn't going to change the mind of one single real American no matter how you twist the facts." He gulped the last of his beer.

Apparently my bet had inspired some sort of interest in beer and mugs. Jennifer slid forward and pushed her little snake-nose against the bottom of Orlando's mug while he still held it to his face, getting the last drops.

"Jesus!" He flung the mug across the room where it smashed against a fake adobe wall.

"She was just wondering about the scent, texture, and temperature of the mug." I suppressed my giggle, but barely. The look on Orlando's face when he'd been looking deep into his beermug and seen the snake's face was priceless.

He fumbled for his gun. "You attempted to attack me."

Not so funny. "Nobody attacked—"

He unbuckled his weapon and pointed it at me. "That's you people's line, isn't it? The wolf that did it, not me. Or your fangs just guided themselves to some poor girl's neck. Or those snakes, which you control fine when you want to win a bet are out of your control. Right?"

"But—"

"Get up and put your hands against the wall. And move slow or, so help me, I'll blow you away."

Not funny at all. I tried to judge the exact speed between frightening him by moving too fast and annoying him by moving too slowly.

A couple of cops, one male and the other female, headed Orlando off before he spattered my brains over the wall.

"We'll take it from here," the woman promised.

"Let me give you a lift home, Billy," the male added. "I'll pick you up this evening for our shift."

"I gotta get that snake woman. She's making a momary, uh, mockaty —"

"Mockery?" I suggested.

"Shut up," the female cop said. "You're making things worse."

Some people say that's what lawyers do. I didn't point that out.

They bundled Orlando out the door, then the female came back.

She pointed her gun at me.

I hadn't pissed myself, but I'd come close. All of a sudden, I got closer.

"You can put your hands down."

"Thanks." I turned and gave the cop a smile.

She didn't smile back. And she didn't put her gun away.

"Can't you perverts leave him alone?" she demanded. "You think you're so magical with your wings and pointed ears and vampire teeth, but you're really a bunch of creeps. Billy's been through enough without you guys making him the villain."

"I'm just trying to find the truth, ma'am," I said. "If you've got a couple of minutes, maybe you could help me."

"Since when has any lawyer cared about the truth? If you want to understand something, understand this, pervert. Most cops are loading with silver bullets. So don't think we can't hunt you down. We'll be watching you."

Common sense told me to keep my mouth shut.

Unfortunately, my mouth rarely listens to the voice of common sense.

"Silver bullets? Now that's a concept in fashion accessorizing."

"You don't think they'll work?" She looked at her weapon like it might have turned traitor, then slammed it into her holster.

I was pretty sure silver bullets would work as well as steel-jacketed bullets. A bullet will hurt whether that metal is cheap iron or precious platinum. Since I'd stubbed my toe that morning, I knew it didn't take magic to hurt me. I suspected the same went for my shape-shifting brothers. Suspected, but wasn't a hundred percent sure.

"Maybe you can use holy water instead of tear gas, too," I said. "Get real. That silver thing is myth."

"You sound pretty positive." The female cop reached into her hair.

I was completely caught off-guard when she pulled something shiny out from behind her head and jabbed me with a pin.

"Ow! Crappola. What the hell was that about?" The tiny poke hurt like a son of a gun, burning as if she'd poured acid on me.

"Hah. You *were* shitting me. Silver works."

"Give me that." Sharon snagged her hairpin before the female cop could pull it back.

I took it from the snake's mouth while the cop reached for her gun. This was getting old.

"Nice," I said, checking out the heavy silver hair clip. "Vintage Mexican silver?"

She forgot about the gun. "You have a good eye."

"Where'd you get it?"

"One of my great-grandmothers was from Mexico." She smiled as she warmed to the topic. "Another descended from one of the original Spanish Land Grant families in California. There's an argument about which side this came from."

"This is so cool. And the silver looks great against your black hair. I'll have to try something like that myself."

I'd been off the mark relating to Orlando. Vintage silver was definitely the way to *this* cop's heart.

"It's hard to find good silver," she explained. "A lot of what passes as antique is really junk, made with something like twenty percent silver. But old silver is highly collectable. A couple of months ago, a guy offered me two hundred dollars for this one hair clip."

I studied it for another moment, then handed it back. "Hang onto it. Money is nice, but you can't just buy family heirlooms. One day you might have kids and you'll be able to pass it down to another generation."

"If they wouldn't be embarrassed to have something so old."

Both sides of my family had come to America as refugees. My mother's Irish side had come across a couple of generations earlier, fleeing English oppression. My father's family had left Nepal with the Chinese invasion. In both cases, they'd gotten away with their skins and not much else. I would have run up my Visa bill to its not-so-distant limit to buy a memory of the families they had left behind.

"Why would that embarrass them?"

"Who'd want to be reminded their family was wetbacks?"

I didn't slap her, but I was tempted. A similar attitude had haunted me my whole life. People wondered out loud why I didn't go back to China, why I was taking a law school slot that should have gone to an *American.* Maybe that's why I was sometimes abrasive.

"There aren't very many of us who don't have immigrant blood."

She sighed, then clipped the pin back in her long dark hair. "I guess that's right."

I took out one of my business cards and handed it to her. "You ever need a lawyer, give me a call."

"I'm not one of you magic types."

"You seem magic enough for me."

Chapter 15

Cal was waiting outside the bar.

A chill went down my spine. "Are you stalking me?"

"Your mother called, worried that you'd be stranded."

Santa Cruz is not that big a city. My mother knew I could walk, take the bus, or call her on my cell.

Either Cal was lying, or my mother was matchmaking. Knowing my mother, matchmaking seemed likely.

It was my fault, of course. I'd told her Cal was taking me on a date. I'd never dreamed she would leave Florida, so I hadn't thought I was taking a risk. I'd been wrong.

What can I say? Me being wrong happened a lot.

"It's nice of you to drop everything and be my chauffeur."

"Even college professors need to eat. I figured I'd take you to lunch. That would handle the eating thing and give me a chance to pick your brain."

"I still don't speak ancient Libyan."

He shrugged and grinned at me. "It turns out, the only vampires who speak Romanian are from Transylvania. Elves don't speak any strange language out of Tolkien. Becoming transformed into a mythic being doesn't give you the ability to speak different languages."

"Well, duh."

Cal had a pleasant, self-deprecating laugh. I wondered if I could have gotten to like this guy if I'd met him under different circumstances. Of course, I never would have met him under different circumstances. His world and mine met only where divorces were being contested.

"It's obvious in retrospect. Language is not an innate capability. You'd have to be taught Greek the same as someone born in Greece would have to be."

I followed him toward his car, then stopped abruptly when he held the passenger-side door open for me.

"Are you sure you want to take me to lunch? You didn't have much luck last time you took me out to eat."

"How about I take you to my place?"

"Did my mother suggest that?"

He gave me his great smile. "She might have mentioned it."

"I suppose you're planning on burning a slab of meat."

He looked disappointed in me. "I remember that you're a

vegetarian."

I nodded. "You win. I'd love to have lunch with you, Cal."

As we drove, he shared stories about how transformation that impacted the insular world of U.C. Santa Cruz. A rabidly anti-gay student had been transformed into a literal fairy and was facing even more derision from his classmates. A particularly devout student had grown little goat horns and cloven hooves and had to be assured she was a satyr rather than Satan himself, or herself. Cal, with his background in myth, was sought out by students, the administration, and the government.

He even gave me an update of the scientific side. "I was right. An ancient virus eliminated the magical way back when. It twisted the DNA and moved a section of switches into a junk fragment. Looks like another virus has reversed that, meaning people are developing what they would have had all along if it hadn't been for that long-ago disease. Best guessing is, it was around the time of the Trojan wars or the Mycenaean meltdown when the virus hit. After that, myth evaporated."

I got so engrossed in his stories that I lost track of where we were going—until he made a sharp turn into a driveway. Costal redwoods scaled the sky. A stone and glass home blended with a stark mountaintop. Far below, the Pacific Ocean glistened gray-green. Wind whipped whitecaps across the ocean's surface and a distant freighter ploughed through the sea.

They must pay professors more than I'd thought. "Nice."

"I made some lucky investments."

Really lucky. But Cal was a researcher, so he'd probably given himself every advantage. Unlike me, whose big investment was paying down student loans.

Cal's place was nice, with no evidence of either women or decorators. Black and white photographs of snow-covered mountains and tumbledown temples covered the few open spaces on bookcase-lined walls. Native American rugs covered polished redwood floors. A table piled high with books separated a couple of cushy armchairs. Most of those books were Greek to me, literally, but I recognized the Gorgon's head on several.

He's not interested in you, I reminded myself. *He's researching.* There was a big difference. Cal's kick-ass body and quick sense of humor made me want to forget the difference and persuade myself that Cal would go for a too-smart Eurasian woman with a figure like the proverbial board and a genetic inability to giggle and coo.

Cal offered iced tea or a glass of wine, seemed content when I picked the tea, and futzed in his kitchen for a few minutes while I checked out his books.

I had to give him credit. He didn't have a single book I'd be caught dead reading. And I read a lot. About the closest I could find to readable was a collection of military-based alternate history fantasies. That wasn't close at all.

"If you wouldn't mind grabbing a couple of tomatoes off the vine, I'll finish the salads." Cal pointed out his back door where half an acre of garden gradually transitioned to first-growth Costal Sequoia forest.

Cal hadn't just had a *little* luck in his investments. I couldn't even imagine how much a piece of property like this would set someone back. Property taxes alone were probably as much as I'd made at Hale, Storm, and Stunk.

"Coming up."

I slipped off the Jimmy Choo's my mother had bought me and padded out to Cal's backyard in bare feet.

Sure enough, Cal had staked up a dozen tomato plants. Santa Cruz soil had become too precious for agricultural use, but it was among the most fertile in the world. The tomato plants vied for space with grapevines, neat rows of lettuce, cauliflower, zucchini, artichokes, and, grossly, Brussels sprouts. A massive avocado tree climbed toward the sky, dark fruit bending the branches under its weight.

I picked two of the ripest looking tomatoes and carried them back into Cal's kitchen. "You don't actually eat the Brussels sprouts, do you?"

"You don't like Brussels sprouts?"

"It's my understanding that they were invented by some cruel botanists solely for the purpose of torturing children."

"My mother used canned Brussels sprouts to reward me when I'd done something especially brilliant." He almost pulled off that cruel lie, but his lip twitched just the slightest bit.

"Evidence in the nature vs. nurture debate. You grew up sick because of the perverse things done to you as a child."

"I picked up a honey-poppy-seed dressing at Trader Joe's. You don't have to take a drug test anytime soon, do you? The poppy-seeds might set it off."

"No job interviews on the horizon."

"They wanted to do random drug testing at the University but they realized they'd have to fire most of their professors. You sure I can't interest you in a glass of wine?"

"Let me guess. You brew it from your own grapes."

"Save that wine for special occasions."

"I'll stick with the tea."

Lunch, the salad, a nutty-flavored bread with olive oil to dip it in and a blueberry cheesecake for dessert, was to die for. If Cal wanted to ravage me, this would be the time.

* * * *

He pulled his chair closer to mine. "So, can we talk about snakes?"

Bummer. It wasn't ravaging, but he had fed me. "Talk away."

I would have said 'talk is cheap,' but I'm a lawyer. Talk costs by the minute.

"You first noticed the snakes when?"

I told him about my experience in the courtroom and how I'd tried to get rid of them.

He wrinkled his forehead. "Your mother said something about an operation."

"My mother talks too much."

"You aren't interested in losing them any more?"

"Of course not. They're part of me."

He scribbled something in a palmtop computer. "They've cost you your job, and landed you in jail. A simple operation would return you to your previous state, but you won't even consider it. You wouldn't refuse to have a cancerous tumor removed, would you? Even though the cancer would be part of you?"

Cal's words hit me like a surprise witness. I'd adjusted to the snakes too quickly. I'd accepted living things with minds of their own extruding from my skull as if this was perfectly normal.

"Have you heard of anyone having their new, uh, features removed?"

Cal shrugged. "I haven't heard of any."

Interesting. I excused myself and called Becky to see if she had heard of any.

She promised to look into any sudden increase in cosmetic surgery, demanded to know what I was up to. When I just happened to mention Cal's mountaintop home, she told me I'd be an idiot if I let him get away and hung up on me.

The rest of Cal's questions centered on how the snakes worked—and proved that Cal was about as interested in my non-snake side as he was in cottage cheese.

So, I talked about snakes.

When I said I could communicate with them, he got excited. When I told him about blowing up the air mattress, he jumped up and started pulling books out of his cases, flipping through, shoving in bookmarks, and generally having that weird kind of fun that appeals only to academics.

If another man had asked to blindfold me, I would have looked forward to wild sex. With Cal it was more of the tricks I'd pulled in the cop-bar. Okay, Cal might not be Mr. Right. Would it be so horrible if he'd at least tried to take advantage of my blindfolded state to steal a kiss?

He finally did kiss me, after three hours of cross-examination any lawyer would have been proud of. But kisses on my cheek didn't count. The girls liked it, though. Maybe they thought taking it slow was romantic.

"I'll call you," he said as we loaded into his car and headed down toward my apartment.

"Sure." Was he going to call and ask for a boy-girl date, rather than a scholar-subject date? I let myself hope.

"I may need to confirm some details."

That answered the question. No boy-girl dates.

Sharon wound her little snake body around my neck and sent reassuring thoughts my way. She thought I was wonderful, smart, sexy, and a great catch—even if no human males did.

If I ever ran into a male snake, I just might get lucky. The thought didn't fill me with elation.

"Thanks for lunch," I told Cal when he pulled up in front of my apartment.

"This is just the start. You're going to make my career."

Just what a girl wants to hear, right? I shook his hand, got out, and went up to my apartment.

* * * *

I'd decorated my apartment in a Japanese minimalist style, featuring a couple of large calligraphy posters I'd made myself, back when I'd studied Kendo and learned that Japanese penmanship uses the same exact strokes as Japanese swordsmanship.

Cool, huh?

Then there was my Japanese tea table and its stools—a.k.a. launching pad for Lisa. Add in the futon and that was pretty much it. Stark, clean, uncluttered. Just the way I wanted it. The sleeping bag and air mattress went into a closet after I woke up.

I didn't recognize it when I walked in.

"Surprise." My mother and Lisa applauded themselves and yanked me through the now bright yellow living-dining area and then into what had once been my bedroom. My now-bubblegum pink bedroom. It was just as well my mother was living there because I'd never get to sleep with all that pink. The frilly white princess frame they'd put around my bed might obscure some of the color, but it had its own problems. This was so not me.

"I made Lisa's lowlife ex-boyfriend turn over her stuff," my mother announced. "That's where the sofa and loveseat came from. And Lisa had a real dining room set instead of that sawed-off table of yours. How could you even sit at that—it was so short? I had no idea you were living like a pauper, Erin. The only TV you had was a four-inch screen job designed for people to watch while they're driving. And your bed? You always wanted a princess bed. Ta-da."

Actually, *she* had always wanted a princess bed. Since she was sleeping in it, you might argue this was fair. Except, much as I loved her, I hoped that my mother hadn't permanently moved in with me. For one thing, I didn't think my father would be happy about that.

They'd fixed what they saw as my TV issue. A flat panel screen now dominated my living room, huge speakers blared out 24-hour news to either side of the TV.

"Your apartment décor was more right for a jail cell than for a young woman," my mother continued. "I got rid of those ugly Chinese scribbles and bought Monet prints. And finally we replaced your funky plates with Target stoneware. What did you do, pick up seconds at the Good Will?"

I heard a scrabbling sound from my office. The nightmare wasn't over.

My perfect sister stalked out, her five-year-old son in tow.

"Hi, Jade," I said.

"You didn't even tell me mother was coming." My sister's motto was, never greet when you can attack.

"She surprised me."

"Come in and take a look at your office."

I wanted to cry. Instead I let my sister drag me into my office, which now resembled a Hollywood set. "I got the law books on sale by the foot," Jade effused. "I asked for a mix of red and green and it's perfect. Anyone who visits you here will think you're supersuccessful."

A huge mahogany-colored desk, equipped with an oversized leather executive chair, dominated the room. Bookcases lined all the walls with a slim break for the window. Lisa's futon was shoved into a corner. I didn't think she'd be able to open it and the door at the same time.

"We know you're going through a tough time, Aunt Erin," my nephew Franky said. "Mom and grandma thought you'd feel better if they fixed up your house."

I let out the breath I'd been holding for a scream session, and closed my mouth. I was so not going to lose it in front of my nephew. I was going to be gracious. I'd find a way to pay them back for all this stuff and replace it with something to my own taste, some day.

"You guys have been working hard."

"I told that nice Cal boy to keep you occupied a little longer," my mother said. "But we were able to get just about everything the way we knew you'd want it."

Gracious is one thing. Stupid is something else. "The old plates you replaced with nice stoneware? They were eighteenth century Kakiemon from Japan. You did keep them, didn't you? I paid two thousand dollars for the set and that was a bargain."

"Oops." Franky's eyes filled with tears. "Grandma put them in a box and I tried to carry them to my mom in your closet. Except they were heavy. I sort of," he scuffed his sneakered foot on the floor. "Okay, I fell."

Oh, shit. Let's just ruin everyone's day, Erin.

"That's why they invented glue," I told my nephew.

From the look on my mother's face, I'd given the wrong answer. Again.

"We took the trash out to the dumpster," my mother reported. "I'm afraid that the collectors came."

Which meant my tea table was also gone.

I reminded myself of the reasoning behind Japanese simplicity—getting hung up on possessions, even beautiful and sparse possessions, was contrary to Zen.

My self-lecture didn't help.

"I cooked a roast for dinner," my mother proclaimed. "Once we eat, we'll all feel better."

Fortunately, I was still full from lunch, because my mother's roasts involved cooking everything in one pot. I couldn't even eat potatoes after they'd stewed for hours in meat juice.

I turned off the television, overriding objections from both Franky and Jade, then joined my family and Lisa at the table.

Mother served up huge chunks of meat. I put a couple of asparagus stalks on my plate so I would look like part of the celebration.

My mother insisted on a prayer: for once, she kept it mercifully short. Afterwards, we had blissful silence as the house demolition crew replaced the calories they'd spent turning my carefully balanced apartment into a monster home.

"You're not eating meat." Franky's whisper was loud enough, and wet enough, I had to back away from him.

"I don't eat meat," I explained.

"Sort of like I won't eat lima beans?"

Franky was pretty smart for a five-year-old, but I didn't know how to explain vegetarianism to him.

"It's a little like that," I admitted.

"But what about them?"

"You mean your mom and grandmom?"

He giggled. "Not them, the snakes. Don't they like meat?"

His mom had cut his beef into bite-sized chunks and he fished one up with his fingers and held it close to my head.

Jennifer flicked out and grabbed it.

Jade screamed and yanked Franky away from me, clutching him to her breast.

"Sorry, Jade. Maybe this isn't such a good—"

"Get those creatures away from my baby." Jade didn't drop the decibel level, but she switched from pure noise to words. "I knew there was something wrong with you, Erin. But I wouldn't guess you'd attack your own nephew."

"The girls didn't—"

"Is that what you call them? The girls? Like they're your *children*? That is so disgusting. They're snakes, Erin. Snakes. You know, slimy crawly creatures that live under rocks and kill people. Who persuaded Eve to eat the apple? Remember? Snakes, that's who. And mom says you won't even get them cut off. I can't believe I wasted my entire day trying to make things nicer for you. I felt sorry for you. Sorry? What a laugh. You are one of them, aren't you?"

"Jade, I—"

"I don't need to talk to you." She yanked the protesting Franky to the door. "I'm glad Franky broke your stupid Kikkoman china."

"Kakiemon," I said. "Kikkoman is a brand of soy sauce."

That answer didn't heal our family difficulties. Jade slammed my door hard enough to knock a Monet print from the wall.

"What a shame," my mother said. "You really have to learn to control your animals if you're going to keep them."

I was tempted to slam the door too, except I lived here.

"We can't expect normal people to understand," Lisa said. "People like us are different. Everyone is afraid of differences."

"She's my sister."

"She's also a mom," my mother reminded me. "To a mom, everything is about her baby's safety. Think about how you felt about your dog, how you feel about those snakes. Now imagine if it was a helpless little human baby."

Okay, my mother was right. My sister's reaction had been wrong, but understandable. And Lisa was right, too. People were going to fear differences, no matter what the law said.

"Maybe we should settle down, have some ice cream, and watch TV," my mother said.

TV sounded about as attractive as having a dentist drill my teeth without Novocain, but I didn't have anything better to suggest.

The super-expensive flat-screen plasma television gave us a choice between a continuous showing of replays of old Buffy the Vampire Slayer segments and the 24-hour news.

It turned out that 24-hour news was pretty much the same as Buffy. Except Buffy had more sympathy for the vampires.

Chapter 16

The D.A. took only three weeks to get ready to try Vic the Vampire.

The judge dropped the gag order and Andrew Deat, the District Attorney, went on television pontificating about protecting citizens from vampires, werewolves, and other once-mythical monsters. Deat looked to be unopposed in the upcoming election, but he was a politician. He saw a chance to play on popular fears to garner himself extra votes—always a winning strategy.

Deat's speech was a masterpiece of innuendo. He mouthed hypocritical verbiage about the *possibility* that Vic was non-representative, that this was *not* a case against all of the vampires—not against every person impacted by this mysterious disease that had turned formerly law-abiding citizens into magical creatures. But he used words like 'might,' 'maybe,' and 'we aren't saying at this time.' His listeners were supposed to be suspicious of all the transformed, no matter how law abiding they might appear to be.

The first day of the proceedings, Vic Ventoro, heavily manacled and in his prison jump suit despite our protests, was half-dragged into court. Two bailiffs, their sidearms drawn and ready, stood behind him.

We protested again, of course. It would be hard to imagine a way to prejudice a jury more, but Judge Hilz rejected our arguments. He wasn't going to have any escapes from his courtroom.

At least the jury draw was encouraging. There were three obviously transformed members, as well as couple I wasn't sure about. Several were traditional ethnic minorities—people whose experience with prejudice might incline them toward giving Vic a fair hearing.

I had mixed feelings about the women in the draw. Women tend to be reasonable and better listeners than men. But sexual assault hits close to home for most women. Mona and I could only keep our eyes and ears open during *voir dire*.

We needn't have bothered.

Deat, playing lead prosecutor although he hadn't led a case in a decade, demanded that the transformed be stricken before *voir dire* began.

Mona reminded the judge that their transformation had in no way stopped them from being citizens with full rights and responsibilities. Excluding them from the trial would be equivalent to excluding blacks from the trial of a black, or women from the trial of another woman.

I liked her speech better than Deat's, but Judge Hilz didn't ask my opinion. He excused the three obvious, the two questionable, and one more I wouldn't have guessed was transformed at all, leaving the jury pool a far more homogeneous set of non-transformed Santa Cruz residents. Taking Mona's message, if not her intent, to heart, he also asked the two black members whether serving in a jury would inconvenience them. One admitted it would, and he was excused as well.

Mona let me ask the *voir dire* questions so that she could watch the potential jurors react to me—snakes on full display.

I'd predicted that reaction wouldn't be good—I was right. One guy seemed interested in the snakes was really checking out my figure. He was excluded almost instantly.

After four hours of questions, Mona and I asked that five of the jurors be excused for cause. They were hateful about the impaired, and had read the newspapers and followed the TV accounts of their case, making up their mind about Vic's guilt before the first witness was brought to the stand.

Hilz denied every one of our arguments.

Which meant we had to use preemptory challenges to eliminate jurors who should never have been brought near the trial. Under the severe limits on the defense's preemptory challenges, we could only eliminate the very worst.

By three o'clock, when the judge finally called a recess, we had our jury. Seven men and five women, including only one Chicana, would judge Vic Ventoro's guilt or innocence.

I couldn't decide whether to hope for a hung jury, or for Hilz to make biased decisions to the point where we could win an appeal. Either way, what should have been an easy case looked impossible.

A hostile crowd of reporters met us as Mona and I left the courthouse. Ventoro's case was the first of a number of feeble cases brought, nationwide, against the transformed, and the media seemed intent on playing it up. Reporters from both national networks and local stations played interview-ambush on us. Most of their questions followed the line of, "how dare you protect a vampire rapist?"

Mona outdid herself. She spoke of California's tradition of accepting individual choice, reminded them that consent by the alleged victim nullified rape, and said she trusted the jury to do their duty, regardless of their personal fears.

If Mona believed that, she was the only person within a thousand miles who did. Naturally, her speech never made it past the studios. She certainly didn't convince anyone out there in TV-land.

When Deat came out, the reporters dropped us like yesterday's newspaper. The D.A.'s take on the jury selection had a different a slant from Mona's. He emphasized that jurors are responsible for keeping our streets are safe and our woman protected. From there, he launched into an election speech, with statistics on all the criminals and monsters *he'd* convicted and on how we needed stability in these difficult times. With Deat as distraction, Mona and I ducked away.

"I'm still working on the money thing," she told me when we were far enough from the shouting to make ourselves heard. "Hilz isn't being cooperative."

"Based on today, you're fighting a lost battle. He doesn't want to help us, period."

"You missed the last bar association meeting. We have some support there. Even your ex-boss backed me up."

I appreciated all the support I could get. I just wish it came with money attached.

"I've gotten calls from other transformed individuals," I admitted. "The Ventoro case has helped me with publicity."

"Any of them have enough money to pay for a lawyer?"

I shook my head. That was my problem. Transformed with money kept out of the way of the cops. I had all the business I could stand and would lose money on every case.

"I'll keep working on it," she said.

I shook the hand she offered, told her I'd see her in the morning when the prosecution would call Billy Orlando as its first witness, and hoofed it home. I was walking more since I'd lost my job. I couldn't afford to drive.

Cal's yellow Mustang cut across three lanes before I'd made it a block from the courthouse. "Come on. We've got to celebrate."

The sun was out and he had the convertible top down. His short-sleeved golf-style shirt showed impressive arm muscles. Damn, the man was hot.

What can I say? I jumped into the car before I'd even thought about his words.

He was moving again before I put it together. "Celebrate what? I got stuck with a jury of hateful bigots, and a judge intent on ignoring precedent, legal authority and decency."

Cal shrugged. "Oh. Were you in trial?"

I wanted to lay into him for being insensitive, for thinking everything was about him. On the other hand, hadn't I just assumed everything was about me?

My logical side won. "I'm glad one of us got good news. Let's hear it."

* * * *

Cal was celebrating the acceptance of two articles based on what he called 'the return of so-called magical demi-human characteristics.' Which was academic-speak for what I'd named the transformation. For his own peculiar reasons, I was the star of Cal's scholarly universe. I suspected it was because he was obsessed with the Greek myths. If he'd been interested in Celtic myths, the fairies and brownies could have done. Trolls and shapechangers fit with the Eastern European tradition. But Cal wouldn't listen. As far as he was concerned, I was his inspiration. Which meant we had to go out and party.

Going out conjured negative memories. The last time Cal had tried to take me out on anything like a date, I'd ended up in jail and with a roommate I couldn't afford. This time, Cal had done his research. He'd found a place that served good food and welcomed the transformed.

And played hot jazz.

In most of the world, jazz warms up after midnight, really gets cranking around four in the morning, and where the players, dancers, and simple appreciators roll into bed well after sunrise to sleep away the rest of the day.

According to the newly painted sign outside the jazz club, this had changed in Santa Cruz. You could now get jazz, twenty-four/seven.

The foursome playing when we went in was hot.

Cal got a much-needed drink into me, then dragged me out on the dance floor for some serious jitterbug.

Moments later, I realized I'd missed something spending high school dancing with my girlfriends. Dancing with a guy is better. Of course, in high school, most of the guys had been shorter than me, awkward as it's possible to be, and deathly afraid of the dance floor. A guy who knows what he's doing was a different experience entirely.

Cal twirled me around until I got dizzy, pulled me into his arms until I got hot, and draped me over his arms, legs, and body like I was a limp dishrag.

I had a blast.

We got looks from a leather-clad mix of pale-skinned and furry hoodlum- types in the back corner nursing beers, but hey, if they wanted to fly over the floor, they could take dance lessons.

By the time the band took a break, I'd worked up an appetite.

Our dinner arrived just as another band stepped in, playing a series of softer improvisations that weren't much for dancing, but that it possible to talk without being overheard by people sitting in adjacent tables.

I scored up the mental points for Cal. He'd gone all-out to find a place that served the kind of food I liked. He'd danced me into the ground. And he'd come back even after he hadn't gotten lucky the first few times we'd been together.

Then I realized that tonight's dinner and dancing equaled our third date. In my world, three dates made us a couple, of sorts. Better, it meant it was okay to follow my libido. Cal had it coming, if he wanted it.

One thing for sure: being with Cal, dancing with Cal had my body revved and ready.

I leaned back in my chair, slipped my foot out of the kitten-heeled pumps I'd worn to court, and ran my bare toes up Cal's calf.

He jerked back like I'd branded him.

That was definitely *not* the reaction I'd been hoping for.

I wanted to knock on my head and say 'hello!' Well, duh. He hasn't made any moves before we reached the three-date limit. Obvious conclusion to anyone other than snake-headed Erin. The man just isn't interested.

I sighed and pasted on a smile. In just about any circumstance, a lawyer can carry on a conversation.

"So," I said. "Tell me about your articles."

Cal's smile came back. He shoved a hunk of dark hair out of his eyes and leaned forward.

"I knew what I had was important. I went all-out and submitted one to the *Journal of Mythological Studies*, even though they'd rejected the previous seventeen articles I'd sent them. I submitted the second to *The Annals of the American Mythological Association*. *JMS* accepted me as the lead paper in a special issue they're putting out next month. And The AMA invited me to give a keynote at the annual meeting. Can you believe that? A keynote! Nobody else in the UCSC Literature Department has *ever* keynoted for a major academic society."

"I'm not surprised," I said. "You're the one who's been saying the myths were real, right? They want to recognize that."

He shook his head at my naiveté. "They've been contemptuous of me for so long, it would have been easy for them to laugh this off and move on. You should have seen some of the rejections I've gotten over the years. Phrases like 'paranoid and baffling attempts to mingle scholarship with teenage fantasy belong on obscure websites, not major peer-reviewed journals' come to mind"

"Wow. So why do you think they changed?"

He grinned. "Because of you. Werewolves and vampires are generic. Like giants. Sure there are stories about vampires, but so what? It's not directly connected to any particular myth. They would claim I had just gotten lucky. Like if I'd claimed that the David and Goliath story was true, then backed it up with a basketball player.

"Gorgons were specific," he continued. "There are fixed depictions of the Gorgons. They couldn't argue that there have always been Gorgons wandering around but nobody noticed. Wouldn't fly. So, I owe it all to you."

I bit back my reflex, which was to tell him that if he owed me so much, he could repay me by taking me to bed and showing me a good time.

After we'd eaten, Cal asked me if I wanted to dance again.

Considering how he'd reacted to my touch, I turned him down. I needed to be in court again the next morning, and if I got my hormones back in an uproar with no satisfaction in sight, I'd never sleep.

Cal had the grace to look disappointed. But he settled the bill and took me home.

Once parked in my lot, he walked me to my door. *That* was datelike.

I was waffling again. I'm not an expert on the gay male, although I've had several gay friends, but Cal didn't exude any stereotypical gay mannerisms. Maybe he was just shy? If so, I could take care of that because one thing I wasn't was shy.

At my door, he made a bit of a wavy motion, like he couldn't decide whether he had to kiss me or not.

I projected the sort of mental commands at him that I used to talk to the girls. *Kiss me, idiot.*

It worked. He did.

His lips felt good against mine and for just a moment I thought there might actually be some tongue.

Before I could tell for sure, my apartment door swung open and my mother popped out.

"Oh. Sorry. I didn't know you were—let me just go back inside—uh."

If she'd just done it without all the talking, or even immediately after talking, who knew what might have happened. But she just stood there flapping her gums. By the time she'd finished, neither Cal nor I were in the mood for tongue-tangling.

He made his excuses and fled down to his car.

My mother watched him. "Nice car."

"Yeah."

"Guy has a car like that, it would get me all hot."

"I'm starting to feel like this is a too much information kind of conversation, Mother."

"Before your dad, of course. If you want a good-looking guy like that to come back, you've got to take matters into your own hands. And into your own mouth."

I was getting where she was heading, but I was sure when she giggled and winked at me. "Give a guy a blowjob, and that's a guy who's coming back for more."

This so wasn't a conversation I wanted with my mother.

* * * *

I surprised myself by falling to sleep instantly, wakening refreshed and ready to tackle Andrew Deat, Judge Hilz, and twelve angry jurists.

When I saw my car, my better-than-average mood fell like a carelessly placed coffin.

The front hood had been pried open and every wire and hose was cut. Fluids of different consistency and color had sprayed and dripped everywhere until the ground looked like Jackson Pollock painting. The tires were slashed to ribbons, and someone had taken a sledgehammer to every one of my windows.

Stylized graffiti, spraypainted over the warped and dented passenger-side door, called me a traitor. A note crammed into the ripped upholstery of my driver's seat said I'd sold out to the normals, that dating a mundane professor showed I didn't give a damn what happened to 'my people.'

I stood beside the shattered body of the first new car I'd ever owned, and cried.

Lisa came down a few minutes later, her wings pierced all along their upper lengths and fitted with rhinestones so she glistened like a rainbow.

"Oh, shit."

"Yeah." I handed her the note.

"But you're helping Vic. Why would our people turn against you?"

"We're all our own people, Lisa. Just because you have wings doesn't make you inhuman. No more than having blue eyes does. We're all just people."

She waved that argument away. "*They* think there's a difference, so there is a difference. But why come after you? I can't believe you're not doing your best in the trial."

I admitted that the trial wasn't going well. This, although the prosecution had no case.

"But is that *your* fault?"

I gestured at my car. "Somebody thinks so."

I couldn't get the image of those guys in the jazz club out of my head. The way they'd glared at me when I'd come off the dance floor with Cal. The way they'd kept looking at me when I'd laughed and chatted with him over dinner. Could they have followed me home?

It wasn't much of a lead, but it gave me something to work on. After the trial.

Lisa backed away from me, alarm written across her pretty face.

"What?"

"You looked like you were going to tear my head off. And Jennifer showed me her fangs."

"Jennifer! You know I'm not mad at Lisa."

Properly chastised, the snake growing out of my forehead drooped. Boss-snake Sharon made a hissing laugh at her sibling's discomfort. Who knew I had a little competition going between the girls?

"Uh, don't you have to be in court?"

I glanced at my watch and saw that I'd wasted too much time mourning the loss of my once-beautiful Toyota. I wasn't going to have time for the review Mona wanted. And I didn't think Judge Hilz would cut me any slack for the personal trauma of losing my car. He probably thought transformed people didn't need cars anyway.

Chapter 17

Deat had been warming up when he'd blistered the reporters' ears the previous afternoon. In his opening statement, he let Ventoro, and every transformed person, have it.

Mona gave our position in her statement—that it's not rape if both want it, that Ventoro should be judged on the facts rather than on his social status, and that the police had botched the investigation so completely, or rather never even bothered with an investigation, that it would be impossible to return anything other than a 'not guilty' verdict.

Every time she started to get rolling, though, Deat popped up with an objection. It isn't unprecedented for the prosecutor to object to the defense's opening statement. For example, the judge may have ruled that certain defenses were out of order and the defense attorney may still sneak them into their statement. That said, it's unusual and unpleasant to put up with that kind of abuse and Mona withered under the assault. Especially since Judge Hilz started sustaining Deat's objections without even requiring the D.A. to give any logic for them.

Mona finally petered out and gestured for me to get up and finish for her.

"Objection." Deat was on his feet before I even opened my mouth.

I looked to the judge. "Seems like he has to give me a chance to say something before he can object to it."

"A snake-haired female makes a mockery out of this court," Deat roared. "This is a trial, not a circus side-show."

Since Deat was the one to make a big deal of Ventoro's otherness, this wasn't fair. But then, nothing in the trial had been fair.

"Ms. Tsong?" At least Hilz was giving me a chance to respond, although I would have preferred for him to slap Deat down on his own.

"I am a member of the California and Santa Cruz bar," I said. "My hair color, style, or configuration has no bearing on the case."

"Judge Hilz. If I could—"

"You've had your say, Deat. So sit down. Tsong, you may complete your statement, but I suggest you remember my instructions to your colleague. Take one step outside the lines I've drawn, and you'll be looking at a contempt charge."

"Yes, your honor."

Being a lawyer means sucking up to judges. Deat had forgotten that. I was just glad I'd kept up my dues to the local bar association. No judge wants to offend the bar, especially since judges raise their campaign contributions from lawyers who practice in front of them.

"Objection overruled."

I summarized our case. That Ventoro and Cornelison had not engaged in *any* activity, legal or otherwise, and that Ventoro had not used force or intimidation to encourage Cornelison's agreement to engage in any said non-activity.

It was a bit of a legalistic argument, but I tried to make it plain. If there's no crime, you shouldn't convict.

After our statements, the judge called a break for lunch, and I got to buck Mona up. Her disintegration had *not* been part of the plan.

We headed for her car with food on her mind and psychological reinforcements on mine.

My breath caught in my throat when we arrived at Mona's car and spotted an envelope under Mona's windshield wiper. My name, in black crayon, was scrawled over the envelope.

I opened the envelope, took out the laser-printed note, read it, and passed it to Mona.

You're not even faking it. Treasure your thirty pieces of silver, bitch, because payback is coming.

Mona squinted at it, as if she might have read it wrong. "I don't get it. Judge Hilz has tied our hands behind our backs and it's supposed to be *your* sell-out? Why aren't they mad at him?"

"Wow, the world's just not fair. Why didn't anyone warn us that it wouldn't be easy back in law school?"

That got the faintest hint of a grin from my partner's face. That'd been the first lesson drilled into our heads.

She glanced at the note. "Think we should turn this over to the police?"

"And that would help us, how?"

"Right. Come on. Lunch is on me."

Free lunch *sounded* good. Reality was less than my ideal. She drove us to a ratty all-you-can-eat pizza place with a large *No Giants, Trolls, or 300+ Pound Humans Allowed* sign posted.

I looked at her.

"I do not weigh three hundred pounds."

"I won't patronize places that exclude the transformed."

"They only care about people who eat too much for them to make money."

Which didn't include me since every pizza they offered had meat on it.

Here's the deal. Santa Cruz is the heart of one of the most fertile agricultural areas on the planet. When I was a kid, I'd planted some lettuce seeds I got in a Raisin Bran box, and forgot them. A few weeks later, I had more lettuce than I could give away. The suckers just popped up and grew. So, a Santa Cruz restaurant had to work pretty hard to serve a salad that consisted of near-liquid brown iceberg lettuce, rock-hard beige tomatoes, and stale croutons. Oh, and a ranch dressing that tasted more like something out of a chemical plant than a ranch.

I told Mona I thought they should change their name to all-you-can-make-yourself-eat pizza.

She was predictably unsympathetic. And her pizza looked great. "Close your eyes, don't watch, and let the girls eat the meat."

Several little voices in my head whispered agreement.

I watched *her* eat instead.

* * * *

Per Judge Hilz's instructions, we were back in court at one-thirty. The judge and Deat arrived at two. I caught the faint whiff of alcohol on Deat's breath and suspected the two had bonded over a liquid lunch. Deat might have forgotten about sucking up that morning, but he was making up for lost time.

The District Attorney called Officer Billy Orlando to the stand, took him through a version of that night's activities, as far as Billy had seen them, then turned the witness over to us.

Since I'd been the one to interview Billy, I was up for cross-examination.

"Officer Orlando. You just told the jury that you arrived in time to see Mr. Ventoro rip at Ms. Cornelison's attire. Is that correct?"

"Correct."

"And you were alerted to the alleged crime by citizens who observed what is alleged to have been an attempted abduction. Correct?"

"I wouldn't say 'alleged.' Ventoro is a vampire. He deserves to be locked up."

A smattering of applause had Orlando nodding his head like he was the ringmaster at the circus.

Hilz hammered his gavel. He intended to be the only star on his show. "Answer the question, Officer Orlando."

"Uh, what was the question?"

The court reporter read back my question and Orlando wrinkled his forehead trying to hold it all in at once.

Finally he smiled as if he'd seen through a trap I'd set. "Yeah. The good citizens of Santa Cruz alerted me to a crime in progress. I responded instantly and was able to catch that man," he gave an obviously coached whole-hand point at Ventoro, "about to rape poor Ms. Cornelison."

I smiled at him, then at the jury.

"I'm second to no one, Officer Orlando, in my respect for the people of Santa Cruz and their energies to combat violent crime, especially crimes against women. What surprises me is these same citizens did nothing to hinder the horrible crime you allege Ventoro was committing in the streets of our city."

Deat stood. "Objection. Ms. Tsong is grandstanding, not asking a question."

"Sustained."

"My apologies, your honor, Officer Orlando. I'll ask more directly. Was Ventoro continuing with his alleged activities, without hindrance when you arrived?"

I guessed that Orlando hadn't reported our interview to Deat because he looked at the District Attorney, at Mona, at the judge, and at the jury, everywhere but at me while he tried to come up with an answer.

Like a tag-team wrestler whose partner is in trouble, Deat ignored the ropes and stepped in for a rescue. "Objection, your honor. I fail to see the relevance."

"Ms. Tsong?"

Thank God Orlando had enjoyed his moment of playing to the gallery rather than to the judge and jury. Judge Hilz wasn't cutting him any slack.

"Despite numerous discovery motions by defense, the prosecution has failed to produce names of any citizens who notified Officer Orlando who might have assisted in stopping the alleged crime. If such witnesses exist, we have a right to know of them, and to understand why they were not questioned by the police as part of the investigation."

"I'll allow the question."

Orlando gave me another grin. He thought he'd figured out the right answer. "When I arrived, there was only the rapist," he gave Ventoro another full-handed point, "and the poor victim."

Mona handed me an envelope. I took out the 8 by 11 photo of Ventoro, in the cop car on his way to jail.

"I'd like to introduce this police photo as defense exhibit one, your honor."

We'd vetted it through discovery so there was nothing Deat could do but steam.

I turned back to Orlando. "In your testimony, Officer Orlando, you said Ventoro came with you peacefully after the arrest. Yet you'll observe that his face shows contusions in these photos. If there was no one else there, who injured my client?"

Deat roared back, arguing that Ventoro could have been injured at a lot of times, that Cornelison could have injured him herself, that he might have self-inflicted those wounds, that I was asking Orlando for speculation rather than evidence.

I felt good about demonstrating that Orlando was lying and setting the stage for our own testimony.

Hilz called it a night, the bailiffs dragged Ventoro back to his cell, and we lawyers ran the gauntlet of the television reporters.

The major networks came down hard on me, accusing me of undermining the people's faith in the integrity of law enforcement in a time of national crisis. But a vampire-type with a microphone sneered at me. "How does it feel to be the *token magical* in Vic the Vampire's sellout, Ms. Tsong?"

His voice must have penetrated because all of a sudden, I had dozens of cameras pointing at me, and boom microphones waving in the air near my head.

"People, whether transformed or not, are people," I said. "Some are criminals. Some aren't. Fortunately, Ms. Hapsburg and I represent an innocent man. His innocence, however, has nothing to do with the strange transformation that occurred to him, as it did to millions of other citizens, including me. He's innocent not *because* he's a vampire, not despite being a vampire, but because he did not commit the crime. And that's all I'm going to say."

Telling reporters that you're done answering their questions is like throwing chum to sharks. They swarmed.

Once again, Deat let me off the hook. His bellowing about how the guilty always blame the police attracted the reporters' attention. I got away during the distraction.

I made sure Cal was nowhere in sight before launching my plan. I didn't want to drag him into the mess I suspected I'd find at the jazz club, but it certainly would have done my ego some good if he'd been waiting for me after court.

He wasn't though. So, I caught a bus.

The jazz club was between Watsonville and Corralitos, which meant I had to change buses a few times, but I'd mapped out my route the previous evening. Eventually I got there.

I couldn't help noticing a profusion of moving vans and broken-down pickup trucks hauling furniture. The closer I got to the jazz club, the more it seemed that the moving vans were moving out, and the broken-down pickups moving in.

Graffiti on low commercial buildings claimed territory for gangs whose names made me suspect they were affiliated with werewolves or vampires.

While I could understand the temptation to move closer to people like you, I hated to see it. We transformed needed to share our differences with the people left behind. We needed to mingle, needed to assert our fundamental humanity. The last thing we needed was a ghetto, an island of the weird and wonderful in a sea of plain vanilla people.

I was already feeling depressed when I got off the bus and walked the three blocks toward the jazz club.

The sky glowed red and purple as the sun plunged into the Pacific. The mountains to the east loomed dark and forbidding, with occasional electrical lights glistening like stars. The moon, huge in *harvest* phase, flirted with the mountains, occasionally hiding behind them as I walked.

Five guys on motorcycles zoomed past me, their engines roaring so loudly it shook the pavement and forced me to cover my ears.

A minute later, they were back, approaching me from behind.

The lead biker revved his engine as he pulled up, and I involuntarily jumped.

The engines cut off, leaving echoes ringing in my ears.

"Well if it isn't the lawyer, snake-girl."

I'd been mad about my car. So mad I'd wanted to go after the jerks who'd trashed it. It took until I faced the helmeted and massively large motorcycle punk that I realized coming here alone, without even letting anyone know, was dumb. It was so stupid, even the motorcycle punks probably wouldn't believe it.

I pasted on a smile. "You guys going to the jazz club, too?"

It was hard to tell under his helmet, but the biker looked like he might be one of the guys who'd been at the back of the bar the previous evening.

"Where's your boyfriend? He get tired of slumming with a magical?"

"What's this 'magical' business?"

"Oh? You think we should call ourselves impaired, like the tube says."

"I like *transformed*."

"If you like transformed so much, how come you're dating a normal?"

It would have been mortifying to explain that I wasn't actually *dating*

Cal, that I was just his research material, or that none of the transformed had asked me out. So I ignored his question. Lawyers learn to be good at ignoring questions they don't want to answer.

"Cool bikes. I've been thinking about getting myself a scooter. Vespas seem high, though. Any suggestions?"

The leader pulled off his helmet and I saw that my suspicions were right. He had been at the jazz club.

Helmet removal was part of an intimidation plan. He hurled it to the ground, stomped up to me, and stuck his chest against mine, breathed cheap wine into my face.

"You've got a lot of nerve coming around here. Don't you see the signs? This territory belongs to the Bloodsuckers."

"Bloodsuckers?" I scratched my head and used that motion to step off a bit to the side. Biker-vamp would like nothing better than to get into a shoving contest with me—especially since he outweighed me by better than a hundred pounds.

"Oh, I get it," I continued. "Vampires, they suck blood, don't they. And riding motorcycles so you're a gang. Boy, that's original. Did you go to one of the boutique branding firms in San Francisco, or did a local marketing genius come up with it?"

Even before I'd said anything, I knew keeping my mouth shut would be smart. Unfortunately, I'd already proven that I was going through a phase of the dumbs.

"That sarcastic lip of yours is going to get you into trouble." He exposed his fangs and closed the distance again, his hands in tight fists.

A hissing sound filled the air and I felt my girls strain at my head.

"Hey, cool," a new voice said. "Check out the headdress action. She's got fangs too. I vote we make her an honorary bloodsucker. That'll take care of any territory issues."

The speaker was an adult, but no one would mistake him for a stereotypical vampire. He displayed a full head of bright red hair, a facefull of freckles, and buckteeth that extended nearly as long as his diminutive fangs. His voice sounded ready to crack at a moment's notice.

The vampire who'd menaced me pulled back. "You kidding, Benny? She's got snakes in her *hair*, she doesn't suck blood, and she's letting down our brother, Vic. For that, we make her an honorary bloodsucker?"

"She's got fangs."

"My cat has fangs, but she's not a bloodsucker."

"Yeah, Justin. But—"

"But nothing. We vampires stick together. She's not one of us, so she's one of them. With the half-assed way she's defending Vic, she's not even a friendly."

"Maybe we could make her an auxiliary, man. We've got lots of non-vampire auxiliaries. That's the cool thing about being a vampire. Chicks everywhere." Benny's voice sounded wistful. Chicks might be *almost* everywhere, but I doubted that many swung Benny's way. He'd probably been the classic nerd before the transformation. He still was.

"Sure, Benny. *You* make her an auxiliary. You want to bite her with those things dripping off her head? Go right ahead. Me, I'd rather not worry about her biting me back."

Benny looked at me, then looked away. "An honorary auxiliary, then."

I should have left well alone with them talking, not acting. But I hadn't come to run away. I'd come to find out who'd trashed my car and to do something about it.

"I'm a vegetarian so I don't want to be a bloodsucker. I do want to know who thinks I'm not doing my job for Ventoro."

Justin, the big vampire grinned. "That would be easy, snake-girl. Look around. Not just the eight of us. I mean, look around the neighborhood. Down the street, see that woman peeking out the door? She's out on bail, supposedly for biting a cop. Across the street are two of the cutest little vamps you'd ever want to meet—Hector and Hermione. Twins. They're only three, but their dad's in the lockup and their mother ran away from them because they were vampires and she wasn't. They're living with their grandmother but I don't know if they're going to make it because only about one out of twenty of us still has a job and it's getting tough making ends meet.

"Want more? How about Benny, here? Benny, want to tell her about your sister? She wasn't a vamp, she was a shifter. A little werelynx, wasn't she? Out in the Cowell Redwoods, a cop shot her with a silver bullet. Just for fun. Killed her dead. I could list more, but it wouldn't matter to you, would it? Because you're special. You're like a normal except you've got snakes in your hair. You're fancy, not common. You've got a college professor who thinks you hung the moon while the rest of us are trash.

"Short answer. *Everyone* here thinks you're doing a lousy job. Because, guess what? You're doing a lousy job. Does Deat cut you a paycheck, or does he bribe you out of petty cash?"

I hadn't guessed Justin would have something of the poet in him: he'd looked like a loser. Then again, he *had* trashed my car. Poet or not, he was a loser.

"That's so much bull."

"Is it, snake-girl? How come the other chick, Mona, and I'd like a few hours with her mona-ing under me, has spent more time with Vic than you have? And how come you're out partying and cutting up the floor with some normal when you should be getting ready for the first day of the trial? How come the only time you spend with vampires is when you're slumming in their club?"

I could tell him the truth—that I'd been out with Cal because he'd asked me, but how desperate did that sound? The only alternative was to go on the offensive.

"Who died and made you the king of who gets to date what? You guys date who you want and call them auxiliaries, but if I go out on one date with an untransformed guy, that's not okay? Now that's really fair."

"Maybe she'd go out with you if you asked her," Benny suggested.

Justin pulled back from me like I'd developed a fatal case of halitosis. "Are you kidding? Imagine opening your eyes in the morning and having one of those snakes staring down at you. And they're poisonous, right? One wrong move and she doesn't throw a flowerpot at you, she lets the snakes bite you and you die. I don't think so."

That was when it finally dawned on me that Cal's problem wasn't that he was gay. I mean, hello. The gay thing had just been *my* excuse for him not hitting on me—like, any guy who doesn't want me must be gay. Cal didn't want me because he didn't want to wake up with the girls. I was used to scaring guys away with my sarcasm and what some dates had called my *snarky manner*. Those hadn't gone away—the snakes had added another hurdle to the list.

"I want to talk about my car," I said. "You guys trashed it. I want you to fix it. You owe me."

Justin tried a manly laugh, but it came out a giggle, which was seriously non-intimidating. "Why should we fix your car? What are you going to do, turn us over to the police?"

The girls wove a little dance on my head and Justin stepped back further.

"Sorry that your car got cut up, snake-girl," one of the other vampires said. "But it wasn't us who did it. We were busy last night. Even if we did it, we're not in the car repair business."

"If you didn't do it, how did you know it was cut? I said it was trashed, not that someone had gone after it with a knife."

I was pretty proud of my catch. It was the kind of thing Matlock would have caught on that old TV show.

Justin grinned. "Busted. It *was* us who tore your car apart. And guess why? To send you a warning. Since you came all the way out here, I'll give you one more warning. Stop hanging around with non-magicals. We see you dating one of them, it's not your car that gets cut. Maybe one of the boys will take your mom for a ride. She is living with you, isn't she? Or that little fairy you hang out with. She'd look good as a hood ornament on my truck. So, no more dating normals. And shape up at the trial. If Ventoro goes up the river, you're going to be fitted with concrete boots."

"That's—"

"Sonofabitch, you can't shut up, can you?" He shook his head. "Take her home, Benny. Speaking of auxiliaries, you haven't gotten any lately. And I don't think snake-girl wants to listen to jazz tonight after all."

Benny's reaction was not what a girl wants to see. He wrinkled his nose, sweated, and edged away as if afraid to breath the same air with me. "She's got poisonous snakes."

If Cal was right about me being unique, there wasn't any snake-headed guy out there waiting for me. I was alone.

"I think I have some say in this."

"Take her home, Benny."

"But—"

"Hey, you're the one who wanted to make her a member."

Chapter 18

I felt upbeat as I walked to court the next morning. I'd put some serious doubt on Orlando's testimony, I'd faced down the vampires who'd trashed my car—and lived to tell about it—I'd gotten a ride home from a vampire who seemed pathetically glad I didn't poison him, and my car was gone from the apartment parking lot—obviously Justin had reconsidered his refusal to take responsibility for the damage he and his blood-sucking brotherhood had done.

My good mood continued through the morning's testimony.

Deat called additional witnesses to testify that no police brutality had taken place, responding to my not-so-subtle hints the previous day.

Mona and I let him parade the so-called evidence without much objection or harsh cross-examination. Deat had fallen into our trap. We didn't plan to make a case for brutality. We were trying to demonstrate that Ventoro had been beaten *before* the cops arrived—which meant that Orlando had lied about coming on Ventoro in the process of committing assault and rape on Cornelison. Orlando should have stuck to his original story that civilians had already broken up any romantic interlude, except then he would have had to justify his neglect in not catching any witness names.

Just before lunch, Deat called the sergeant in charge of admissions to the county lockup. He testified that Ventoro had arrived with injuries.

Mona handled cross-examination for this.

"So, Sergeant, you are saying that Ventoro did *not* receive injuries while in your custody. None?"

He hemmed and hawed at that, finally admitting the possibility that some inmates might have objected to the horrible crime Ventoro committed, but that Ventoro had definitely been beat up before he'd arrived.

"And you heard the testimony by the other officers indicating that Mr. Ventoro had already suffered those injuries before coming into their custody, is that correct?"

"I heard them."

"Then where, sergeant, did Mr. Ventoro suffer those injuries? Who beat him up? If it wasn't the police, and it wasn't the inmates in your jail, and if there was no one else there when Officer Orlando arrived on the scene, who—"

"Objection. Calls for speculation on the part of the witness. Council is badgering the witness. I completely object to this line of questioning."

"Mr. Deat established the line of questioning, your honor. I'm merely attempting to—"

"Sustained. Ms. Hapsburg, please confine your questions to what the witness properly can or should know and do not ask for speculation."

"No further questions at this time, your honor. Although I would ask that the Sergeant make himself available for follow-up questioning regarding Mr. Ventoro's mistreatment, excuse me, treatment, while in the custody of the County Jail."

"Objection."

"Sustained. The term 'mistreatment' will be stricken from the record. The jury will disregard Ms. Hapsburg's slip of the tongue. And Hapsburg?"

"Your honor?"

"Another slip of the tongue like that and you're looking at a five hundred dollar fine for contempt. Got it?"

"Yes, your honor. Sorry, your honor." But when she turned back to me, she gave me a big wink. As my snakes would say, 'Yesh!'

After lunch, Deat sprung a surprise witness on us.

"Your honor, I apologize for not introducing this witness during discovery. At that time, the Federal Bureau of Investigations had not created its Office of Impaired Individuals. I received word over lunch that the FBI OII has made the Chief of their Vampires and Vampire Terrorism branch available to us. Special Agent Samuels is an expert on vampires and vampire terrorism, or VVT as they call it. His evidence will demonstrate that Ventoro's criminal acts are no aberration but are, exactly what the people of Santa Cruz must face if vampires are allowed to mingle with the unprotected."

"I object." Both Mona and I were all over this one. Mona sat back down, deferring to me as the expert on the transformed.

Hilz nodded at me to go ahead. Another example of showboating coming back to bite the prosecution.

"Your honor, we are trying an alleged crime, not some statistical pattern. Mr. Deat could bring in an expert to show that men are more likely to commit rape than women and it would be laughed out of the court. Although it might be statistically true, it's hardly relevant to the guilt or innocence of one particular man. The question is not whether *some* vampires may have committed *some* crimes, but whether Mr. Ventoro has committed the alleged assault and attempted rape of Ms. Cornelison. Mr. Deat has given us no reason to believe that Agent Samuels has any knowledge of the alleged incident, of the alleged perpetrator, or any useful information regarding vampires at large, given that they have only existed for a few weeks. Then there's the issue of jurisdiction. Assault and attempted rape are state crimes, and I fail to see how the FBI has any relevance to these alleged incidents. Finally, if Mr. Deat had intended to pursue this line of investigation, he should have included the FBI on his witness list, even if he had not been prepared to enumerate which agent might be available."

"Mr. Deat?"

Deat danced for a few minutes, basically repeating what he'd already said. When we'd been in discovery, this resource hadn't been available. Given that the FBI now had such experts, it seemed stupid not to take advantage of the information our federal tax dollars were paying for.

"I'll allow this witness," Judge Hilz decided. "But I warn you, Mr. Deat, don't make a practice out of surprises. This isn't Perry Mason."

"No, your honor."

Agent Samuels trashed vampires as blood-sucking criminals.

Mona and I objected until we'd each rang up a couple of thousand in contempt fines. Then we sat on our hands while Deat took a showboating trial and turned it into a church revival meeting. Agent Samuels finished his statistical analysis of vampire crime and launched a bizarre theory that the vampires actually evicted the souls of the humans who had resided in their bodies before the transformation and replaced them with demon souls. From what I could tell, his evidence came from the old *Buffy the Vampire Slayer* TV series.

I couldn't hold back and got myself another five-hundred dollar fine for objecting too strongly.

Judge Hilz and the jury ate it up.

* * * *

We were packing up our stuff for the day when Ventoro grabbed me. "What does it take to appeal a conviction based on incompetence by the defense team?"

I felt like I'd been slapped in the face. I was defending this jerk for free, had just been fined twenty-five hundred dollars I didn't have for trying to stop a railroading, and now my client was accusing me of incompetence.

"What the hell is that about?" Mona might have developed psychic powers because she plucked the words directly from my head.

"I've been talking to the other vamps in the lockup. They agree that neither of you is up to this job." He gestured at Mona. "You're not magical." He stuck a thumb in my direction. "And nobody knows about you. I mean, a Gorgon? Just what is *that* nonsense? Did anyone ever make a horror movie about a Gorgon?"

"We're lawyers," I reminded him. "Which happens to be what you need right now. And there are plenty of horror movies about lawyers. We're doing our best to make sure you get a fair shake, but if you think you could do better with another legal team, I suggest you talk to the judge. Because by the time an appeal based on incompetent defense makes its way through the courts, you'll be old and gray."

The bailiffs led Ventoro out, and Mona stuffed the rest of her papers into her oversized briefcase—a briefcase, that could contain a full-sized pizza with no more problems than a few extra grease stains on the nearby legal papers.

"Want to go out for a drink?"

I considered my alternatives. I could go out drinking with Mona, or I could go home and see what new disasters my mother and Lisa had inflicted on my apartment.

"A drink sounds great."

Mona led the way to The Catalyst, a Santa Cruz tradition that, I discovered shortly after we walked in, was now an outlet for Pleasure Pizza. No mystery why Mona picked the club.

My partner ordered a beer and a large pie. I settled for a Margarita and found what I hoped would be a quiet corner.

I didn't see any signs banning the transformed, and the bouncer hadn't looked twice at my snake-hair, but the crowd ran mostly to normals. I'd been tossed out by both normals and vampires, so I was gun-shy and prepared to lay low if I had the chance. At the very least, I wanted to see whoever was attacking me first.

"I hit Hilz up about paying you again." Mona returned from the hundred-foot-long bar with a beer so big, I'd be up all night peeing if I drank it. "He asked why should he pay you when you're doing it for free?"

"Figures." Maybe I should have gone home to Mother. At least she'd pay for dinner.

"But you're doing a good job. And I'm sorry about the fines."

"I got an A in my bankruptcy class."

"But you can't use bankruptcy to get out of—oh, I get it. A joke. Very funny."

Hey, I knew I was humor impaired.

If my joke wasn't funny, the man I saw looming behind Mona wasn't even funnier.

"Agent Samuels. Isn't this a surprise?"

"Don't make it out of San Francisco often. I've heard of this place but never been here," the FBI agent said. He was drinking Coke. God forbid that he violate the FBI clean-cut image by having a beer. But he also carried a super-giant deluxe extra-everything pizza. "Mind if I join you?"

"You sure you want to sit with the team that's going to cut your liver out and feed it to the jury in cross tomorrow?"

He put the pizza on the table, close to Mona. "No problem. You know the nation *needs* to win this one, and that it's going to win this one. The President himself called Hilz last night."

I hadn't voted for the incumbent President, but that didn't mean I though he'd stoop low enough to interfere in a criminal trial. Which is what I told Samuels.

"You're pretty funny," he said. "This disease is the biggest political story since the Civil War. Of course he's involved."

Samuels mentioned, almost as a throwaway, that he'd gotten an early look at one of Cal's articles. The FBI was funding Cal's work, and planned to use his information to criminally profile the impaired. "Fairies don't seem inclined toward criminal behavior," he explained. "We're having the most problems with vampires and shapeshifters."

"Maybe because fairies are too wimpy to cause problems."

He shrugged. "That's not what the statistics show. We've got population subgroups who just enjoy being criminals."

"I ran into a vampire last night who told me that the unemployment rate for vampires is ninety-five percent. Wouldn't that explain criminal activity more than some genetic flaw?"

Samuels made a patting move in the direction of my shoulder, but I noticed he kept out of range of the girls. "Save your sympathy for someone who appreciates it. Of course they're unemployed—vampires don't *want* to work. They read books where all the vampires are rich and elegant and want to be like that."

I'd already spent too long listening to Samuels' nonsense, but I had a barely touched Margarita. Walking away from a drink I couldn't afford was tough. I decided I'd rather waste my money than listen to Samuels. "I've got to go. Mona, you coming?"

"Uh, I think I'll stay and talk to Agent Samuels."

I didn't look back as I walked toward the door, but I didn't have to. My brain was getting used to the signals that the girls sent. So, I saw Mona slide closer to Samuels. Gross.

It got me thinking, though. What were the odds that the FBI had just happened to send a sexy young Agent who exactly fit what Mona was looking for in a man, considering she'd given up on men?

I didn't think it was coincidence.

* * * *

My mother and Lisa were wallpapering the living room when I got home—red wallpaper with large raised gold flowers. I failed to suppress my shudder. It wasn't just not Zen—that part of my apartment was gone. It was horrible.

My mother assured me that it was 1960s retro. I suspected it was a mistake someone had left on the rack until my mother had discovered it.

She forced me to admire the gaudy wallpaper before popping out with her big news. "Cal called."

"He say what he wanted?"

"We both know what he *wants*, darling. Oh, and the apartment manager called, too. Maybe he's ready to fix the toilet."

Wouldn't that be nice? When I stopped by to visit him, though, that wasn't it. He was very sorry but that we had to move out. Since my apartment was on month-to-month, he'd leased it out to someone else.

He looked embarrassed, and he should have. We both knew this wasn't about leases. This was about a woman with snakes in her hair and her fairy roommate.

"I hear there are some nice places over between Watsonville and Corralitos," he said. "You can get some real bargains."

"Serve me valid eviction papers and then watch out. I'm a lawyer and I'm sick of getting pushed around."

I concentrated hard on keeping the girls under control—they wanted to join in the attack, but I managed to keep their movement down to a couple of small twitches. Still, the apartment manager spasmed almost in time with the girls. Sue me, but it felt good to be scary.

He looked away and ignored me until I went home.

"Is he coming to fix the toilet?" my mother asked.

"Once we move out."

"That's absurd. I've spent thousands of dollars turning this dump into something you can be proud to live in, sweetheart."

I didn't have anything to say. I spent my first eighteen years explaining myself to my mother, trying to help her understand why I was different, why I didn't appreciate some of the things she did for me. That effort had made both of us miserable and hadn't changed anything. My mother could no more stop 'helping me' than she could fly to the moon.

"Uh, the toilet stopped dripping," Lisa said.

"Great. You had to have your little joke, didn't you, Erin," my mother said. "Very funny. You got me."

"But I'm not getting any water out of the sink either."

The manager was being sneaky. Rather than evict us, he'd make things unpleasant. Three women sharing an apartment with no running water would get highly unpleasant, in a hurry.

"I'm unemployed, losing a case that should be a no-brainer, my partner is flirting with an FBI Agent on the other side, the only guy to date me in months only kissed me because of psychic commands, and now we have no running water and the manager is trying to force us to move to the werewolf ghetto where I almost got mugged last night. At least things can't get any worse."

"Oh, I almost forgot to tell you," my mother said. "You got something from the city or county or something. An official-looking letter. Maybe they've decided to pay you after all."

My fingers fumbled as I opened the letter. Could I really have hit bottom?

Nope. Things were still going downhill, maybe even accelerating. The vampires hadn't collected my car for repair after all. The city had picked it up as a hazard and wanted me to pay an eight hundred dollar towing and storage fee.

Three minutes later, the lights went out.

I lit a candle. I'd talked big to the apartment manager, but I wasn't going to be able to do this.

I wondered how long it would be before the electric company cut service to the entire areas where the county was pushing us?

I had the feeling I wasn't even in the *To Kill a Mockingbird* universe any more. *Aliens vs. Predators*, maybe.

"I'll be back in a minute." My mother took the candle into what had once been my bedroom leaving Lisa and me in darkness.

I dug up an oil lamp. I didn't have any lamp oil, but the canola oil I found in my kitchen did the job, and made the apartment smell like popcorn.

As Lisa pointed out, smelling like popcorn was better than it was going to smell if we living there with no running water in the shower, the toilet, or the sink.

It didn't bear thinking of.

I put my head in my hands and tried not to cry.

Sharon curled around my neck and made comforting little hisses. I stroked her cool, smooth skin. To my surprise, it helped a little. Not much, though. The world was still falling apart.

My mother emerged from my bedroom when her candle had diminished into a small nub.

"Your sister says no and none of the area motels will accept what they're calling *impaired people*, but Cal will take us in." My mother closed her cell with a snap. "He'll pick us up in ten minutes. And darling, remember what I told you about—" she made a disgusting face with her mouth in a circle around an invisible cock, as if saying it out loud in front of Lisa would be bad but acting it out was socially acceptable.

"I'm not going to give a guy a blowjob so he'll let us stay with him."

"*I* could do it," Lisa said. "If you hadn't taken me in, I'd be out on the street anyway. No big deal?"

"You keep your goddamned mouth off of him."

My mother patted me on the head. "I knew you were getting the message, dear."

* * * *

We stuffed the Mustang's small trunk with our essentials and piled in. Cal offered to have a moving company put the rest of the stuff into storage and I couldn't figure out a way to say that I hoped someone *would* steal it. So I just promised I'd pay him back, eventually.

My mother was way too obvious making sure I got into the front seat with Cal while she and Lisa squeezed in back with a couple of suitcases that didn't fit in the trunk.

"You guys eaten yet?"

"Why don't we call out for a pizza," my mother suggested.

I groaned. "Anything but pizza."

"How about Chinese?" Cal suggested. He looked at me and trailed off.

I was used to that. Because I was partially of Asian ancestry, I was supposed to be offended by someone wanting to eat Chinese food? I didn't understand it, but I'd seen it.

"Great."

He got preferences, called ahead, and then drove through a takeout Chinese place.

"You don't want to leave all of your stuff in the car while we eat," he said. "So, we'll bring the food to my place."

I suspected the drive-through approach had as much to do with not having time to find a restaurant that let transformed people sit with their 'normal' customers as with making sure our stuff didn't get stolen. But I couldn't complain. He was being thoughtful again.

I hated that I owed him. I mean, so far our relationship was mostly in my mind—that and my mother's mind. I wasn't an expert on relationships, but working at Hale, Storm, and Stunk did make me an expert on divorce. Most of the divorces I'd contested were about unfair power relationships. Well, that and a bunch of guys who had problems keeping their dicks in their pants. If Cal and I ever moved beyond my one-sided attraction, I didn't want him thinking I owed him.

Getting what I wanted didn't seem likely.

My mother and Lisa went gaga over Cal's home, his view of the city of Santa Cruz below, the Pacific Ocean beyond that, and the redwood forests just to the east. Then they went gaga again over his vegetable gardens.

While my mother and Lisa ran around picking stuff for a salad, I thought about my mother's tacky advice. Would taking Cal to bed repay him for what he was doing and get our relationship back on an equal footing?

I decided I wouldn't be whoring if I really *wanted* to go to bed with him, which I did. He looked wonderful in tight jeans and a nubby cotton sweater. His bare feet reminded me that my mother had pulled him from a relaxing evening to rescue us from darkness and no bathwater.

He put out the salad my mother and Lisa had made and the food he'd bought and invited us to serve ourselves.

After eating, he helped carry our stuff in from the car, and turned over one guest room to my mother, and a second to Lisa and me.

At least he had enough beds for all of us. I wouldn't need my sleeping bag.

When he pulled out clean sheets and towels, I had to wonder why this guy wasn't taken. Most guys I knew were lucky to have one extra set of sheets, but Cal had enough for a house-full of guests. He didn't even need a stop at the washing machine.

I logged on to the web to check on the bus schedule for Cal's neighborhood, then took a fast shower and headed for the bedroom Cal had assigned Lisa and me.

"He's really cute." Lisa's figure had grown even more buxom with the hours she now spent swimming.

"He's a peach. Do you think he might be gay?"

She laughed. "You're kidding, right?"

"He keeps his house clean, has extra sheets, and he hasn't made a move on me. Or maybe he hates snakes."

Lisa put her hands on her hips and glared at me. "He's not gay. He's a grownup with a decent job. You and I spent too much time dating losers trying to hold onto their adolescence to recognize a good one when he comes along. But that's a big part of why things didn't work out for us with other guys. Cal is different."

I'd been nursing this crazy wish that maybe I was the only one who could recognize that Cal was a catch. But Lisa saw it too.

If I'd been a good girlfriend to Lisa, I would have told her to go for it. If he didn't want me, why should I stand in her way?

But I couldn't make back off. I wasn't good at sharing and, dammit, I wanted him.

"I'm not making any moves on him," she promised.

"You reading my mind or something?"

"I guess it would count as an 'or something.' When you think too hard, the girls wiggle. That one looked like the wiggle they give when your mom does her lecture on not letting guys get away."

"Think she's right? You know, about that mouth thing."

Lisa considered, then shook her head. "No way. There isn't anything sexual I didn't do to keep my old boyfriend. And he still dumped me. Maybe back when your mom and dad were dating a lot of girls wouldn't do it, but a guy like Cal probably gets three offers a day. I mean, he's a college professor and he's what, maybe thirty? College girls have got to be throwing themselves at him all the time."

"But you don't think—"

Lisa rolled her eyes. "He's so not gay."

I went through my suitcase and pulled out some of my clothes, hanging the pantsuit I planned to wear to court the next day and putting my underwear in a drawer.

At the bottom of the suitcase, I found a skimpy emerald green satin nightgown, baby-doll style. I didn't wear things like that when I wasn't dating, so why had I packed it? Cal might hate Freudian stuff, but I suspected my subconscious was telling me something.

I held it up to Lisa. "Think I should go for it?"

"Bad idea. Let *him* make the first move."

I'd get old waiting for him to make the first move. It was time for the lawyer side of me to take over.

I pulled off my nightshirt, slipped into satin, and left the matching tap pants behind to make sure my message didn't get missed.

"Wish me luck."

"You're crazy but, good luck."

I closed the door and headed down the hall.

Chapter 19

Redwood floorboards creaked under my feet. Golden light gleamed under Cal's bedroom door. He was still awake.

I knocked, then opened his door immediately.

He lay in bed, a leather-bound book in his large, strong hands. A single bedside lamp cast a halo of light around him.

A sheet covered his lower body, but Cal's chest was naked.

A handsome man, a naked and muscular chest, even the book he closed over one finger to mark his place as he looked my way, it added up to a complete turn-on.

"Do you need something else, Erin?"

I couldn't have asked for a better lead-in. "This time it's about what you need. I owe you for everything you've done and I've come to pay you back."

He didn't smile. I was pretty sure that the quick intake of breath was solely in my imagination. "You figure a little sex and we're even, do you?"

Shit. This was my sexiest nightgown. He wasn't supposed to be thinking, let alone asking tough questions. By this time, he was supposed to have leapt out of bed and jumped my bones.

"That isn't exactly—"

"Tell me if I'm wrong," he interrupted, "but haven't I treated you with respect and courtesy. I was actually feeling good about myself. Helping those who need a hand puts positive energy back into the universe. Turning it into a commercial relationship would kill that feeling."

"You aren't gay, are you?"

He looked at me stonily. "Is that what this is about? I'm a challenge and you thought maybe you could be the perfect woman to cure me?"

"It's nothing like that."

"How lucky. I'm not gay."

"Oh." Shit. Lisa was right. It wasn't him. It was me. As long as I had snakes in my hair, I wasn't going to be getting Cal. Even the vampires had backed up, and none of the Bloodsucker gang had been anything close to a good catch.

I turned and ran back to our room. I wasn't going to let him see the tears.

Sharon snuffled.

"Snakes don't cry," I told her sternly.

"I guess it didn't—"

"You told me so. So don't push it."

I might need a lecture on how to catch a guy, hell, I *needed* a college curriculum, but I didn't *want* one. I wanted to be by myself, in my own Zen apartment, waking up to find out that all of this was a horrible nightmare.

Sharon swooped around my ear, then doubled back so she could look me right in the eye. Her inquisitive glance made me feel as guilty as sin.

Okay, I wouldn't want to wake up from all of this. The girls weren't doing anything for my love life, but it wasn't their fault. They were my pals and they were part of me. I wouldn't want to wake up and find them gone.

Not even if that meant you could have wild monkey-sex with Cal?

Ooh, cool. That was the first time one of the girls had talked to me so directly.

"Definitely not even for monkey-sex," I answered out loud.

"I'm too tired for monkey-sex," Lisa said, yawning. "Ask me again tomorrow."

I was pretty sure she was kidding.

"Just go back to sleep."

Which was easy to say. I had a rough time falling asleep. I kept thinking of Cal's sexy chest, the scent of soap and citrus aftershave in his room, and the way he'd rejected me. Or maybe it was the way I'd turned myself into a whore that nagged at my conscience.

* * * *

I didn't look my best when I showed up in court.

Mona, in contrast, was radiant.

I'd suspected she'd be a Marilyn Monroe-style sexpot if she gave herself a chance. She had, and she was.

Her skirt was slit to show yards of long curvy legs. Her bra made a huge difference—literally huge. She practically burst out of the jacket and blouse.

Black seams up the back of her stockings proved that she wasn't just dressing for the judge.

Someone had enjoyed wild monkey-sex the previous night, and it hadn't been me.

I smiled at her, happy for her success despite my own problems, until reality—or maybe it was Sharon—slapped me upside the head. I'd left Mona at The Catalyst, munching on pizza and drinking beer with the prince of darkness, FBI Agent Samuels. If Mona had gotten laid, and she had, Samuels was the best bet.

I turned the smile into a glare. After meeting my gaze for a second or two, she looked away.

"Mona, how could you?"

She had the grace to look embarrassed. "I haven't felt this way since I was fourteen and fell in love with Carlos on *A Changing World*. I know it messes up the case, but I'm moving to San Francisco to be with Samuels. We're leaving today, after he finishes his testimony. Now come on back to the judge's chambers. We've got paperwork to handle."

"But we're in the middle of the case."

"I've been waiting for this all my life. I can't afford to wait any longer."

She dragged me back to where Hilz and Deat waited. "There *is* some good news," she said. "I persuaded Hilz to pay you. You need to fill out the forms now."

"But—"

She surprised me by kissing me on both cheeks, shook hands with Hilz and Deat, and vanished from my life.

I was practically numb as I signed the paperwork Hilz had sat on for the past month, making me an official court-appointed attorney and earning the County's barely-better-than-minimum-wage payout.

I was glad to have an income, especially after what I'd seen when I'd visited the Bloodsucker area east of Watsonville. Unemployment sucks as bad as any vampire. Still, I felt overwhelmed. I wasn't second seat any more, I was lead.

I was certain the FBI had intended things to work this way, They must have decided Mona was too effective, and that they could walk all over me.

Since I'd seen the jurors react to the girls, I couldn't argue with their conclusions.

"I'll just garnish your wages until you've paid off the contempt charges," Hilz said as I handed back the forms. "But you're doing a good job for your client, Tsong. If you keep down your histrionics, I'd be willing to see you in my court on future cases as well."

"Thanks, your honor."

"And call me Arnie when we're in chambers, Erin."

"Right, uh, Arnie. I appreciate that."

Deat glared at me. Under the judge's watching eyes, he made himself shake my hand again and offer his own congratulations.

"Lucky for you," he grumbled. "I was hoping you'd serve our your contempt fines in the county lock-up. At a hundred bucks a day. You were looking at a month of baloney sandwiches."

"I was afraid of that too," I admitted. Deat was being a jerk but after talking with Agent Samuels the previous evening, I knew it wasn't all Deat's fault. He was under orders. Besides, it didn't hurt me to be polite to him in the judge's chambers. I'd tear him apart in front of the jury, where it counted.

I did my best to do just that once Samuels got back in the witness box.

"Agent Samuels, you testified yesterday that Vampires are prone to acts of violence, is this correct?"

"Yes, ma'am."

"But you never met Mr. Ventoro before. Isn't that true?"

"I hadn't—"

"It's a yes or no question, Agent Samuels."

"Objection. Badgering the witness."

"Overruled. It was a yes or no question."

I nodded to Judge Hilz, then glared at Samuels. A pinhead of sweat formed on his perfectly shaved upper lip.

"Well, no. I hadn't actually—"

"Thank you. So you have no data on whether Mr. Ventoro is typical of the vampires covered in your statistical data?"

"The probabilities—"

"Agent Samuels, I'm sure the jury members have lives they would like to get back to. So, if you'd answer the questions, yes or no, it would help us all."

"I can't say for certain that Mr. Ventoro is typical. But the data—"

"In the course of your duties with the FBI, how many vampires had you met before, say, three months ago?"

"But there weren't any vampires—"

"So, your answer is zero?"

"Of course."

"And how many vampires have you personally interviewed in the small number of days since the transformation?"

I was taking a chance with this one, breaking law-school rule #1 by asking a question I didn't already know the answer for. But I felt I needed to take a chance.

Samuels mumbled something.

"Could you repeat that," the court reporter asked.

"Six."

"Six? It seems a small number to make up a sweeping conclusion about an entire group. Oddly, I was talking with six vampires two nights ago. One of them was a shy redhead who reminded me of Howdy-Doody. How does he fit your statistical profile?"

He was sweating harder now. "The profile reflects averages and probabilities. Not every vampire will match the profile in every respect."

"But you're certain that Mr. Ventoro does? After all, you spoke with, uh, six whole people. No further questions."

* * * *

Deat gave the jury some nonsense about not asking the victim to testify to spare her embarrassment and humiliation, and ended the prosecution case.

It was smart tactics, and horribly unethical. He was poisoning the jury against me. When I called Leone Cornelison, I'd be the one who forced her to endure embarrassment and humiliation. Well, the jury could get over that when they heard what she had to say.

"Are you ready to begin your defense?" Hilz asked.

"I move to dismiss the case," I said. "The prosecution has not offered evidence that would support its recommended guilty verdict."

"I'll consider your motion over lunch. In the meantime, be prepared to begin your defense case at two."

"Yes, your honor."

The defense almost always moves to dismiss or direct a verdict of not guilty after the prosecution completes its case. While the motion is almost always rejected, the law was on my side on this one. Other than a discredited story by Officer Orlando, the prosecution had provided no evidence that a crime had taken place, and not much to argue that Vic had been the one to do it. I didn't that mattered, though. No judge would take the political heat of ruling for a vampire, innocent or not. Any justice for Vic, the Vampire, Ventoro would come from the jury.

I'd gotten used to having lunch with Mona. But Mona was off for her new life in San Francisco. So, I called my friend Becky to rescue me.

She picked me up three minutes later.

"What are you doing, stranger?"

"Very funny. I just saw you last weekend."

"And now you need me to buy you lunch?"

"Actually, I'm getting paid again." I gave her a toothy smile. "We can go Dutch."

"Wow, the last of the big spenders. Must be a great job."

"If what I saw down near Watsonville is typical, it's a fabulous job for anyone who's been transformed."

"You've been checking out the vampire zone." Becky wrinkled her nose. "There's no shopping there at all. But you can buy great organic vegetables."

For Becky, shopping mattered as much as social movements and injustice. The funny thing was, if everyone had her attitude, maybe we wouldn't need so many social movements and there wouldn't be so much injustice.

She drove me to a deli on Pacific where we ordered sandwiches. There wasn't a sign, but no transformed people were eating in and I didn't have the energy to see what happened if I sat with the normals.

We took our sandwiches and chips down to the Boardwalk.

Like most teenagers in Santa Cruz, I'd worked at the Boardwalk during high school summer vacations. The scents of cotton candy, saltwater taffy, and seawater carried memories of first kisses, first betrayals, and massive sunburns.

We sat on a bench and watched middle-aged men with metal detectors sift through the sand, looking for lost treasures but finding rusty brass rings from the merry-go-round, beer pull-tabs, and the occasional penny. Now that was a high-tech metaphor for my dating life. I wanted a treasure, but all I'd ever found were trash and rusty brass rings. The metaphor broke down when I considered Cal. I mean, none of the treasures the metal detectors turned up actually fought back.

"Scientists are working on a crash program to cure this magic plague," Becky said. "With luck, we'll get the impaired back to normal."

The girls shivered despite the sun beating down on us.

"We're not sick, Becky. We're just different. You said yourself that most of the DNA that's causing this has been there all along. According to Cal, we're recovering from a disease that hit thousands of years ago."

She shook her head. "The world needs a cure. Check out what it's done just around here. I know you're attached to the snakes, but can't you see that you're the exception? People are hurting and hitting back. They're even hitting back at you, and you're one of them. Look what happened to your car."

She was wrong. I wrestled for a way to explain it, marshalling talents honed by years of arguing divorce cases. Because if I couldn't convince my best friend, who could I expect to persuade?

"They're mad because they're being treated unfairly, because they can't get jobs. That doesn't mean they'd give up their talents. At least not most of them."

Becky shuddered. "Talents? Sometimes I just don't get you. Sucking blood, turning canine, or going troll-ugly are not talents. Those are horrible handicaps. I heard that FBI Agent on the radio on my way to pick you up. He says the vampires are out of control. If that isn't a disease, what is?"

"He also said vampire souls are replaced by demons. Samuels doesn't have a clue."

Becky's eyes widened. "Ohmigod, what if he's right? What if their souls had been replaced? What if *your* soul is at risk?"

"What if their souls had been replaced by demons with identical memories, feelings, actions, and friendships? Think about this, girlfriend. How could Samuels know? Do you think the FBI has soul detectors? It took them thirty years to put in a new database system. It's about elections, Becky, not science."

"You didn't used to be paranoid." Becky took a bite out of her sandwich and turned to watch the surfers, their black wetsuits glistening like the sea otters they shared the ocean with.

I wondered if my friend from the sporting goods store was out there.

I'd given myself a test—to persuade my best friend. And I'd failed. Good thing the case against Ventoro was so bad, because if I couldn't persuade Becky that Samuels was nuts, I was going to have trouble persuading anyone of anything.

"Okay, enough political stuff. Let's talk about something that matters."

Becky's eyes widened. "You want to talk about shopping?"

"Not *that* important." She was making a joke, but she really did think shopping was the purpose of existence. "I've got guy problems."

She perked up. "The college professor, right?"

"Yeah, Cal. I put on a Victoria's Secrets nightgowns and threw myself at him last night. He told me to get lost."

"Not good. Had you used mouthwash?"

"He didn't let me get close enough for smell."

"More bad news." She considered, then got a *lightbulb* look. Maybe he's afraid of your snakes."

I tried not to roll my eyes. "Of course he's afraid of the snakes. Even my mother's afraid of the snakes. But what if that's not the *only* issue?"

I'd been sort of veering around this in my mind, not wanting to come to grips with the possibility, but now I had to.

"Everyone blames the transformation for what's wrong in their lives. Normals blame the vampires and shapeshifters. The vampires blame me. And I've been blaming the girls for Cal not responding to me—when I wasn't trying to persuade myself it wasn't about him being gay. Which he isn't. But the dirty secret is, I haven't had a serious boyfriend in over a year."

"What about Johnny Fredricks?"

I'd forgotten about Johnny. No big surprise. The guy was completely forgettable. I couldn't even think what had possessed me to believe he might be better than a night alone. "Johnny was a loser, and he was also more than a year ago."

"You went to bed with him."

"Which proves I'm a slut, I was horny, and Johnny wasn't fussy. And that raises another point. Even Johnny didn't come back around for seconds."

Becky looked at her watch. "I've got to get back to work, so I want you to listen to this without interrupting me, without cross-examining me, and without shutting off your ears because you don't want to hear it. Okay?"

I nodded.

"You're pretty. You've always had an inferiority complex about being half Asian and half Irish, but it makes you exotic. Guys go for that.

"But you're smart. That intimidates some guys. Especially guys, like Johnny, who don't have that much going on between their ears. But being smart and funny attracts other guys. Like guys you'd want to spend time with when you weren't making the sign of the two-humped camel in your bed.

"But best of all, you've got a good heart, despite the whole lawyer thing. You care about people and animals and shit like that. Which makes jerks back off because they know you'll figure them out and they'd rather reject you first. You need a special kind of guy. If Cal is special enough, he'll figure a way to get to you. If you don't scare him away first."

"But what if I'm too special? So special there's no one for me." I hated that my voice got whiney, but I couldn't help it.

She sighed. "Then I'll just have to track down this college professor of yours and feed him to the werewolves. Okay?"

I blinked back a couple of tears. "Right. No more feeling sorry for myself."

"You know what your problem is?"

"Snakes?"

"Of course not snakes. I've even gotten used to them."

Sharon jutted out a little, looking for affection, and Becky jerked back in a hurry. "Got me, I lied? No, your big problem is, you haven't done any serious shopping in ages."

"Once I figure out a place to live, I'll take you up on it. Because I can't go on living with Cal. If I was sleeping with him, it would be one thing. But taking advantage of him is something different."

"It wouldn't be taking advantage of him if you lived with him and made him have sex with you all the time?"

Becky said it like a throwaway. But hadn't Cal said the same thing? I acted as if sex with me was so wonderful that it would pay him back for whatever. That Cal would owe *me* if I put out for him.

"Talk to your college professor," Becky suggested. "Find out if he thinks you're racking up a debt. He's smart, Erin. Give him some credit. He can use his words to tell you what he wants."

And what he didn't want, unfortunately.

We got into her car and headed back toward the courthouse. "You know what, Becky? I think you're pretty smart, too."

Chapter 20

Before she'd left, Mona had found one of the civilians involved in roughing Vic up. I'd counted on her to handle the questioning.

We'd had to subpoena him to testify at all, and we'd persuaded Hilz to classify him as a hostile witness.

Orson Swift wore a ratty pair of jeans and a t-shirt favoring legalization of marijuana. His glare, when he stalked up to the witness stand, looked likely to tear Ventoro into pieces.

The bailiff swore Swift in, then turned him over to me.

"You don't like vampires much, do you, Mr. Swift."

"Bloodsuckers want to steal all the women. Just like that FBI Agent said. Bunch of freaks should be put down."

"Is protecting women a high priority of yours, Mr. Swift?"

"Hell, yeah. Can't let lowlifes get them all. Not hardly enough to go around as it is."

"So, if you noticed a vampire having his way with a woman, you'd—"

"Objection. Calls for speculation." Deat sounded tired.

"Sustained. Ms. Tsong, please limit your questions to matters of fact, not opinion or speculation."

"Yes, your honor. I withdraw that question."

I gave Swift what I hoped was a resigned—*I'm beaten*—grin. "Is it true, Mr. Swift, that you saw what appeared to be a vampire having his way with a woman on the night of October Seventeenth of this year?"

"Not what appeared to be. What was. That creature, Vic the Vampire, was mauling at Leone."

"That would be Mr. Ventoro. Mauling at Ms. Cornelison?"

"I said that didn't I?"

"I was repeating for the jury. I'm curious about what you did when you spotted that behavior, Mr. Swift."

"What any real American would do. I went and stopped it."

"Alone?"

"Would have done it alone if I hadta, 'cept there were other guys, felt the same way. We sort of hit him from all sides. From what I hear, it was lucky I had some good'ole American boys for backup. I woulda had to try to stop him anyway, but I hear them vampires can purely tear a man apart. And back at that time, I wasn't carrying anything like this."

He reached into the crotch of his baggy jeans yanked.

I thought I was about to get flashed and took half a step back, which turned out to be lucky. Instead of the one-eyed snake, he pulled out a sharp two-foot long fire-charred wooden stake and jabbed it in Ventoro's direction.

My step back hadn't been quite big enough, and I was between him and Ventoro.

The sharp tip of the stake ripped through my top, exposing my distressingly boring beige bra to the world.

With all my power, I willed the girls to stay calm. This was theater, and I'd completely mess it up if one of my snakes struck at Swift, let alone killed him.

Hilz gaveled the court to order, had the bailiff take the stake away from Swift, and asked me if I was able to continue.

I inspected my ruined top, my exposed cup, and the bloody scrape down my side.

"If I could have a few moments to pull myself back together, your honor, I believe I can continue.

"Court is in recess for one hour. And Mr. Swift, you may consider yourself in contempt of court."

Swift pulled out his wallet and started counting out hundred dollar bills. "Just tell me when to stop, your judgeness."

"Stop counting when you hit thirty days," the Judge said.

Despite the pain from my scrape, I couldn't help grinning. Good for Hilz.

* * * *

Amelia, from my old office, must have had a spy at the trial, because she arrived with an extra blouse while I was in the woman's room washing up.

"The whole firm is rooting for you," she whispered as she attacked my scrape with a Handiwipe. "I even heard Mr. Hale wonder if we shouldn't get back into criminal law."

"The money is to die for. I'm earning right at minimum wage. Before my contempt-of-court charges, of course."

"You're silly. Now try this blouse. It should work."

When I'd been at Hale, Storm and Stunk, we lawyers speculated that Amelia had dozens of identical outfits since she always looked perfect and always looked the same. This was the first proof I'd seen that she kept clothing at the office, too.

She was shorter than me, and bigger around the bust, so the blouse wasn't a great fit, but it was better than fixing mine with a stapler. I could have asked Hilz to hold over the case until the next day, but I was on a roll with Swift and wanted to finish him before Deat got hold of him.

After taping a gauze bandage over my scrape, Amelia tailored the top with the stapler, and pronounced me good to go.

The hallway outside the restroom was filled with cops and reporters, with camera crews fighting for space and shouting out questions to anyone who would answer them.

Amelia elbowed a pathway between them and led me back to the courtroom where a reinforced group of bailiffs limited access to a suddenly overflowing room.

As I took my seat at the defense table, Ventoro grabbed my arm.

"You took a shot for me. I know you didn't mean to, but you did it and I won't forget that."

Wow. Was that why I'd become a lawyer? In all the years I'd done divorce work, I couldn't remember a single time a client had thanked me. No matter how good a deal I got them, they deserved more. Maybe I'd stick to this criminal stuff. Of course, the problem with criminal work is, a lot of the time your clients are criminals. How fun would that be?

Hilz returned from his chambers, ushered a red-faced Deat back to his seat, inquired politely about my health, and then let me proceed.

I had the court reporter read back the last statement Swift had made, partly to remind the jury what a creep he was, and partly to get everyone reset. Swift might not like me, and he definitely didn't like Ventoro, but he'd flat-out contradicted the prosecution's primary witness. And his testimony provided a match for the supposedly mysterious abrasions on Ventoro's face.

I could handle this.

I took a deep breath and told the girls to stay calm. We were going to get Swift, and we didn't need snake venom to do the job.

"Mr. Swift, you testified that you and a group of unknown others stopped Mr. Ventoro before he could have his way with Ms. Cornelison, is that correct?"

"Damned right we did. The pervert."

"And when the police arrived, you turned Mr. Ventoro over to them?"

"Right. Slick as snake-sh—"

"No further questions."

Deat got up, stomped to the witness box, then turned on his heel and walked back to his table. "No questions."

"You don't want to cross-examine this witness?" Judge Hilz sounded like he'd bitten into a chocolate and discovered a dill pickle center.

"The jury will decide whether to believe a sworn officer of the law or an admitted vigilante, your honor. I feel confident that they can make the right choice without any coaching from me."

I raised an eyebrow at him and let Sharon spread her hood.

Deat had the grace to look embarrassed. He shuffled his feet a little as he got himself situated at his table, but the man was a politician after all, smooth. Rather than charge ahead and give my witness credibility, he'd done his best to saw the legs out under my case.

"Given the violent activities of the day, I'm going to call an early recess," Hilz announced. "Bailiff, please remand Mr. Swift to the County Jail where he can begin serving his thirty days for contempt of court immediately."

"What is this bullshit?"

"Mr. Swift, you've tried my patience. If you'd like to add more time to your penalty, please continue. Otherwise, shut your mouth."

Swift shut his mouth.

* * * *

Cal waited for me, his Mustang's convertible top down despite the December chill.

"Heard you had a rough day. Come on, get in."

"I've had better."

"Anything I can do to help?"

He'd turned down what I really wanted.

"I already owe you too much to ask for more favors. Although I appreciate the ride home." I got in and sat back as Cal accelerated away from the curb.

"You're caught up in this 'who owes whom what' thing, aren't you?"

"I have no idea what you're talking about."

"Maybe an example would help." He paused theatrically. "Oh, I know. How about that you tried to seduce me last night because you feel guilty about mooching off of me."

"You're a big one to talk. The only reason you took me out the other night was to pay me back for all the help you say I gave you on your papers."

He painted an imaginary line in the air. "Point for you. I would have sworn, though, it was celebration, not payback."

And I'd been thinking my seduction offer was more than payback, too. Except I wasn't positive. Could Cal have recognized more about me than I knew myself?

He turned his car north—we weren't going home.

"Is this some sort of complicated kidnapping?"

"I wanted to talk about this payback system of yours."

"You make it sound like I run a pawnshop for favors. I ran up serious student loans when I was at Stanford and I realized it would be easy to use them as an excuse to take a free ride off other people. So I try not to go into debt anymore, that's all."

He followed Mission Street where it turned into Coast Road and continued north. Everyone in California wants to live near the beach, but there were still some beautiful expanses of open space—nothing but road, waves and mountains.

"Sex as a payback makes me feel cheap," Cal admitted. "Of course, you have to see it as payback or else you aren't in control. Right?"

"You don't know what you're talking about." I turned on his sound system and found a CD I liked—an upbeat jazz combo that reminded me of the dance music we'd listened to at that club.

He let the CD play for about five minutes, then reached over and turned the volume way down. "Your mother is worried about you."

"Newsbreak! The only way to stop my mother from worrying would be to move to a suburb somewhere, marry a doctor, give up my career, and have two point seven children. Mom is going to have to keep worrying."

"She said you hadn't made any money from the Vic the Vampire trial."

"Don't call him that. He's Vic Ventoro."

"He calls himself Vic the Vampire, doesn't he? Why should he be ashamed of what he is?"

"Because he's not just a vampire. He's a person. It would be like you calling yourself Cal the Mustang Man. As if all you are is someone who owns a car." Ventoro wasn't the sharpest knife in the drawer, but he'd been a person before he'd become a vampire. There was more to even him than a pair of sharp fangs. Unfortunately, Ventoro and everyone else had a tendency to forget it.

"I can see that. But I can also see you're using my misstatement to help you avoid my question. Are you broke?"

"I'll be fine. With Mona gone, I'm the official court-appointed."

"Your mom will be relieved." He drove on for another couple of minutes. "Can I talk you into dinner? There's a Buddhist Monastery at Martins Beach that's supposed to serve incredible vegetarian food."

I looked at him for a moment, then decided to do what lawyers hardly ever do—put all my cards out on the table.

"Why are you doing this, Cal? I get the message that you aren't looking for sex from me. Fine, I can accept that. If you just want to pay me back for the little help I gave you on your research, you've already done it, and you're doing it again by letting us stay with you. So, what's this trip about?"

"Don't you have any friends, Erin?"

"Hell yes, I've got friends. You go shopping with friends. You go to lunch with friends. You might even go clubbing with friends." I waved my hand at the ocean to our left. "But a drive and dinner isn't friend stuff. It's date stuff. You can see how that would confuse me."

"And dating is about sex?"

Trust a college professor to respond to my openness by asking a question. "Of course dating is about sex. What else?"

He shook his head slowly. "I can't give you an answer you'd understand, Erin. So, why not relax and enjoy the process."

"Yeah, sure. Sounds Zen to me."

I'd never heard of it, but Cal proved his research skills again. A Buddhist temple nestled along the oceanfront cliffs, halfway between Santa Cruz and San Francisco. The temple supported itself by offering vegetarian food to anyone who wanted it. I wasn't sure how they afforded a location that looked over the ocean when they charged so little for their dinners, but I wasn't going to complain.

I resisted temptation and didn't even complain when they noticed my snakes and suggested that I might feel more comfortable eating on a picnic table overlooking the ocean.

When he looked like arguing, I grabbed Cal arm and dragged him out. It had taken me weeks to get a paycheck after the last restaurant disaster. All I needed was to get arrested for causing trouble in a Buddhist temple. I'd never hear the end of that, or see my first check.

* * * *

Despite the rocky beginning, dinner was fun.

The orange California sunset looked like the entire sky was on fire. As the sun touched the horizon, it cut a golden road across the ocean waves heading back toward me.

I almost felt I could walk that path across the waves, keep going until I found a golden treasure at the.

The sun dropped below the horizon, leaving behind a deep rose glow in the sky that competed with the stars that flickered into life in the slowly increasing darkness.

Cal joined me in admiring the view. Then he entertained me with more stories about what was going on at the University. Although the students were riled up about the transformation, the faculty was taking it in stride. Partly, I thought, because many members of the faculty were already stranger than any werewolf or vampire.

When he sensed I'd heard enough about the, admittedly hilarious, goings-on of a bunch of people I'd never met, Cal switched channels. Using questioning skills I wished I could manage in the courtroom, he pumped me about how the trial was going, what I was going to do without Mona to handle her share of the work, and how I dealt with my mother.

His hands twitched when I told him about Swift and the stake.

"I got it bandaged up," I assured him. "And put Neosporin on it so I won't get infected."

"I hadn't realized being a lawyer was a dangerous job."

A star shot across the sky, plunging toward the Pacific. I wondered what I should wish for. My life was a wreck, but I didn't know what I'd change, even if magic did work. And I was no longer prepared to say it didn't.

"Lawyers interact with people—same as in teaching. And some people are a little crazy. Of course, criminal lawyers interact with a slightly more dangerous group of crazies."

"Considering some of the students I've had, the emphasis should be on slightly, as in *very* slightly."

"Anyway, I don't think Swift was trying to hurt me. He just wanted to show himself he wasn't afraid. That's tough when you're convulsed with panic."

Cal nodded, squeezed my hand for a moment, then stood. "We should get back. I don't want your mother and Lisa chasing after us."

Walking back to his car I took the chance to admire the way his jeans fit around his tight butt. He was a college professor, for goodness sake. How'd he get a body like that?

He didn't kiss me when we got home. Again.

* * * *

Putting your client on the stand is risky.

No matter how the judge instructs them, juries assume that an innocent man would take the stand to protect himself. Little things like the Fifth Amendment don't get in the way of their logic. But, once you put a witness on the stand, Fifth Amendment protections go away and you open the door to all sorts of questioning. Innocent or not, Vic Ventoro was not exactly the most articulate guy in the world. Plus, his fangs gave him a lisp.

Mona and I had gone back and forth on the issue since day one. But Mona wasn't there to help, which meant it was up to me. And up to Vic, of course. And Vic wanted to testify. I would have felt better if he'd just been a little less willing.

I decided to go for it. My client was innocent. That should count for something.

Direct examination went pretty well. Vic took me through meeting Cornelison, their agreement to go off together, and how the vigilantes jumping him before he could do more than hold her hand. Ending with the late arrival of Officer Orlando.

I went for the hard sell.

"Would you say, Mr. Ventoro, that your intentions were to engage in voluntary adult activity, and that you were stopped before any of these activities had taken place?"

"That's what I said isn't it? Why would I force her when so many girls are willing to pay for it?"

I spent a couple of minutes trying to undo that before finally turning to the prosecution.

"Your witness." Ventoro had already been far too much Deat's witness. He'd probably been an arrogant bastard before the transformation—becoming a vampire hadn't helped his personality any.

I didn't like Deat's wink or the big grin smeared over his face.

He stalked to the witness box like a tiger approaching a staked sheep.

"Would you mind if I called you Vic the Vampire, Mr. Ventoro?"

"Objection—"

Ventoro didn't give me the chance to say more. "It's what everyone calls me. Go ahead."

"In that case, I'll overrule," Judge Hilz said.

"How does this vampire stuff work, Vic the Vampire?"

"You know. It's just blood."

"*Just* blood." Deat repeated Ventoro's phrase with a twist, emphasizing the word *just*, in case anyone in the jury didn't get it the first time. "So, you what? Bite into someone's carotid artery and suck?"

"Objection. Relevance."

Deat faced the judge. "Your honor, the prosecution has maintained that Mr. Vic the Vampire Ventoro assaulted Ms. Corneilison, and that, even if he had been stopped in his attempt, the attempt constitutes an unlawful assault. This is true even if Ms. Cornelison had agreed to the assault. My current line of questioning is designed to help the jury understand the nature of the vampire technique and demonstrate that the prosecution's theory is consistent with the facts."

It took Hilz about two seconds to wade through Deat's answer. "Overruled."

"Vampire techniques," Deat reminded Ventoro.

"What you said is the basic idea." Vic's pale face took on a flush as he recounted the details of blood-sucking. "My fangs are hollow. Blood just flows up into my throat. Biting and sucking is a piece of cake. But the fangs also release a blood-thinning chemical. That's what feels so great for the victim. Sort of like a drug high."

Oh, shit. How many times had I coached him not to use the word victim? Or drug?

Deat frowned at the jury. "That's fascinating, Mr. Vic the Vampire. Can you explain more about the drug high?"

"Objection. Mr. Ventoro's knowledge or lack of knowledge of drugs is hardly on trial here."

"Your honor," Deat argued, "Vic the Vampire brought up the subject. I was merely asking for elaboration."

Hilz considered, then nodded. "Overruled. But be careful, Mr. Deat. This trial is not about recreational use of banned substances."

Considering that this was Santa Cruz, and that most of the jury probably indulged in an occasional joint, Deat shouldn't need Hilz's caution.

"Please continue, Mr. Vic the Vampire."

"It works like this. The vampire gets the blood and the vic—uh, the person receiving the bite gets a jolt. It's sort of sexy. That's one reason chicks dig vampires. We satisfy them in a way that ordinary guys can't."

"Fascinating. You satisfy in a way no *normal* guy can. No further questions," Deat said.

Deat thought he'd scored some points with the last dig, but I wasn't so sure. There were women on the jury. They might just sympathize with a guy who could give women some satisfaction. Considering the crime Ventoro had been accused of, getting sympathy from the women on the jury was my big problem.

On re-direct, I asked Ventoro a couple of easy questions. He assured me, and the jury, that he had a lot of respect for women; that he had never, and would never, engage in behavior that the woman didn't agree to; and that he was single.

Deat shook his head when he had his chance to follow up, so Ventoro got off the witness stand and shuffled back to the defense table.

"Was I great or what?" His stage whisper could probably be heard in San Francisco.

"You have no idea," I told him.

Despite my efforts, the case was getting away from me and I had no idea how to get it back.

Chapter 21

Thanks to her newfound swimming abilities, Lisa had gotten a job at a surfboard shop located on the Boardwalk.

It was Saturday and the trial was off for the weekend. So, we caught a bus down to the beach and went for a swim before the shop opened— me in a little pink wetsuit she'd given to me as a birthday present in thanks for all I'd done for her. The employee discount helped, but I still felt that I owed her.

She didn't need a wetsuit herself, luckily, since nobody had invented wetsuits with wing-holes. Despite the Pacific's frigid cold, Lisa's fast-beating wings warmed her metabolism.

I swam about two miles and Lisa swam at least three times that far before climbing out of the water.

A couple of big dogs squatted where we'd left our towels on the sand.

"Werewolves," Lisa whispered to me. "Jeez. Why can't they leave you alone?"

"You guys have something to say to me?"

"The alpha male growled, then raised a leg and whizzed on my towel.

"Ohh, that's classy. Now come on you guys. Shoo!"

Shooing them probably wasn't my brightest idea yet. But this being terrorized by my own kind was starting to blow.

The alpha half-transformed so he could talk. "You made our buddy Vic the Vampire look like an idiot yesterday. The vamps wanted you to get the message. Start doing your part or we'll turn your life to shit." He transformed back to full wolf and demonstrated by taking a dump on my towel.

"You really know how to win friends and influence people," I said. "Now get out of here."

The wolves left, and I wadded up my towel, bought at a discount at Lisa's shop, and tossed it into the trash.

"Sounds like you need help," Lisa said as we walked across the sand to the boardwalk.

"Maybe I'll buy a silver dagger."

"I meant with the trial. Deat's theory is that it's assault even if Cornelison and Ventoro wanted it. How can you fight that?"

"I spent four hours in the law library last night and I'm going to spend the rest of today there. I'm on my own while Deat has the entire

County Prosecutor staff backing him up. I can only do so much."

"So you need help. Uh, didn't I say that?"

"Very funny. There isn't another lawyer in the county who'll help with the case. Believe me, Mona checked. And I followed up after she quit. Still nothing."

Lisa smiled. "If only we knew someone who was a great researcher, who loved pawing through ancient books looking for just the right information, who could be trusted."

I sighed. "Yeah. A good paralegal would come in handy. But I can't ask Kay. Or rather, I did ask her even though I felt guilty about it because I can't pay her much. Unfortunately, Hale, Storm, and Stunk have her working overtime."

"I had someone else in mind." She unlocked the surf shop door, went in, and tossed me a new towel. "Dry off."

I wiped sand off my legs and drops of salt water from my face, arms, and legs where the wet suit didn't cover. "Who?"

"This isn't tough. And you're good at guessing. Who do we know who loves research and who likes doing things for you?"

An uncomfortable prickle went down my back. "Not Cal?"

She shook her head theatrically. "Oh, I forgot. That would be taking favors, wouldn't it?"

"You're not as funny as you think."

She fluttered her wings at me. "And you're not as autonomous as you think."

Whatever that meant.

* * * *

I had a hard time ignoring what Lisa had said. I was living in Cal's house. I was riding the taxpayer supported bus rather than my own car. Even the towel I had wrapped around my hair, keeping the girls warm, had come from Lisa. If I wanted to be autonomous, I wasn't doing a very good job at it.

Lisa had to be crazy. I almost managed to convince myself of that. I didn't mind asking for help, I just didn't want to humiliate myself with Cal. That was my story and I intended to stick her with it the next time I saw her.

Unfortunately, I saw Cal first.

The professor was installing photoelectric panels on his roof when I stepped off the bus.

He looked down at me, a big stack of the panels in his arms, and almost lost his balance.

"Need some help?" I asked.

"Why don't you get changed first? If I'm still up here, that means I need help."

I didn't want to snag my wet suit, so I went along with Cal's request, but I couldn't help feeling a little sad. I mean, he could have at least checked out the body under the form-fitting wetsuit. As it was, he'd sent me away so fast I was practically dizzy.

Wearing jeans and a faded Banana Slug sweatshirt, I joined him on his roof a few minutes later.

He gestured to the other side of one of the solar panels and together we lifted it into place.

"Think these will help with the electric bill?"

He nodded. "Should help me some. And it helps everyone else, too. If enough of us do it, the power company doesn't need to build a new power plant. That's something I learned from the classics. Society is all about people pulling together."

Yeah, yeah. I got the message. There's no such thing as autonomous. And Erin Tsong was a self-centered loser.

Jennifer twisted herself around my neck. The rest of the world might have problems with me, but the girls thought I was terrific.

If things continued the way they had been going, who knew? I might be able to figure out a way to make them mad at me, too.

"I don't suppose that all of the extra electricity you're using because of three unexpected houseguests has anything to do with needing more of these solar widgets."

He gave me that sexy grin. "Solar panels are long-term investments, Erin. Do you think I'm counting on you sticking around long enough to pay them off?"

"Sorry."

It took many hours before I realized he'd been asking a question. As in, how long was I sticking around?

Although it was December, the sun was out and the top of Cal's house got toasty warm.

After half an hour of hard work, Cal stripped off his flannel shirt, exposing his impressive chest, his sculpted six-pack abdominals, and his great shoulders.

"Do guys do that on purpose to distract women?"

"Hum?" He bent over a drawing of an electrical circuit, making sure he plugged the right dohickies together.

I gestured at his naked chest.

"Oh. You shirts? Probably goes back to when we played shirts and skins in basketball. I can put it back on if you want. I was just hot."

Well, yeah he was hot all right.

"Make yourself comfortable." And I'd pray for more sunshine and thank heaven for California where a guy could go topless all year round.

"You want to hand me that cable?"

"Umm." I realized I'd been staring at the way the muscles in his back splayed when he lifted the panels, completely zoned from reality and unaware that he had been holding out his hand waiting for me to hand him the plug. He could have been standing like that for ten minutes, for all I knew. I definitely would have been able to watch his naked back that long.

I handed it over and watched him plug the wires together.

Nothing happened.

The girls drooped in disappointment. "It didn't work?"

"You expected an explosion? It's working. Solar energy gets converted into current, goes through a DC-AC inverter, and then feeds into the grid. Hard to notice any difference until I get the electric bill at the end of the month."

He'd lost me somewhere around the word current. But I kept nodding because he'd turned to face me and I got a close-up look at his chest. Damn. It was a rule that guys can have intelligence or great bodies, but not both. Cal was a rule breaker.

He gathered up his tools, putting each neatly in its compartment.

Wanting to be helpful, I picked up his shirt. The fabric felt warm in my hands. Warm from the sun, maybe, but also warm from his body. I worked very hard at ignoring the tingle down my spine. I'd learned my lessons when it came to Cal. Friend, not boyfriend. Look, don't touch.

Unfortunately, keeping those lessons in mind meant that I forgot older lessons. Like, watching where I was going.

I put one foot down and it kept going.

"Oh, sh—"

Cal moved faster than anyone I'd ever seen, grabbing me before I fell off the roof and hauled me away from the edge.

"It's okay, Erin. We're getting down now."

The warm wall I was pressed against moved.

I couldn't make myself open my eyes, but the girls had no fear. They let me know that the worst had happened.

I hadn't fallen off Cal's roof. That would have been bad, but at least maybe I'd have a broken leg or something to show for my embarrassment. Instead, I was holding him so tight my entire body was draped all over him. The best I could hope for now was that, when I fell, he'd fall on top of me and I'd be the only person who got killed.

"I can't let go." My voice was a squeak.

"It's all right, Erin. We're only about twenty feet off the ground. Nobody is going to get hurt."

But it wasn't all right. I was draping my body all over Cal's naked chest, and I was so filled with panic, I couldn't even enjoy the moment.

The word *ironic* didn't begin to describe my situation.

I looked down and vertigo swept over me. "Scared."

"I'll go down and hold the ladder for you." He unwrapped my arms from around him. As he freed himself from each of my clutching claws, he gently placed them on a dormer where I resumed my death grip.

"Just hold on for now. I'll take down those tools you didn't already toss, then I'll hold the ladder for you. I promise you'll be okay."

"You won't leave me up here, will you?" My sister had stolen the ladder from our tree fort once when I'd been five, and nobody had noticed I was missing for hours. I'd been certain I would starve there in the trees.

"I'll be right here. I'll even catch you if you fall."

If I hadn't been such a chicken, I would have taken him up on that offer, making sure I fell into his strong arms.

As it was, once he'd reached the bottom and told me he was holding the ladder steady, I had to pry my fingers off the dormer window to put them on the ladder.

The girls thought this was a great game. They wrapped their bodies around the rails of the ladder to help me hold on, or maybe to speed my frightened descent.

They just made me feel worse. If I fell, I wouldn't just hurt myself, I'd hurt the girls too. What kind of a mother was I that I couldn't even overcome a stupid neurosis like height fright when the lives of her girls were at stake?

Lecturing myself didn't help, but it distracted me a bit.

Sharon draped Cal's shirt over my shoulders and I held onto the top of the ladder and looked down.

Cal smiled at me from a million miles below, clearly unaware that I was guaranteed to fall on him, puke on him, or both. Probably both.

Tiny drops of blood gathered on his chest where my clawing hands had grabbed naked skin in a desperate bid for safety.

"I'm sorry. You should just leave me up here. You can toss me some food once in a while."

"You'll feel better once you're down. Fear of heights is common, nothing to be ashamed of. But it does mean I won't ask you along on my trip to Mount Olympus this summer."

"I'm coming down."

I'd thought getting to the ladder would be the hard part. Wrong. Getting onto the ladder and actually starting down was far worse. I couldn't figure out how to turn around and ended up sitting on my butt, flopping my legs over the edge, and then going down facing away from the building. Which meant, when I finally reached the bottom, my entire body pressed up against Cal's naked chest.

The girls, having picked up on my desire and not having my level of discretion, wrapped themselves around him.

At least Cal had been right about one thing. I did feel better once I'd reached the ground. And once I was down on solid earth, I could actually appreciate Cal's fine chest. If I hadn't known better, I would have guessed Cal enjoyed it too—something was definitely pressing against my thigh.

* * * *

Predictably, my mother broke the mood by coming out of Cal's house with a platter of sandwiches.

"I made lunch. How does roast beef sound, Cal?"

She was in heaven sharing a home with someone who ate meat.

"Great, Mary. I worked up an appetite installing these solar panels. I'll bet Erin is starving as well."

"Ohh," my mother said. "You must eat a lot of protein to maintain muscles like that."

"Mother, you're embarrassing him."

"I don't mind."

Yeah, right. My mother and Cal had developed a mutual admiration society.

I noticed, though, that he stripped his shirt from my shoulders and put it on. Fortunately, he didn't bother to button it up so the view was only partially obscured.

My mother had forgotten that I was a vegetarian, something she'd forgotten regularly for the past decade. Once we were inside, sitting in the open-air atrium in the middle of Cal's home, she insisted on rushing back to the kitchen and making me sandwiches.

Cal buttoned a couple of the buttons on his shirt. But his eyes were on me, rather than on the buttons and he looked as if he had never seen me before.

"What?"

"I've been thinking about another research paper."

"Great. Maybe the FBI will pay you for that one, too."

"I told you that Agent Samuels mischaracterized my findings."

He *had* told me that. And I'd even considered putting him on the stand to refute the Agent, except I thought it would only call more attention to Samuel's weird theories. Besides, I had spent all those years in law school listening to complex arguments and I still sometimes had trouble following Cal's logic. I feared he'd confuse the jury.

"Sorry. You didn't deserve that."

"Actually, you've inspired my current research idea."

"Well that's a switch."

He laughed easily. "Yeah, I've given you credit for inspiring my earlier research, but it wasn't really you. Not individually, anyway. I mean, it could have been anyone with the Gorgon transformation. Those papers were about the Gorgon. The idea I'm bouncing around now is about Erin."

"Let me guess. You're writing about a legendary bitch-queen who's afraid of heights."

"Is that how you think about yourself?"

How to answer a question like that? I *didn't* think of myself as a bitch-queen. In court, I have to be tough and mean, otherwise the other lawyers would walk over me like I was grass. But that wasn't me.

I non-answered. "Maybe not a bitch-queen? And I'm all ears. What *is* your newest project?"

Cal took a bite of his sandwich and his eyes got that far-away look I was coming to recognize as his way of communing with his college-professor self. It probably was similar to the look I got when I talked to the girls, except on him it looked wise. On me, it looked like I had gone too long without sleep.

"It's long been recognized that most legends show ordinary humans in confrontation with magical creatures," he said. "Sure there are occasional benevolent gods, angels, or other powers. But mostly, the magical must be confronted or survived as part of a challenge. My thesis is that modern society is trying to force today's transformed individuals into that antagonistic model, with the transformed replacing traditional racial or political bugaboos."

I stared at him for a moment. "That's actually sort of profound."

Cal spent enough time outside to have a decent tan on him, but I was watching closely. I swear he flushed.

"It seemed the next logical step in developing and demonstrating the link between classical mythology and reality."

"There's only one problem. It has nothing to do with me. And you did say I inspired it, didn't you?"

My mother burst back into the atrium with another stack of roast beef sandwiches. "Oh, Erin. Sorry. I was going to make you something vegetarian, wasn't I? I forgot."

"Don't worry about it, mother. I'll take off the meat and eat the bread and butter."

I'd checked that Cal's butter was organic and came from non-feedlot milk cows. I wasn't a strict vegan, but I liked to be confident that no animals had been hurt for what I ate.

"We'll eat the beef," the girls hissed into my skull.

My mother sniffed. "Wouldn't hurt to put a little meat on your bones. Men like women with some curve to them."

That would have been a great opportunity for Cal to tell her how great he thought I looked without adding rolls of fat.

Instead, he seemed completely engrossed in studying a roast beef sandwich.

Mother didn't seem disappointed by Cal's lack of response, but I thought she was by mine. After giving me a full twenty seconds of stare, she left to catch the reality show she and Lisa were watching. Since Lisa had gotten her job, she counted on my mother to keep her up to date.

Cal's eyes were dancing when she left.

"It's no secret she thinks I need a man," I said. "So don't give me a hard time about her."

"Maybe both you and your mother need to learn the difference between needing and just wanting something."

"I'm pretty clear on that distinction."

"Nope. She thinks that because you like men, you need one. You think, because you don't *need* one, you *shouldn't* want one. Mirror images of the same problem."

"I'd be happy to find the right guy. I think the ideal for me would be someone who isn't too smart. Someone with a lot of experience with animal handling. The circus is coming to town next week and I'll meet up with the snake wrangler and see if we could make some magic together. So, there."

He just looked at me, so I blathered on.

"Besides, I've got a case. Once I finish this sandwich I'm back at the law library working. And I really *need* to do that if I'm going to have a chance in this case."

"I thought everything would sort of go puff when Leone Cornelison testified that she was a willing participant."

"I thought that too. But I'm not so I anymore. Deat isn't stupid. He'll know her story. If he didn't feel confident he would win anyway, he would have turned the case over to whichever of his assistant D.A.s might run against him in the next election.

Cal grabbed a bunch of grapes, then pushed back from the table. "Okay, then. What are we waiting for?"

* * * *

Cal wasn't a lawyer, but he sure knew his way around libraries. And around women.

In ten minutes, he'd charmed the county law librarian, a dour-faced woman who hadn't spared me more than a sour glare in the weeks since I'd been cut off from the library at Hale, Storm, and Stunk and had to use the County's services.

She explained the library's organizational system to Cal and preened when he complimented her on how everything was in its place. Before either she, or I, knew what was happening, she was running around the library and around the County Building fetching him casebooks different lawyers had checked out, and tracking down citations from *Westlaw*.

She even sat down with him and brainstormed new areas to research, then disappeared into the stacks to dig up ancient case law from the days of the witch trials in England and in colonial America.

"What's that about?" I demanded when she came back from somewhere, her breasts heaving with effort, and a trickle of sweat running through the cobwebs on her face. The look of triumph in her expression made it clear she'd been that the thick, leather-bound volume clutched in her arms was a prize.

"Barbara and I see an analogy between Ventoro's case and the Salem Witch trials," Cal explained.

"It can only be because this magic plague thing is so new that no one has noticed," the librarian gushed.

Cal smiled at her. "I wouldn't have thought of it either if Barbara hadn't reminded me of some of the Salem accusations."

The librarian was named Barbara? Who knew? I'd thought she was just Mrs. Schlachtaxt.

"Huh?" I sometimes get so articulate it makes me sick.

"Think about it." Cal ran a long finger across the leather cover of the old law book and both Barbara and I inhaled sharply. The man was too sexy to be safe around women.

He didn't notice our reaction, or maybe he was so used to women acting like idiots around him that he just shrugged it off. He went on talking as if we hadn't both just about orgasmed while we were sitting there.

"The claimed crimes behind Salem trials, and the witchcraft trials in England that formed the legal basis for the Salem trials, weren't religious at all. The supposed witches were alleged to have committed criminal acts, not blasphemy."

"That was a long time ago, before we were even a country."

"If what you've told me about law is correct, the legal precedents in those cases are still valid, unless they were superseded by specific legislation."

That was a big exception. "I've got some bad news, then. There is legislation on assault and attempted rape. Even in the current paranoid environment, Deat would make a laughingstock out of himself if he announced he was going after Ventoro based on ancient witchcraft case law. Besides, the Salem trials were a horrible injustice, everyone knows that."

"You think? Did you hear that Hollywood is doing a remake of *The Crucible*? They're turning it into a horror film with the witches acting out what they were accused of."

"That's absurd."

"If you say so." He turned away from me. "Come on, Barbara. Let's see where this takes us."

I knew where Barbara *hoped* it would take them. And it had nothing to do with Colonial American history. I also knew where I thought Cal was going, which was nowhere. I let him continue. He was at least helpful in distracting the librarian so she couldn't work for Deat.

I didn't exactly tune him out. I kept my eyes on the computer screen, but the girls made sure I was posted—when Cal went down the hall for a cup of coffee, when the librarian leaned over him and not-so-accidentally brushed her breasts against his back, when he smiled at her and thanked her for bringing him another moldy tome.

So, I wasn't completely surprised when she stood up, crossed her arms across her formidable chest, and scowled.

"We're closed."

They were the first words the librarian had spoken to me in hours.

"Huh?"

"It's five o'clock. Some of us have lives."

"Sorry. I lost track of the time." I gathered my papers, forked over a few bucks for the copies I'd made, and collected Cal.

"I'd like to come in next week and keep working on this," he told the librarian. "But I'd hate to trouble you with digging all these books up again."

"I'll keep them under my desk," she said.

"That's very kind."

She preened like a self-involved cockatiel.

"I suddenly feel like vomiting," I said. "Let's get out of here."

"Barbara is very pleasant." Cal grinned as he opened the door to his Mustang and let me in. "Keeping those books under her desk means no one else can read them. We might be able to steal a march on Deat."

"Ole Barbara is a regular sweetheart." She probably wished she could keep Cal under her desk. His books were the next best thing.

"Oh, my. I almost detect the slightest tinge of jealousy."

"You wish."

He turned west, heading toward the ocean.

"You kidnapping me again?"

He waggled an eyebrow. "Tempting. But, since we're close, I thought we'd pick up Lisa and save her bus fare. Those surf-shop guys pay her a pittance."

"They gave a job to a transformed. She's not complaining."

He swept around a couple of cars that had abruptly stopped in the middle of the road and pulled up at the boardwalk. "That's exactly the point I'm making in my paper, Erin. In classical and pre-classical myths, the magical were described as if they were incredibly powerful. But read between the lines and the social stigma comes through. Consider the Perseus legend since it's the closest to you. Perseus sought Medusa, but first had to find Atlas and the three Graiae—all magical creatures. Where was Atlas? At the end of the world. Where were the Graiae? In a dismal cave. Where were the Gorgons? So far away from civilization that he needed the Graiae to locate them and Hermes's winged sandals to reach them. All were in remote areas, separated from ordinary humans and cut off from culture.

"What's your point?"

"Could it be coincidence that the first thing people do when confronted by the return of magical creatures, is push them away, return them to the deserts and abandoned territories that they dwelt in mythologically? I don't think so."

Chapter 22

"The defense calls Leone Cornelison."

"Objection, your honor." Deat was on his feet, his voice raised in mock horror. "California protects its citizens from the blame-the-victim defense."

"Your honor," I said, "there is a dispute as to the facts of the case. The prosecution has argued that the police intervened while an assault was taking place. Two witnesses, as well as the physical evidence of assault on my client's body, show that the prosecution's so-called facts are pure fiction. Ms. Cornelison is best-placed to help the jury discern between the facts and the prosecution's fabrications."

Judge Hilz glared at me. "Let me make this warning very clear. The questioning of Ms. Cornelison will be limited to the facts of the case. There will be no examination of her background. No discussion of her sexual habits, if any. No questioning of the clothing she chose to wear. If your questioning strays from these guidelines, Ms. Tsong, you will join Mr. Swift in the county lockup."

"Understood, your honor. I assume that the same rules apply to cross-examination by Mr. Deat?" Not that I thought Deat would badger the alleged victim. But I wanted to let the jury Deat receive the same instructions I had just gotten. Otherwise, they'd think I was the bully here.

"Exactly the same." Hilz didn't instruct Deat, but I'd made at least a partial point.

The bailiff swore Leone in, then it was my turn.

I studied her, noting that she wouldn't meet my gaze. A bad sign.

She wore a black pantsuit with a duster-style overcoat that covered her from hand to foot, neatly obscuring the tattoos and piercings I'd noticed when I'd interviewed her. A large crucifix hung around her neck and she even wore one of those little hats with the wisps of veil like the one Becky had bought me. Maybe it was retro enough to be in.

"Ms. Cornelison, I'd like to thank you for coming before the court. I know this has been a difficult time for you."

She nodded ever so slightly, still not meeting my eyes.

"I'd like you to tell the jury, in your own words, what you told me."

"I don't remember what I told you."

"Let's just go through it point-by-point, then. You met Mr. Ventoro at the Fast-Times club in downtown Santa Cruz, is that correct?"

She nodded again.

"I'm afraid you'll have to answer out loud," I said.

"Yes. That's where I met him."

"The prosecution has stipulated that you left that club with Mr. Ventoro voluntarily. Is this stipulation correct?"

"Yes." Her voice was barely discernable.

"Had you agreed to engage in any particular activity with Mr. Ventoro?"

"Objection. A victim's initial agreement has no bearing on the crimes perpetrated by Vic the Vampire. A woman's right to say no is not diminished by her earlier agreement."

"Sustained. You've been warned, Ms. Tsong. More questions like that and you're looking at a contempt citation."

"Sorry, your honor."

I turned back to Cornelison. "After you left the club, you and Mr. Ventoro walked to the alley behind Fast-Times. Correct?"

"Yes."

"At that time, did some number of civilians, not members of the police force, intervene?"

"I—I can't remember." Her voice squeaked so badly I could barely understand her. Or maybe I just didn't want to understand her.

"I'm sorry. Could you repeat that answer?"

"I don't remember what happened next. We were walking away from the club, and then things went hazy. I don't remember anything until Officer Orlando told me that I was all right."

I looked at the Crucifix on Cornelison's chest, then willed her to look me in the eyes. She continued to look away.

"You have no memory of a group of men who assaulted Mr. Ventoro before he was able to kiss you? You've forgotten the details of what the prosecution allege is a horrible crime? How is that possible, Ms. Cornelison?"

"I can only think it was hypnotism. I've seen the old Dracula movies, and—"

It took Judge Hilz better than a minute of gaveling to quiet the shouts, the buzz of conversation, and the galloping exodus of reporters as they headed for their cell phones and wireless networks.

I walked to the defense table and got a drink of water.

When faced with a witness who simply out-and-out lied, I'd normally go on the offensive, pointing out the differences between what that witness had claimed in the initial interview and what she was claiming now.

But I was used to dealing with divorcing people. Nobody had much sympathy for a lying divorcing skunk. Attacking the alleged victim of an alleged assault was trickier, regardless of her lies.

Also, Judge Hilz wouldn't let me attack for long, and I'd spend some time in jail if I did.

But being a lawyer means taking chances for your client. And I couldn't let Cornelison get away with the fabrication unchallenged.

The really horrible thing was, I'd brought her in as a defense witness.

"Do you have further questions for this witness?" Hilz demanded.

"Only one, your honor." I strolled back to the witness box trying to look calm and collected. The girls thrashed a bit, which detracted from the look, but I keeping my voice from shaking and my knees from quaking sucked all of my energy. I didn't have the strength left to bring the snakes under control.

"Isn't it true, Ms. Cornelison, that you remember exactly what happened? That you're simply ashamed you agreed to let a vampire suck your blood in exchange for the sexual high you would have gotten from it, and that you've made up this story of hyp—"

"Objection." I could barely hear Deat's shout over the roar of the onlookers.

"Sustained. Ms. Tsong, you will meet me in my chambers now. Bailiff, clear the courtroom. The jury will disregard Ms. Tsong's question. Ms. Cornelison, you may not answer that question."

* * * *

"Do you believe me now?" Cal demanded.

Hilz had recessed the trial for three days to let me serve out my contempt charge. Incredibly, Cal picked me up, and didn't even put drop cloths on the Mustang's nice cloth seats to keep my prison stench from soaking into the fabric.

"I don't know what you're talking about."

Cal accelerated into traffic. "Cornelison didn't forget anything, someone got to her. If Ventoro had hypnotized her, she wouldn't have remembered when she first talked to you."

"Of course I know that. What I don't know is what the hell *you're* talking about. You never warned me she'd come up with a hypnotism story." Three days in the lockup hadn't improved my mood. And I'd had plenty of listening to angry men give me orders there, too.

"Hypnotism is the modern terminology for what was called possession in Salem Witch Trials. Deat will argue that Ventoro really did assault her, of course. Even if the jury decides to buy your version of the facts, it doesn't matter. Because the only reason a nice girl like Leone

Cornelison would agree to do something disgusting with a vampire was that he'd controlled her mind. That kind of mind control would be an assault as serious as any on her body."

"Mind control is a myth. You've spent too much time reading *X-Men* comics."

We picked up Lisa and headed home, continuing the conversation when Lisa plugged into her iPod and tuned us out.

"Hypnotism, or possession, ties into the separation myth I'm working on. Why do powerful but semi-human creatures inhabit the outskirts of the world? Because these magical beings have strange powers. Powers that make them dangerous when they come too close to the world of the ordinary. Locking them on the outside is necessary if the mundane are to be protected."

I was tired, hungry, and mad, but I wasn't stupid. Cal was right. It didn't matter if Deat's theory was impossible. What mattered was whether he could get twelve jurors to buy it. Since I'd brought in Cornelison as a defense witness, he was within his rights to bring rebuttal witnesses to argue the plausibility of the possession theory.

"Can I admit you have a point without it going to your head?"

"Too late. If I didn't have a job, I'd apply for a position as a paralegal right now."

"Very funny. So, what do we do about this possession theory?"

Cal shrugged. "People are scared. They'll believe anything Deat and his experts throw at Vic. You might lose this case."

I felt the girls gritting their teeth in a reflection of my own gesture and forced myself to relax. "Not without giving it my best shot."

"I'll do what I can to help. Oh, by the way, have you talked to your mother lately?"

I shook my head. Even when she was nowhere in sight, somehow my mother always interfered just when I thought I was getting closer to Cal.

"She went back to Florida," Cal informed me. "She missed your dad. I'm surprised she didn't let you know."

"She's self-trained to do what makes me feel most guilty. It's the Catholic way—part of what a mother has to do."

He pulled into his driveway and pressed the button to raise his convertible top. "The house will seem empty without her."

"Yeah. You'll have to make your own sandwiches now. Unless you can get Barbara Schlachtaxt to swing by from the law library to help out."

His laughter was like smooth Kentucky whiskey. "You are jealous, aren't you? That is actually kind of flattering."

I refused to talk to him for the rest of the day.

* * * *

Cal probably didn't notice my silent treatment. Becky swung by and took me and Lisa shopping.

Becky reminded me that I'd already worn the same outfit three times during the trial. That alone would make the jury unwilling to trust me.

Lisa nodded in agreement.

Logic like that that always gets me in trouble. It's so close to being reasonable that you can't argue with it.

"You need spiked heels," Lisa put in. "It'll give you a dominant look. And don't worry about the rent. I've saved most of what I've made at the surf shop. I'll cover us if you fall short."

She had a wary look in her eyes, as if waiting for me to reject her, to tell her to get her own place.

That look reminded me of Cal's new theory. Lisa had faced enough rejection to push her into a psychic wilderness. Just as the vampires had created their own wilderness in their new ghetto.

"Spike heels aren't for girls who top five nine in socks."

"Clothes make the woman," Lisa argued. "And believe me, legs can't be too long. Spiked heels will sway jurors your way and make Deat think twice before challenging you. Guaranteed."

"The only person they'll sway will be me—before I fall down. Not to mention, I'll look like a stork."

The girls wiggled and said they could help me keep my balance.

The mental image gave me my first laugh in days. It would almost be worth it to see Deat's face when I walked out in five-inch heels, with the girls spread out like rays from a halo, helping steady me.

But my laughter died pretty quickly when we actually hit the Eastridge Mall in San Jose.

The Christmas decorations were out in force, the Salvation Army Santa Claus rang her bell in front, big wrapped presents decorating the courtyards, and a huge fake Christmas tree stuck through the middle of the skating rink.

Becky ushered us into a shoe store so exclusive that the prices were written in words rather than numerals. Big words. Like 'Seven Hundred,' or 'Two Thousand.'

I couldn't get anyone to wait on me.

Becky and Lisa dug through stacks of shoes, even heading into the storage room behind the store, to bring me a selection of overpriced scraps of fabric and leather.

"Leather is made out of dead cow," I reminded Becky.

"It's a byproduct. If you don't use it, it'll be wasted."

"I wouldn't feel comfortable."

"They're shoes," Lisa said. "You're not supposed to feel comfortable. You're supposed to feel powerful."

"Three dollars to use our shorty-socks." The sales clerk, who hadn't said boo to us before, was in our faces when it came time to try on shoes.

"Good thing I brought my own socks then."

"You can't use those," she sniffed. "These are five-hundred-dollar shoes. Humans won't touch them if they know one of you impaired touched them first."

"They don't mind your impairment?" I recognized the tremble in Lisa's wings. My friend was seriously pissed.

The clerk sputtered. "What impairment? There's nothing wrong with me."

"Other than that you're a shapeshifter, you mean?"

"I'm not—"

"Not a wolf. You're a bitch."

The clerk opened her mouth a couple of times, then her brain finally caught Lisa's slam and she hustled away.

"I don't want to shop here," I said.

"Shut up and try on shoes," Becky said.

Becky and Lisa decided on a pair of emerald-green shoes that glistened like an iridescent oil slick. "Now we need to find you the perfect outfit to go with them," Becky announced.

The clerk bustled back, a shoebox in her hands.

"I found the perfect shoes for you. Please take a look before you go."

It was a big box—six inches deep, and at least a foot on either side.

I opened it carefully, fearing something might jump at me.

The clerk's grin split her face like a swordstroke.

Western boots gleamed with scales.

Someone had made cowboy boots out of the skins of black snakes.

I dropped the box like it was on fire and told Sharon to *sic* her.

The clerk's grin vanished when Sharon lurched across the distance, nearly catching the putative werebitch's nose with her fangs.

"We'd better get out of here before they call the police."

Becky shook her head. "No police. The manager wants to make a five-hundred-dollar sale."

We didn't get any apologies from the manager at the cash register, but she took our money.

Becky was happy because she was spending money, but seeing those abused little snakeskins had sucked all the pleasure out of shopping. And the clerk had been laughing at me, daring me to make a scene.

Still, neither Becky nor Lisa were ready to call quits to shopping trip after coming so far. So Becky led me on the hunt for the perfect outfit to go with the green shoes.

* * * *

"You're wearing that to court?" Cal was doing a T'ai Chi pattern, but he looked up when I clattered across his tile floors in my new shoes.

The formfitting jade-colored silk dress was a change from my usual suits, but I thought it looked professional.

The other dress Lisa had suggested was slit up to my crotch with cutouts that showed bits of waist, cleavage, and shoulder. Not at all professional, although I knew that the right dress could hypnotize a man, even one like Cal.

I hadn't thought he'd react strongly to a fairly traditional Chinese look. I was Eurasian, after all. If I couldn't wear something to show off my Asian side, something was wrong here.

"Of course I'm wearing it. I wore the same boring suit three times already. I need to make a change before the jury decides I had no credibility."

"Deat only wears two suits."

"Deat is a guy. Rules are different."

He sighed. "Give me a couple of minutes. I'll drive you."

"I can take the bus."

He stared at me, then shook his head as if he couldn't get the mental picture out of his brain quickly enough. "You aren't getting on a bus dressed like that."

"What's going to stop me? You, with your t'ai chi action?"

He sighed. "Don't knock it. Those shoes aren't practical, and the dress is so tight you can barely totter a couple of inches a step. You'd have to yank it up over your hips even to climb up the bus steps. Besides, I was hoping you'd invite me to sit at the defense table with you. There are some things I want to see."

"You can't watch on TV like everyone else?"

"I might be able to help you."

I owed him. Besides, who knew? It might even help with the jury if they saw someone who wasn't transformed on Ventoro's side. And it wasn't like we didn't have room. The tables were designed to allow at least three lawyers to sit and work together. Lawyers overflowed at Deat's table. Ventoro and I had the defense side all to ourselves.

"You'll have to dress up."

"You can take me out in public, Erin. Trust me."

Lack of trust had never been my problem. My problem was a lack of interest—on his part.

Five minutes later, he was showered, shaved, and dressed in a suit that had to have been custom tailored for his body.

Jennifer whipped down and wrapped around my jaw to shut my mouth before I started drooling, otherwise I might have stood there looking at him for hours.

The guy was sexy with no shirt on. He was sexy in jeans and flannels. And he was to-die-for in a tailored suit. And I was living with him. If it hadn't been for the little issue of him treating me like I was his sister, I could be in hog heaven.

I still didn't know whether it was the snakes or the rest of me he had problems with, but I guess it didn't particularly matter. The girls and I were attached. Nothing, not even a guy, was going to pull us apart.

Chapter 23

I'd imagined intimidating Deat with my dragon-queen look. No such luck. He glanced up from his last-minute strategy session with his co-counsels when I came in and gave me the slightest nod of recognition. He hid any fear too well.

I swallowed my disappointment, nodded back, then gestured toward the judge's chambers.

Deat followed and I introduced Cal to the judge and Deat, explaining that he was a researcher and expert on the transformation and leaving it at that. Cal wasn't going to be talking and they didn't have to know all of the details of my private life. Like, that I didn't have one.

"Write me notes if you've got anything to say," I told Cal as we settled down at the defense table before Hilz's entrance.

"Got it. No talking."

Jennifer thrashed a little, letting out some of the laughter the rest of me had to suppress. What fun when a guy has to listen, has to ask permission to speak, and has to write little notes to get any attention. The guys I'd dated always tried to steal center stage for themselves.

Of course, it would have been even funnier if Cal and I *were* dating. Then again, a lot of things would be more fun if we were dating.

Hilz arrived and we went through the *all rise* ritual.

Hilz pretended that I hadn't spent several days in the custody of the County and asked me if I had further witnesses to call.

I admitted that I had no further witnesses. Swift hadn't identified any other civilians involved in breaking up Cornelison and Ventoro, and I'd already put Swift, Ventoro, and Cornelison on the stand. For all the good it had done us.

"Rebuttal witnesses, Mr. Deat?"

Deat stood. "Your honor, Ms. Tsong's questioning opened a theory that The People feel they must address."

Cal handed me a note. *The possession thing.*

I scribbled back, *Don't bother me if it's obvious.*

As Cal predicted, Deat had a list of witnesses to discuss hypnotism and possession. "The People definitely do not accept the version of reality proposed by the defense, your honor. But even if events took place just as the defense claims, it would in no way alter the nature of the crime or justify acquittal."

"Objection. Your honor, the Prosecution can't be allowed to provide a flawed version of the facts and then act as if the facts don't matter because of something out of a Stephen King horror novel."

"Considering that the world we live in is inhabited by werewolves, vampires, trolls, elves, and dwarves," Deat paused and stared at me for a moment, then continued, "as well as Gorgons, dismissing the study of possession as a horror novel plot device misses the point. Besides, Ms. Tsong's witness opened this line of questioning. The People of the State of California are entitled to address these fallacious arguments."

Hilz studied the witness list Deat had provided him and I took a moment to do the same.

Cal leaned close to me, reading the list at the same time. His muscular shoulder brushed my silk dress, warming my skin through the fabric.

He ticked three names on the list. "These three. They'll stab you in the back."

* * * *

Cal had whispered. I still put my finger to my lips and gestured to the note pad. I'd already put time and money into Hilz's contempt of court bucket. I didn't want to spend more time behind bars just because Cal couldn't keep his mouth shut.

"If you can't make whatever point you want to make with three witnesses, the point isn't there," Hilz announced. "Pick no more than three and let's get started."

Proving that his longer list was a negotiating tactic, Deat picked the three men Cal had identified.

Since Cal knew more than I did, I asked Cal to jot down everything he knew about them while Deat started questioning.

The first was a Catholic priest from a group that thought the church had made a horrible mistake when it abandoned the inquisition.

The priest, Father Ortman, cheerfully assured Deat and the jury that demonic possession was a very real threat, with hundreds of proven instances over the centuries. He claimed that the church had recorded numerous occasions where a demon-ridden human had gained temporary control over others, and where the controlled individual had a loss of memory for the period of time while under that demon's control.

"I see." Deat nodded seriously, pretending to take notes on a little pad he carried with him. "Father Ortman, did you hear Agent Samuels' testimony that vampires are actually possessed by a demon, rather than holding an individual soul of their own?"

Dammit, Cal was right. The dress did get in my way. I should have been on my feet before Deat was halfway into his question. As it was, he got the whole thing out.

"Objection. Hearsay. And irrelevant. This issue in this trial is not the soul or lack of soul of my client, it is whether he performed the acts the prosecution alleges."

Hilz considered, briefly. "Overruled. I'm interested in this theory of demonic possession. You may answer the question, Father Ortman."

"Agent Samuels' testimony is consistent with the teachings of the Church. The forces of evil are everywhere and must be fought where they are found."

"No further questions at this time," Deat said.

Cal had spent most of the time Deat had been examining the priest using his handheld computer and a wireless connection. He handed me a scrap of paper as Deat finished.

I glanced at it and nodded.

I approached the witness box and studied the priest as he drew back from me. He grasped the crucifix around his neck, apparently preparing to ward me off with it.

Unfortunately for the priest, the Cross didn't scare me, or the girls.

He was sweating, so I took my time, shuffling my notes and giving just that little extra switch in my hips to see if he responded to me as a female.

Nothing. Which didn't prove *anything*, unfortunately. My recent record with guys was off the bottom of the scale. Given what Cal had found, this helped confirm that Father Ortman was either a very good priest, or a very bad one. If Cal was correct, he was a very bad one.

The priest wiped the sweat off his forehead and I chose that moment to attack.

"Father Ortman, have you ever met Mr. Ventoro? Have you ever spoken to him? Have you examined him as either priest or counselor?"

Ortman looked Deat's way, but Deat just shrugged. He didn't care about this line of questioning.

"No. Of course not."

"So, you have no way of knowing whether this *particular* man might has any sort of demonic possession and, if he does, whether it's the type of demonic possession that can induce false memories or cause amnesia. Isn't this correct?"

"Although I've not examined—"

"Please answer the question, Father."

"If the first ninety-nine are found demon-ridden, you can assume that of the one-hundredth."

Gotcha. I strode away from him and addressed the jury directly. "Fortunately for all of us, Father Ortman's version of theology is not the

American way of determining innocence or guilt. If nine, or ninety-nine, or ninety-nine thousand men were consecutively brought here before a jury, accused of crime and convicted, the American system holds that the next is still considered innocent until proven guilty. I'll admit it's been a while since my confirmation, but I thought that the Catholic Church had similar inclusive—"

"Objection. Counsel is making her arguments, not examining the witness."

"Sustained. Although Ms. Tsong's points are well taken."

Judge Hilz didn't tell the jury to disregard my statement, so I felt vindicated. I turned my attention back to the priest.

"A couple more questions, Father Ortman. From the answers you gave Mr. Deat, it seems to me that you've been concerned with demonic possession for some time now. Your research goes back for years, long before the transformation that we experienced some weeks ago. Is this correct?"

Father Ortman smiled at me. "Quite. Which is why I offered my services to the prosecution."

"Very noble." I glanced at the note Cal had written for me, made sure I had everything right. "You've offered your expert services in court before, haven't you?"

"Perhaps."

"According to the records turned over to me by my research assistant, you have offered expert services in seventeen different trials over a period of years. In each case, you testified that every single young man who testified that priests had taken advantage of them were, instead, demon-possessed. That none of their memories were valid. Do I have my number correct, Father? Seventeen times. Or did my researcher miss some?"

"Objection. Relevance. The facts of some long-ago—"

I wasn't going to let Deat win this one without an argument. "Father Ortman's nose for demons is precisely relevant, considering that Mr. Deat has held him up as an expert on the field. And it seems to me that Father Ortman finds demons wherever he looks."

Judge Hilz gaveled the suddenly raucous courtroom to order. When he got some quiet, he summoned the two of us to his bench.

I couldn't help myself. I kissed Cal on the cheek as I went past. Deat had tried a fast one on us, trying for killer testimony before we could find the skeleton in the priest's closet. But super-Cal had called his bluff and together we'd nailed the priest's sorry carcass to the floor, dragging Deat along with him.

"This testimony has gotten completely out of hand." The courtroom was still full, but it was all Hilz could do to keep from screaming at us. His face had turned a purple so deep, I worried that he'd collapse right there.

"I'm sorry, your honor," I said. "I thought—"

"If you knew about this, this, this," Hilz stuttered for exactly the right word finally settling on, "monster of a priest, why didn't you bring it to my attention before we put him on the stand?"

"I just—"

By the time I'd opened my mouth, Hilz was jumping down Deat's throat.

"And you, Deat. What the hell were you thinking? Are you intentionally trying to blow this case? That crazy priest opened the appeals doors so wide a halfway competent lawyer could drive an aircraft carrier through it. And Ms. Tsong is way more than halfway competent. There may be political ramifications to this case, but this is a by-god trial of a by-god alleged crime. Even if that priest hadn't been a wackjob, his testimony, as Ms. Tsong so eloquently pointed out, is hardly relevant. As it is, he's made you, and me, look like idiots."

It was Deat's turn to turn purple. "Sorry, judge."

"You damn-well should be sorry, Deat. If your next two witnesses are as bogus as your priest, I suggest that you cancel them right now."

"They aren't, your honor. I promise."

Deat was groveling, but it wasn't enough for Judge Hilz.

"Ms. Tsong has spent some time enjoying the hospitality of the Santa Cruz County jail. If you want to find how seriously I take contempt of court, just continue in your current direction, Deat. Because you're *that* close." He held his finger and thumb out, the distance between them roughly enough to slide a thin sheet of paper between.

Deat glared at me, as if this was my fault, and I sent another wave of psychic thanks toward Cal. When the jury came back and we won this case, I'd remember this moment as the turning point.

Hilz sent us back to our tables, told the priest to get lost, and instructed the jury to ignore everything they'd heard that morning with the exception of my statement about American law. They could take that as an instruction from the court, he explained, if Deat had any objections.

Deat shook his head. He wasn't purple any more, but he was unnaturally pale. The guy didn't mind sending other people to prison. When it came to spending time there himself, he was a weenie.

* * * *

Cal and I made a great team.

Night after night, he and I stayed up late, tracking down cases where Deat's witnesses had contradicted the testimony they offered in the Ventoro case and places where case law restricted the use of the 'hypnosis' theory. Cal even persuaded a psychology professor from the University to come down the hill and give us an expert rebuttal to the guys Deat had put on the stand.

When it came time to make our closing arguments, I felt pretty good about our chances. It would have been nice if I'd found more of the civilians who'd mugged Ventoro, but anyone who'd listened would doubt the prosecution's version of events. And with Cal's help, I'd demolished the witnesses who'd put forth the silly demonic possession story.

On a personal note, it might have been my imagination but the time I gave Cal a hug for all of his help, I swore his hand slipped down to my butt. I didn't think guys did that by accident. Of course, I was crazy in lust with the guy and wanted to believe he was feeling something for me.

The night before I was going to make my final arguments we went through every witness, listed every contradiction in the prosecution's case, and brainstormed ways to make sure our version of the story rang true despite a jury that had been hand-picked for conviction.

The next morning, I got up early. Becky came over to offer fashion advice, then I had Cal and Lisa sit down at the breakfast table and practiced my pitch.

By the time I'd finished, Lisa's wings were beating so fast that the breeze from them sent my notes flying.

Cal was harder to please, but he complimented me on the clear way I'd gone through the arguments.

I felt like I'd won a war.

I felt that way all the way until Deat stood to give his final statement.

The prosecution goes first, of course. Hell, the prosecution has all of the advantages. They have the cops on their side, and the FBI, homeland security, and State Police available to help out with labs and expert testimony. Most important, they have a presumption of *guilt* from the jury.

It isn't supposed to work this way, but it does. Jurors know that the police arrested someone and assume they had a reason. They know that the grand jury was presented sufficient evidence to indict. They know that the accused will lie to protect themselves and assume that the police would have less motivation to lie.

The only advantage the defense has is the legal presumption of innocence. If I could get the jury to remember that presumption, Ventoro should walk free by the end of the day.

Deat didn't mention any presumption of innocence as he went through his statement.

In most prosecution summaries, the prosecutor re-tells his story, trying to help the jury understand why that particular story is the only one that meets the facts. Deat hardly mentioned the facts of the case.

Instead, he reminded the jurors that *they* were the thin line between civilization and barbarism, that the whole world was waiting for the example they would establish in this battle against evil.

Sure he mentioned Officer Orlando's testimony and the feeble case he'd built against Ventoro, but mostly, he stressed fear. Fear of the transformed. Fear of males forcing innocent women. Fear of a mind control that could, he said, sap a woman's will. He likened a vampire's *demonic* powers to date-rape drugs, reminding the jury that a victim need not actively resist rape if her will had been undermined by fear or drugs.

"Like the drugs Ventoro admitted using to trick women into his arms, to gain advantage of their life-blood," Deat concluded.

As a legal argument, Deat's sucked.

From the looks the jury shot my client, he'd done what he'd set out to do. He'd done his best to persuade them to convict, even if they thought my man was innocent. It wasn't fair, it wasn't right, and it wasn't the law.

But it *was* my turn.

I'd worn the dragon-lady dress again.

I'd decided to go hatless, but I had my hair in braids, and tied the braids off in jade fasteners that looked a little like snakeeyes. If I kept calm, the girls would lay still and they might just look like more braids. After all, the jury knew I was a Gorgon. If I wore a hat, I'd look like I was just trying to hide it from them.

Cal gave me a pat on my butt as I stood. Just like I was a player on his team, about to run out onto the field.

I liked being on Cal's team, but I'd like it better if the team engaged in some intramural skirmishing. In bed.

I took a couple of deep breaths, reminded the girls to stay calm, and stepped close to the jury.

"District Attorney Deat has reminded you of something important," I admitted. "You *are* the thin line between civilization and barbarism. Every time a jury meets, they can make the choice to defend the Constitution and the body of law that forms the foundation of our nation. Whenever they accept that challenge, America becomes stronger, serves as a better example to the rest of the world. When they turn from that challenge, vote based on fear or doubt, they strike our nation in a way more vital than any physical attack.

"The law in this case is clear. In every trial, the prosecution has a heavy responsibility. They must prove that an actual crime has taken place. And they must then prove that a particular defendant has actually committed that crime. In the case of Victor Ventoro, the Prosecution has failed on both counts. Indeed, they had to fail. Because no crime was committed. The facts, as demonstrated by sworn testimony before you, are that two individuals, both well over eighteen, decided to engage in some necking. Now, when I was sixteen, my father swore that necking was a crime and he'd go after the boy he caught kissing me. But neither Mr. Ventoro, nor Ms. Cornelison, was sixteen at the time of the alleged incident. Simply put, ladies and gentlemen of the jury, there's no crime here."

I looked into the eyes of the jury foreman. He wasn't convinced, but he was listening.

"The evidence shows that a group of civilians burst onto the scene and prevented my client and Ms. Cornelison from engaging in anything, including the necking they'd agreed to. If they'd been left alone, would Mr. Ventoro have stepped over some line? We don't know the answer to that question, but we have no reason to believe he would have. Surely there must be reasonable doubt that he would abruptly cross a line, break the law. In America, we don't have laws against *thought-crime*."

I went through our case, point by point, hammering the fact that no crime had been committed, that the prosecution's argument was a castle built on air.

I finished with a slightly over-the-top reminder that fear had no place in justice. Fear led to injustice, to wrongful convictions, and to a breakdown in the very civilization they had been asked, by both Deat and myself, to protect.

Several jurors uncrossed arms they'd initially locked across their chests. They were open to persuasion. It was up to me to convince them.

"Do you want to send a message to the transformed?" I was on a roll. "Wrongfully convicting *will* send them a message. And that message will be, *Whether you abide by the laws or not, we're still coming after you. So why not do the things you're going to be accused of? You might as well, your punishment will be the same.* What a horrible message, what a horrible world that would be.

"Or you can send a very different, but no less powerful message by acquitting. That message will be, *abide by the laws and you are safe. Break the laws and you will be punished. The choice is yours.*"

I paused for a moment, partly to catch my breath, and partly to let the jury think.

"But now, members of the jury, the choice is *yours*. The world is listening, decide what you want to tell it. Do you want to strengthen the walls of civilization, or tear them down by succumbing to civilization's greatest enemies—fear and injustice?"

I would have finished a bit stronger if I hadn't fallen off my shoe when I'd turned toward the defense table. But I recovered and tottered back.

Cal shook my hand and even Deat's glare had a bit of respect to it.

The jury got Hilz's instructions. As they marched out, I felt a cold touch, as if someone deadly was watching me.

Chapter 24

Amelia and Kay waited outside the courthouse door. They dragged me to an Indian restaurant where Lisa and Becky joined us.

I invited Cal along, but he shook his head, claiming he had some research to catch up on.

A couple of guys wearing black leather jackets watched as I piled into the back seat of Amelia's Mini and we headed off. Unlike us, they weren't smiling.

"Eeww. Your snakes are thrashing," Kay told me.

"They don't like the way those vampires looked at me."

"You should be their patron saint. Like Joan of Arc."

"Joan of Arc won," I said. "And she also got burned at the stake. The vampires don't think I'm working hard enough for Ventoro."

"It's up to the jury to prove them wrong, huh?" Amelia said. "Hale, Storm, and Stunk shut down all day so we could watch you on *Court TV*. When you said how law is the cornerstone of civilization, Hale gave you a standing ovation. He told the associates that you're the kind of lawyer clients want to have working their case. That he was proud to have mentored you."

"Mentored? That's a laugh."

"No kidding. Want to know the really cool thing?"

We were in the restaurant by then so I swallowed a gulp of Margarita and guessed. "He told you to hire me back, as a full partner? With apologies for ever doubting me."

Kay shook her head. "We did remind him you need a job. I told him if we could ride in the same car as your snakes, he could share a floor with them. He wouldn't even have to take the elevator at the same time as you. He still said no."

Since the transformation, nothing had been easy. "I give up. What's the cool thing?"

"Judge Eagle was hanging out in our offices. About halfway through your statement, he said you were welcome back in his court. You can do divorce again."

Why did I not feel like celebrating?

Despite her wings, Kay and Amelia seemed comfortable about Lisa, but they remained cautious around me, even while pretending argue that I should hire them.

"I can't believe you hired a boy-toy as a researcher when you could have had a certified paralegal like me," Kay said.

"What can I say? Boy-toys do it for me. Besides, you were busy."

"You're not a slut. You're just cheap," Kay said. "You went to one of those will-work-for-sex places, right?"

I tried to kid along, but my heart wasn't in it.

When the vampires from outside the courthouse strolled into the restaurant like they owned it, I decided to get out of there. I reached into my bag for whatever cash I had left, but Amelia pulled out a hundred-dollar bill. "Big-spender Mr. Hale isn't ready to hire you back, but he wanted to buy a round of drinks. The round ends when the hundred bucks is gone."

Lisa cheered and waggled several fingers at the waitress, so I grinned and pretended to relax.

"We're going to have to take taxis home," Amelia proclaimed to the world. "Because we're going to be drunk out of our skulls."

The proverbial blond mating call worked like a charm. When the hundred dollars was gone, guys lined up to buy drinks for the table and plied their pickup lines on Amelia, Kay, and Lisa.

One or two even tried me. Drunk as they were, they backed off quickly when they noticed my hair hissing.

The vampires glared at the guys trying to pick us up, but otherwise sat still, hammering down double Bloody Marys like there was no tomorrow.

When one vampires reached his limit and went to the bathroom to free up some space, I collected Kay's keys so she couldn't change her mind about driving home, and slipped out the back.

* * * *

Two sharp bangs, followed immediately by a bright flash and then, darkness told me I'd walked into trouble.

I reached for the door I'd just walked through, but it had locked me out when it had closed. I was on my own.

My eyes slowly adjusted to the darkness. What had been a lump of shadow down the alley resolved to a canine form.

"I believe my line is 'what big eyes you have,'" I said.

It barked.

I assumed the bark was laughter, perhaps mingled with respect for my ability to fling *bon-mots* while being terrorized.

A few seconds later, a rattletrap pickup truck swung around the corner and headed directly toward me.

There was no way I could reach the second-story window ledge above me. That didn't mean I wouldn't try.

If I'd regularly been able to make that jump, I could have earned a basketball scholarship. Still, my hands barely grasped the brick ledge under the closed window.

I tried pulling myself up, and moved maybe one inch. Gymnasts make that move look easy: it isn't.

The pickup scraped along the wall of the building and I yanked up my legs to keep them from being scraped off.

"Looks like your friends deserted you. Need a ride?"

"That's okay. I'm fine."

Justin, the pack-leader from the Bloodsucker gang, shook his head slowly. "She says she's okay, but she doesn't look okay. She looks like she pissed her panties."

Now, I'm smart enough to be scared when a bunch of angry werewolves and vampires come calling. Maybe I'd been *ready* to pee in my tap pants, but I hadn't done it.

"Guess your night vision isn't as great as you thought."

Recognizing that I wasn't going to make it into the upstairs window, and that I would be a sitting duck if I hung from the ledge, I dropped down onto the hood of the pickup.

The sheet metal was cool—they'd been waiting. At least I'd come out alone. Three drunk girlfriends wouldn't have helped me, and the vampires could have made a mess of them.

"Bitch, you dented my truck."

Sure enough, my spike heels had put deep gouges in the beat-up truck's hood.

"Too bad it was your truck and not your head I landed on."

He shook his head slowly. "You might want to drop the tough-girl thing, counselor. I suggest groveling instead."

I get all the groveling practice I need in court. "You might be right. I'll think about it, all right? See you around."

I scrambled down from his hood—and stopped when the werewolf grabbed my dress and tugged.

Rip!

"Dammit, that dress was expensive."

"Drop it, Ralph. She's not going anywhere."

"If you had something to say to me, one of your flunkies could have delivered the message in the bar. I've got an appointment with the jury tomorrow, so if you'll just back-off, I'll be on my way. And I'll send you the bill for my dress."

"I'd like to let you go, but there are really bad folks out at night. I'm going to insist on giving you a ride."

He insisted by twisting my arm behind me and jerking on it.

Cal had showed me some t'ai chi and I tried a move, but the vampire cranked down on my wrist until I felt something shift.

"You're hurting."

Justin's smile looked hungry. If anything, he tightened his grip. "Really?"

"If you want to persuade the jury that vampires are evil and should be put in jail, you're going about it in exactly the right way."

"As if that jury can be persuaded of anything. You don't get it, do you, lawyer-girl?"

He let up the pressure on my hand, so I pulled it away. "Don't get what, blood-sucker?"

"Your do-gooder stuff doesn't cut it. They want to wipe us out, and you're legitimizing it."

"I'm doing my best to win the case for Vic."

He grabbed me and pushed me into the pickup.

Sharon struck at him but he caught her in mid-strike, squeezing her neck until I told him I'd stop resisting.

"You're validating their oppression," he explained. "They'll say, 'hey, we gave him a fair trial. We even had one of his kind defending him.' Both magical and normals get fooled into thinking this isn't a systematic oppression, that we have a chance—until too late. Haven't you ever heard of divide and conquer?"

When Justin was acting for the members of his gang, he'd seemed a classic low-life. When it was just the two of us, he used bigger words, more complicated thoughts.

The worst part was, he had a point. The trial was rigged. I'd done my best to make sure Ventoro got a fair hearing, but my best didn't mean much when I had to buck the entire legal system. My efforts might not help Ventoro, but they could give the trial an air of legitimacy. That might even explain why Judge Hilz had agreed to pay me as a court-appointed.

If Ventoro were convicted, however wrongfully, that he'd been capably defended would convince people he really was a rapist, and that vampires and other transformed were dangerous.

"I'm a lawyer, Justin, not a politician. All I can do is give my clients the best representation I know how."

"You're a turncoat and a traitor." He shoved at me until I slid over to the passenger side. "And you're sleeping with one of them." He held up a hand when I opened my mouth to rebut his claim. "Don't lie to me, Tsong. I know you moved in with that professor. I know the FBI Agent used his work. I know he's manipulating you, pretending to be on your side."

Justin scraped paint off the stucco building as he pulled his truck away from it and headed into the darkness.

I tried my door, but the latch moved easily, clearly disconnected from any opening mechanism.

"I said I'd take you home. Now why would you want to jump out and risk hurting yourself? I didn't know better, I'd think you were prejudiced against vampires." He paused a beat, then smacked himself in the forehead. "Come to think of it, I don't know better."

"Call me old-fashioned but I get nervous when someone kidnaps and threatens me."

He shook his head in mock sorrow. "You can trust me, Erin. Trust every word I say. I'll spell it out to you nice and simple. Tomorrow, the jury reaches a verdict. That's when we decide who was right: you, with your naïve notions of law and justice, or me with my clear understanding of what the paranoid majority is up to. If the verdict is not guilty, we all party. You'll be the heroine of the magical set, with more law business than you can shake a stick at. If the verdict is guilty, you'll be the heroine of the normals because you tricked us into going along with their system, helped railroad Vic into a prison cell in a way that they can point at and say how fair they were.

"But you won't be invited to *their* parties. Because guess what, you're not normal. So, we'll host a special party just for you. Sort of on their behalf. Either way, you get a party. You'd have to agree that's fair, right?"

"My social schedule is pretty booked up."

Justin dropped his artificial smile and jammed his brakes. "You think you're pretty damned funny. Problem is, I'm not laughing. Don't worry, though. Tomorrow, I'm going to laugh, and laugh hard. But the joke might be on you. Now get the hell out of my truck."

I almost snapped my neck looking around and was surprised to see that I was only a hundred yards or so from Cal's driveway. As he'd promised, Justin had brought me home.

The realization wasn't reassuring. It was a little chilling that Justin knew where I lived and knew ways to get there that I had been unaware of.

"See you tomorrow, babe. At the party. Whichever party we have." He turned off the engine, got out, and yanked me after him.

"Sometimes the law takes time, but it's there to protect the weak." I bleated a little because he was dragging me while I was talking. Still, I needed to be heard. "The appeals process is a part of the law."

"I watched you on Court TV. I heard your message. Tomorrow, the jury will tell us if it's real or just hot air."

Justin dumped me on the ground, hopped into the truck, and took off, sending a storm of gravel over me.

* * * *

The next morning, I wore a conservative suit with a knee-length skirt and kitten-heeled sandals that I could run in if I had to.

My acrobatics, coupled with Justin's rough handling and the werewolf's bites, had ruined my Chinese silk dress. Although spiked heels might work as weapons, I thought I'd do better to run rather than stay and fight.

"Want me to come in with you?" Cal had gotten up early and made waffles with strawberries, using eggs from a nearby farm hosting free-range chickens.

I pretended to consider. "No point. There's not going to be any research. Of course, you've earned it if you want to."

"I've got things I need to do here, but only if you don't mind."

"No problem."

"Good. School will be starting in a few days and I've got to update my lecture notes. You can take the car?"

"Your Mustang? But it's your baby."

He started to say something, then shook his head and tossed the keys to me. "It's a car, not a baby. Besides, I trust you."

"Considering what happened to my last car, trust isn't the issue. The vampires might trash your car, too."

"Then you'd better hurry home after the trial. I made reservations for us at the Casa Espana."

"What's that about?"

"You went out with your girlfriends last night. Tonight's my turn to show how proud I am of all you've done."

Wow. Proud. I would have gotten a swelled head, except I remembered what Justin had said. Agent Samuels had referred to Cal's research. And Cal's new theory, that magical beings identical to the recent crop of the transformed were supposed to be forced to the margins of society, was something our enemies could grab onto.

Of course, Cal *had* bent over backwards to be helpful in the case. He'd been the one who'd found the inside scoop on Father Ortman's questionable morals and legalisms. Justin had given me the answer to that as well. If the County had wanted to put on a showing of a fair trial, they needed to give me something to fight with. Just enough weapons to make it look like a fair fight. Could the entire thing be a setup?

Since it was obvious that Cal didn't want me in his bed, I needed to find some other explanation for his attentions. Having him as a spy in my camp fit the facts, even if it wasn't as satisfying as believing that my charm, long legs and intelligence had proven irresistible.

I drove more carefully than usual as I tried to decide whether I was being paranoid or whether this was one of the times when paranoia offered the best explanation of reality.

* * * *

The courthouse was a crush.

I'd thought the first couple of days of the trial had been bad, but the cameras and reporters had gone on a breeding frenzy, at least tripling their numbers.

Deat gave another campaign speech on the courthouse steps and I had to shout to get one of the sheriff's deputies to open a parking spot for Cal's Mustang.

"Vandals destroyed my last car because of this case," I told him. "I'd appreciate it if nothing happened to this one."

"I thought it was vampires, not vandals who got your car."

"Yeah, whatever." The deputy was younger than me and didn't look completely on the ball. Still, he appreciated a nice car and told me he'd make sure someone kept an eye on the 'pony'.

He didn't offer me an escort through the crush, though.

Saying "excuse me" got me nowhere. Even letting the girls come out from behind the braids and whirl in people's faces didn't help. There were just too many people blocking the courthouse entrance.

"Let me help you through."

My mind had detected just another suited man, but the voice sent shivers down my spine. And not the pleasant kind.

"What are you doing here, Justin?"

"Same as you, darling. Waiting for the verdict."

The vampire lifted people out of his way as easily as if they'd been made of Styrofoam, creating a path that closed almost instantly, but not before I could slip in behind him.

"Kick ass, Erin," someone shouted.

I turned to see my mother, back from Florida, Becky, and Lisa waving tickets as they stood in line for the gallery.

I waved back, pretending to be happy when my stomach felt like Justin had stuck vampire hands into it and tied it into knots.

I was trapped and had nowhere to run.

"Want me to sit with you today?" Justin lifted the last reporter out of the way and shoved me through to the line of armed bailiffs. "I can provide moral support."

I considered. I could signal the judge and get Justin arrested? But I rejected the idea. With no witnesses to his threats, he'd be out in hours, and even more angry.

"I don't need moral support. We're going to win this case."

"You sure you didn't change into an ostrich instead of a Gorgon? You're burying your head in the sand."

"Go away, Justin. You can have your celebration party without me. I've got a date."

"Oh, no, babe. You're the guest of the BloodSuckers. The *very special* guest."

"I won't—" but Justin twisted his hip, blended into the crowd and was gone.

I wiped my sweaty hands on my skirt and stepped through the newly installed next-generation metal detector. It had been ordered right after Orson Swift had gone non-linear with his wooden stake. That the metal detector wouldn't pick up a wooden stake didn't raise anyone else's sense of irony. For once, I'd managed to stay quiet.

Which was more than the metal detector did when I walked through it. The alarm bells, electronic beeps, and flashing red lights made the courthouse atrium look like a cheap disco from an eighties movie.

While an increasingly angry crowd watched, the security guards ushered me back through the detector, making me hand over shoes, laptop case, jewelry and hair clip.

Stripped of everything but my pride, I set it off again.

"Your bra have underwire in it, ma'am?"

Well, yeah. I needed all the help I could get in the chest definition area.

"How could that possibly—"

"The detector picks up concealed metal. Take that thing off and you'll be able to walk through with no problems."

I glanced at my watch and saw that I had two minutes to get to my seat. I didn't *think* Judge Hilz would hold me in contempt if I was outside the courthouse arguing with a metal detector, but I couldn't take the chance.

"There's a bathroom over there, ma'am." The security guard pointed down the packed hall to where a line of women stretched outside a closed door. "Might take a while, though."

"Well, shit." I grabbed a pair of scissors off the security guard's desk, unbuttoned the middle button in my top, slid the scissors in, and cut out the two cups to my bra.

I tossed them onto the desk, dropped the scissors, buttoned myself back up, and walked through.

This time, no alarms went off and I gathered my stuff.

But I looked around at just the wrong time for the security guard and saw him snickering and pointing to a small button on the floor near the desk.

Deat followed me through the metal detector without setting anything off even though he had a big metal belt buckle shaped like the California Golden Bear.

I'd been had.

I shoved the security guard out of the way and mashed the button with my foot.

Sure enough, the alarms all went off.

"You've got two choices," I told the guard. "Keep laughing and I'll see you in court. Or quit at the end of the day and start running, because I'm coming after you."

"Big threats," he answered. "Considering that you're not even human any more, I guess I'm not that scared." He picked up one of my bra cups, brought it to his nose, and sniffed. "Smells like snake."

Chapter 25

Waiting for a jury is stressful.

I glanced at my watch, saw that all of three minutes had gone by since I'd checked it, and turned to Ventoro. "The longer they're out, the better our chances. If they'd gone with their preconceptions, they would have—"

Before he could remind me I'd told him the same thing every five minutes for the last seven hours, the bailiff jumped to his feet, walked over to the jury room door and listened.

Ten minutes later, with Hilz back on the stand, the jury marched in.

I tried to read them, but they wouldn't meet my eyes. That wasn't good, but I couldn't lose hope. It could just be that they didn't want to look at the snake-woman.

Hilz went through the motions, asking the foreman if they had reached a verdict. When the bald guy who'd been appointed foreman agreed they had, Hilz asked for it.

"We find the defendant, Vic, the Vampire, Ventoro, guilty of assault. We find the defendant, Vic, the Vampire, Ventoro, not guilty of attempted rape."

After polling the jury to make sure the foreman hadn't misstated their positions, the judge nodded solemnly.

"Thank you, members of the jury. You have fulfilled your duty as citizens. You are dismissed. Court is recessed until tomorrow. Counsel, be prepared to discuss sentencing at that time. Bailiff, please return Mr. Ventoro to his cell."

My heart had dropped when they'd announced the guilty verdict and had only partially rebounded when they'd found him not guilty of attempted rape. "I'll try to get you out on time served for the assault, Vic. Without the rape charge, you should be free in no time."

"Like that will happen. The guys were right. I should have never agreed to play by their rules."

"Don't do anything stupid, Vic."

He stared at me as if I were a stranger, then his eyes flickered between the approaching bailiff and the courtroom's high, sealed windows.

I grabbed him. "You don't have a chance," I whispered. "If you make a scene, they'll throw the book at you. I've gone to bat for you and I'll keep doing it."

He shook off my grasp, but he didn't move when the bailiffs reached him and grabbed his chains.

"Sure you don't want to try something?" the bailiff growled. "I've got a wooden stake here, and Joey has silver shot in his shotgun. We *think* we could catch you, but hey, we might be wrong. Be your best chance. Think it's worth the gamble?"

I felt blame radiating from Vic's dead-looking eyes.

"We're going to get you free," I promised. "Trust me."

"Nobody should trust you," somebody whispered. "Because you aren't going to be around to be trusted."

I sensed, rather than saw Justin although I knew he hadn't legally entered the courtroom. "Hey," I protested. "I got him off on the attempted rape. That was the big one."

I could only hope that Justin had heard what I'd said. Because when I turned to look, he wasn't there. And the bailiff looked at me like I'd gone crazy and was talking to myself.

* * * *

The end of a case is anticlimax. After weeks of preparation, of attention to the subtlest nuance in a witness's expression or word-choice, of verbally combating the other side, all of a sudden, it's gone.

By the time I'd packed up my stuff, shaken hands with Deat and the dozen or so assistants he'd cycled through during the trail, and gotten Ventoro safely off to the jail, an hour had gone by and I was still in the courthouse.

That was when I realized I was delaying the inevitable. I didn't think Justin had been kidding about the Bloodsucker's reaction to the trial.

I was afraid.

I considered calling the police, but they'd rallied around Officer Orlando. They would probably cheer Justin on. I toyed with the idea of calling Cal. Except, Justin and his gang hated Cal. Getting him killed too would be small thanks for all the help he'd given me. The more I'd thought about it, the more certain I was that Cal had been on my side through the entire case—Justin's paranoid delusions notwithstanding.

I tucked my palmtop in my briefcase, and headed for the door. Time to suck it up and see what happened.

The guard who'd hassled me was still at the entryway.

"Hey, Erin," he shouted. "Be sure to take these bra cups with you. They're too small for me."

He was lucky I didn't have a wooden stake with me because I would have been tempted. But I was a lawyer—words were my weapon.

"A good diet and exercise program would tone your pecs to the point where you wouldn't need to wear a bra at all."

"Why you little—"

"Erin. Over here." Lisa jumped on the base of a pillar and waved.

I left the security guard steaming and headed in Lisa's direction when I felt a sting on my neck.

Jennifer struck at my assailant, but it was too late.

"I've got her. She must have fainted from the crush." I woozed down into Justin's arms, then the world went black.

* * * *

"What about Harry?"

"He'll make it or he won't." I hadn't recognized the first voice, but the second belonged to Justin. "Snake venom is designed to kill small animals and Harry is not exactly small. Besides, vampires are hard to kill."

"He's still out like a light."

"What do you want me to do? I've told you I'll take care of snake-girl. She won't poison anybody else."

I didn't dare open my eyes, so I used the girls to look around. Which didn't help much. It was pitch black and even Sharon's heat-senses didn't pick anything specific. The noise told me I was in a vehicle. Once my brain started working, my cramped position let me guess I was in the trunk of a good-sized sedan.

I was alive, which was more than I had counted on, and I could hope that Lisa had seen what had happened, would contact the police, and would have better luck than I'd had getting them to respond to problems suffered by one of the transformed. The bad news was, I didn't hear any police sirens. The worse news was, I heard sand crunching under tires as the car braked to a stop.

I maneuvered to spring out of the trunk the second the Bloodsuckers opened it, but it was a lost cause. My legs were cramped and I was too tall to bend the way I needed to.

A key scritched into the lock and clunked when it turned the latch. As the trunk hatch opened, I kicked, connecting with the guy holding the key.

"Ooof."

"I knew you were a party girl. Nice panties."

Justin stood a few feet beyond my reach, a nasty looking pistol in his hand.

"The jury found Ventoro innocent of attempted rape," I argued. "Come on, Justin. That proves I was right and you were wrong."

I wasn't counting on winning the argument, but I hoped for a few seconds of distraction.

His arms blurred as he grabbed my legs, and yanked me out.

My suit jacket and blouse both snagged on the trunk's latch and ripped as he pulled, and my head smacked into the beach's hard sand. The man was tough on my wardrobe.

I tried to kick away, but I only succeeded in thrashing my back against the ground, grinding bits of course sand into the scrapes Justin had made when he'd pulled me out.

"Want to dance, do you? I was thinking we'd try water ballet."

I figured I'd pretended to resign myself to my fate and wait for an opportunity, so I relaxed and let him drag me toward the Pacific.

The roar of motorcycle engines announced that the rest of the gang had arrived.

"Spread out and make sure nobody's watching," Justin ordered. "Bennie, come on, this is a party. Get some music going. Charlotte, give me a hand here. But don't get too close to her head. Those snakes bite."

"Like I'm sure they can hurt a vampire?"

"Tell Harry that. He's still unconscious."

"Oh."

Charlotte grabbed one of my legs and she and Justin yanked together.

The salty moisture of wet tidal sand stung my back as they dragged me toward the sea.

They kept walking as they entered the surf.

I concentrated on keeping my head above water. When a mid-sized wave hit the two vampires, I tightened my stomach muscles and twisted for all I was worth.

The water distracted him and Justin's grip loosened. I took advantage of that—and the water's lubrication—and I tore my foot from him, kicking at Charlotte.

Despite the dark, she blocked my kick, caught my ankle, and twisted me over so I was facedown to the water.

"I guess snake-girl had some fight left," Charlotte said.

Justin grunted and grabbed my leg. "I almost feel bad doing this, cause she meant well. But we need an example that we'll fight back, that appeasers are as much the enemy as the oppressors."

I was face down in the water, about to be drowned, and a part of me actually sympathized with Justin. Law was a poor substitute for real justice.

Still, my sympathy was limited, and not just because Justin's cause looked to kill me. Physically fighting back, when the normals controlled the police, the military, every branch of the government, was a recipe for failure and for an escalating violence cycle that could only hurt the transformed. My way was the only sensible course.

With my mouth and nose under the water, I couldn't explain that—not that he'd listen.

"How we going to kill her?" Charlotte asked. "If we get too close to her head, those snakes will bite."

"Keep her face underwater. Once she drowns, the snakes won't cause any trouble."

"Excellent. Because I'd like a necklace made of snakeheads. I mean, nobody is going to mess with a chick with snakeheads around her neck, are they?"

"They didn't help Tsong much. But don't worry about anyone giving you trouble. Once word gets out about what we did, nobody will mess with any vampire."

Justin lifted my leg higher into the air, then reached a hand under my skirt, grabbed my butt, and shoved on it, pushing my upper body deeper into the water.

I arched my back and grabbed a gulp of air when I felt him move but I almost lost it when he pushed so quickly I inhaled as much water as oxygen.

I struggled. I didn't want to die. If I was going to die, I'd rather they shoot me than suffer the slow death of suffocation and drowning.

But vampires are strong and there were two of them and only one of me. No amount of thrashing even brought my head to the surface and the vampires each kept a death grip on the leg they'd selected.

It took me maybe a minute before I realized that while I was hurting for breath, I wasn't dead.

I'd forgotten the girls.

Like the time I'd blown up that air mattress, they were pitching in, supplying my body with as much air as they could filter through their little noses. My struggles were causing the problems, burning more oxygen than the girls could supply.

I slowed down my thrashing, gradually going limp.

The vampires didn't go for it at first. In fact, Justin took my lack of resistance as an opportunity to slide his hand further up my butt and push me deeper.

The supply of oxygen got shorter as my head went deeper, pushing more of the girls below the surface.

"Think she's dead?" Charlotte didn't loosen her grip at all. Her voice was distorted, but I realized I was hearing it through the girls' ears rather than through my own.

"Hard to tell," Justin answered. "Can you find a pulse?"

Charlotte snorted. "You're kidding, right. I'm a vampire. If there's a pulse, I can find it."

"Check her out. She's been under for a while, but she's a lawyer. You know how sneaky they are."

I saw a blur of movement under the water and shuddered. All I needed was a shark to join the party.

Charlotte slid her hands down my leg.

In the weird, false-color view the snakes' eyes provided, the vampire was barely warmer than the icy ocean water. Her lips followed her hands, her fangs protruding as she neared my femoral artery.

One of the girls stretched, moving so slowly that we hoped it might be taken as simply floating in the ocean waves. But Charlotte stayed well away from my head. We couldn't reach her.

With my human eyes, I watched the moving darkness in the water.

The underwater threat struck just as Charlotte's lips created a seal on my upper thigh and her fangs pricked my skin.

My game of possum was up.

I jerked for all I was worth—and the underwater thing grabbed me and yanked at the same time.

Charlotte had been so interested in finding my artery that she'd dropped my foot and was just holding onto my thigh. Given how slippery the water was, that didn't add up to a great grip. Justin only had one hand holding my leg, with his other hand on my butt, pushing me deeper into the water. And my corpse act had both of them convinced I was past fighting.

I brought my knees to my head and then kicked back.

This time, I managed to break away from both of them.

But whatever had grabbed me underwater didn't let go. No matter how slippery I thought I was, the shark had me.

It zoomed me through the water at a pace way faster than either vampire could chase, even assuming they knew which way I was going. Which was good news, I guessed. Being eaten by a shark was marginally more appealing than getting snuffed by a vampire.

It took a few seconds for Justin to recover, but then he started shooting.

Which answered one question. Yep, he knew which way I was heading.

The bullets hit close, curving when they smacked the waves and pulling trails of air behind as they tunneled through the water. The water slowed them quickly, but even so, those bullets could kill.

The shark pulled me deeper, cutting off the last of my oxygen flow.

If this was a shark attack, it was the strangest one I'd ever heard of. Because no teeth ripped at my flesh.

Maybe a sea serpent had come to rescue its distant cousins. Or maybe it was a mermaid, like in the movie *Splash*.

I asked the girls to see if they could make out what was happening, but we were moving so fast they couldn't buck the water pressure, and it was so dark they couldn't see much anyway.

Just as I'd decided I was going to drown, we angled up, bursting through the water's surface. I choked, spit out a salt-water lake, and inhaled sweet air for the first time in what felt like forever.

"Sorry it took me so long."

My brain struggled to make sense of the words. Could a sea serpent talk? "Lisa? Is it you?"

"You were expecting the Loch Ness Monster?"

* * * *

Lisa used her arms to hold me as her wings propelled us both of us through the water.

"Where are we going?"

"Your mom is at the lighthouse with Cal's Mustang. Can you hold on until then?"

I nodded. Although hypothermia wasn't out of the question, I was breathing. Then I noticed the straight-line of luminescence trailing Lisa's passage through the water. That was what Justin had shot at. Now he'd follow it to our destination.

"They'll be there before us. No way you can out-swim their motorcycles."

Lisa shook her head. "You really need to give the rest of us some credit sometimes. That's been taken care of."

She refused to answer any more questions until we reached the cliffs under the lighthouse.

"I'm sorry if I seemed ungrateful," I said as I clamored onto shore. "I just don't want anyone else to get hurt. Not even the vampires."

"You're welcome. Now hang on a second. Here's your mother with a blanket."

Sure enough, Mother wrapped a blanket around me, then she and Lisa half-walked, half-dragged me up the wooden stairway that led from the beach to the cliff top.

"What's happening with the vamps?" I asked my mother.

"Some UCSC students went to talk to them. They're going to be persuasive about not leaving right away."

"Just coincidentally, huh?"

"It has something to do with expressing solidarity with oppressed people. Santa Cruz students are big on that."

Okay, both my mother and Lisa were hiding something.

"It's Cal, isn't it? He organized the students, right?"

My mother smiled. "He's such a nice young man. I can't understand why the two of you haven't, you know, hooked up."

Maybe because of her bad advice? "He could be in trouble. We've got to make sure none of the students gets hurt."

"Cal is taking care of it. We're going shopping," my mother said. "Look at your suit. And Lisa tells me that a vampire ruined that nice new dress you were wearing on Court TV."

"How can you think of shopping at a time like this?"

"Earth to Erin. I'm your mother, the woman you've known for almost thirty years. I always think of shopping. Your father is the Zen master, not me. I'm the shopping master."

I love shopping too, but really. "But—"

"Here." Lisa shoved me her cell. "Push redial."

I did.

"Yeah?" The answer came before I even heard a ring.

"Cal?"

"Erin? Are you okay?"

"I'm fine. The girls breathed for me, and Lisa got away before the vamps could do anything permanent."

"When I heard the gunshots, I feared I was too late." Could that be anguish in his voice? Cool.

"Justin isn't a great shot. But what the hell are you doing? That Bloodsucker gang is a menace."

"They're scared and angry. I had to use my martial arts to disarm a couple of them before they would listen. Now I've got things under control. I've invited Justin to give a guest lecture for my senior seminar next semester. He's got that classic 'I wouldn't want to belong to a club that would have me' mentality."

I heard the *boom-boom* of a portable stereo over the cell. In a weird kind of echo, the wind carried me the actual sound waves a few seconds later.

"Is there a party going on down there?"

"It seemed like the best way to defuse the situation. I kept them distracted and made sure nobody followed you."

"Do you need me to help?" I asked.

His pause left me feeling uncomfortable, especially when I heard a very female-sounding voice near Cal. Did girl-vampires have the same sex-laden abilities that Ventoro had bragged about?

"That is a really *bad* idea. The students and I are trying to bring these guys around," he paused a second. "Oh, right, Charlotte reminded me that it's not all guys. Anyway, we're trying to bring them around to more positive engagement with the normals and the other magical beings. Your confrontational attitude won't help. That and the fact that they'd be reminded they were just trying to kill you. Be a shame to go to all this trouble and still get you killed."

"My confrontational? That's ridiculous. I was the one—"

"Come on, honey. Finish up on the phone already." Charlotte had wasted no time after getting out of the water.

"Fine. Gotta go, then."

"Erin. I'm really glad you're all—"

I hung up on him before he could finish. *Confrontational attitude?* What did that mean? And how was I *supposed* to react?

"Erin, do you think—"

"I think is that Mother is right. We should go shopping."

I handed the phone back to Lisa. "Would you mind calling Becky and asking her if she'd join us? I'm being outgunned by vampires and I want to get more ammunition."

I was financially in the hole over the Ventoro case. I owed more to the county in contempt-of-court charges than I'd made in court-appointed attorney fees, but I'd gotten my severance and I hadn't spent much since moving in with Cal so I could splurge. Besides, as my mother had pointed out, I'd ruined my two newest court outfits in the past two days. I needed something to wear if I was going to work. I'd learned *shopping logic* at an early age.

We met up with Becky at a sushi place where I was able to get some vegetarian spring rolls and fresh edamame. My mother ordered us all pots of sake, so we were feeling no pain by the time we decided to hit the mall.

"I need a new suit," I said. "I was thinking colorful. I'm bored of beige and black."

"Black is the new black," my mother quoted.

"You know, I'm not even sure what that means."

She burst into tears.

Oh, great. I'd put my foot into it again and I hadn't even known I was close.

"You might be a little more empathic," Becky said.

I tried to get my mother to turn around and look at me, but without much luck.

"But—"

My mother pulled a Kleenex from her bag, blew her nose, then repaired her makeup. She managed a trembling smile. "Don't worry about it, darling. I'm fine."

Well, shit. That made me feel even worse. I wished I at least knew what I was supposed to feel bad about.

"We don't have long before the stores close," Becky announced. "So we're going to split up. Mary and Lisa, I want you to handle stuff Erin wouldn't buy for herself. Pretty underwear, something to replace the dress the werewolf tore up. Erin, you're coming with me. We're getting you a killer suit. I was thinking sharkskin."

My mother and Lisa both giggled.

I didn't. "Was that a lawyer joke, Becky?"

She looked at me. "It was an Erin Tsong joke. Come on. We'll meet in front of the mall twenty minutes before closing time to make sure we've got everything. Anyone have questions on their assignment?"

I opened my mouth because I had plenty of questions.

"Not you, Erin. You're here for the ride."

Chapter 26

I hardly noticed the way Becky dragged me into different shops, demanded my credit card to pay for things, and generally took control of my life. I was busy assimilating. Cal had called me confrontational. Then, after I'd forced my mother to tears, Lisa had told me I needed more empathy.

I was the queen of empathy. I never ate meat, insisted on free-range chicken eggs, only consumed milk products when I knew the cows were treated properly, and had been shocked when my mother had suggested murdering the girls. What was I missing?

I grabbed Becky and stopped her.

"Have I changed, Becky?"

"Huh?"

"I need to talk."

She plunked down at a table in the food court. "All right, talk."

"Give me the truth, as my best friend. Has my personality changed since I got the girls? I haven't noticed anything, but—"

Becky laughed. "They're creepy, especially at first. But I think the snakes are a good influence on you."

"But then—"

"It's being a lawyer. You got that kill thing."

"But I *am* a lawyer. I'm supposed to act like one."

"I know that. It's just that since you became a lawyer, you go around like a hired gun, looking for a shootout. With you anymore, it comes down to winning or losing. Like you're a guy."

"But—"

"Most of the time it doesn't bother me. I'm *still* your friend."

I think she was trying to reassure me. It didn't work.

"You don't win cases if you're Little Miss Nice Girl." I knew I sounded defensive but couldn't help it. "I've got to be tough, to go after the liars, to make sure the District Attorney doesn't pull any end-runs around the law."

She got up and shoved her chair between us. "I didn't want to have this conversation, Erin. I told you that it doesn't bother me. Be however you have to be."

I wrapped Jennifer around Becky's arm and tugged her back to the table.

"I'm sorry I got all huffy. It's just that—" I cut myself off before I got defensive again. Sure lawyering was still a male-dominated field, but there were tons of women doing it now. If I'd adopted the male role model, it had been my choice rather than anything I was forced to do.

"Want to tell her she can let go?"

Becky went pale and looked at Jennifer like she was a spawn of Satan.

"It's just Jennifer, Becky. She isn't going to hurt you. It'd be the same as if I stopped you with my arm." If my arm had poisonous fangs, a mind of its own, and could breathe for both of us.

"Still, if you don't mind—"

I asked Jennifer to relax. "Uh, did you really buy me a sharkskin suit? I was distracted."

Becky laughed. "One black, one royal blue."

"Good."

My mother and Lisa spotted us and joined us at the plastic dining-court table. Both were loaded with sacks and boxes.

"Victoria's Secret is having a sale," my mother announced breathlessly. "We saved you hundreds of dollars on bras and panties. With the money we'd saved, we splurged on a couple of nice dresses."

"Thanks, Mother." Shopping logic was still at work.

"Remember that dress you almost bought last time we went shopping?" Lisa sounded about as excited as a fairy can get. "The one with no back and the slit up to you know what? It was on sale too."

I'd get arrested if I wore that to court. "You guys are just too much."

"Come on." My mother grabbed my arm and yanked. "We're staying at the Beachfront Inn tonight. You can model them for us. It'll be a slumber party. Jade is coming in from San Jose. And she's leaving little Franky with his dad."

"But—" I trailed off. Cal was busy with the vampires and the students. The last thing he needed was a confrontational bitch nagging at him. Or trying to seduce him into her bed when he'd made it clear a million times that he wasn't interested.

"I told Cal that this was girls' night out," Lisa explained. "He won't be worried. And we thought it would be safer somewhere the vampires wouldn't suspect, just in case."

Right. And Cal wouldn't care because he had Charlotte to bite his neck and fill him with vampire magic.

We switched to rental car my mother had gotten when she'd landed in San Jose airport that morning and went down to the Beachfront Inn.

A raccoon the size of a St. Bernard crawled out of the sewer as we headed down Riverside and I clutched Becky's arm. "That's a Were. They're onto us."

My mother overheard and laughed. "Those sewer raccoons were here when I was a child. They're not shapeshifters and they're definitely not spying on you."

I was ready for another drink, and my sister arrived just in the nick of time, complete with a trunk-full of liquor and mixers, and a high-powered blender.

She played bartender, serving up head-banging martinis, and big glasses of single-malt Scotch that tasted like something you'd use to remove paint.

After a couple of drinks, my friends insisted that I model my new wardrobe—all very chic and expensive.

I was halfway into the backless, boob-exposing, slit-up-to-my-ass dress when I heard the knock on our door.

I froze. Could the vampires have tracked me? I was going to get my family and friends killed after all.

"You guys hide under the bed," I said. "I'll check who's at the door once you're safe."

"It's Fernando," Lisa said. She brushed past me and opened the door. "Lisa! You look so beautiful."

"Who's he?" I breathed the words to Becky.

"Boyfriend," she breathed back.

Great. More proof that I was a bit lacking on the empathy front. I hadn't even known that Lisa had a new boyfriend.

"I'll be cheering for you in court tomorrow," Lisa said. "But I promised Fernando we'd go out tonight. After we took care of you, of course."

She whipped out the door and I turned to face my mother, sister and Becky with my mouth open.

"Lisa is a person who need a boyfriend," my mother said. "Surely you're not jealous."

* * * *

I felt good. My new royal-blue suit was shorter than I normally liked, showing about four inches above my knees, but fit me like a glove. The lacy bra and tiny thong I wore underneath were just obtrusive enough to make me think of sex.

When I arrived at the courthouse, the security guard mentally undressed me, then he stretched his leg toward the test button I'd discovered the previous day.

I shot him a glance. "Don't even think about it, bozo."

He backed off in a hurry, and drips of sweat popped up on his forehead. Maybe it was just me, or maybe it was because the girls all shot him the same glance at the same time. My love life might suck, but I was getting in touch with my snake side.

"Over here." The whisper hit me as soon as I'd successfully passed the metal detector test. It was close enough to ruffle my eardrum, but neither I, nor the girls, saw anyone nearby. A bit away, Charlotte, in a black leather jacket and a black leather miniskirt that made my skirt look like something a nun would wear, leaned against the wall.

When it came to sleazy sexiness, she outshined me a million times.

Impelled by a bizarre curiosity and a pathetic trust in the court bailiffs, I headed over. "Did you call me?"

"He did."

Justin stepped out of the woodwork. He'd been there the whole time, but he blended in when he wanted to.

He smiled when he saw me, his fangs protruding at least a couple of inches from his lips.

Oh, shit.

"Don't scream."

"I wasn't going to scream. I was looking for a wooden stake."

"I want to tell you something."

"Hey, guess what? Somewhere while I was drowning last night, I got that message."

"Jeez, you never stop arguing, do you?"

I wasn't going to beat myself up for being confrontational with the guy who'd kidnapped and tried to kill me. "So?"

"So, you're off the hook."

That was about the last thing I'd expected.

"Off the hook in what way?"

"We had a long talk with that professor. He's got a clear understanding of dialectical materialism and how it impacts the current situation. How the capitalist system is manipulating the magical to serve the traditional role of the lumpen-proletariat, delaying the revolution. He also beat the shit out of a couple of vampires. Pretty good."

Okay, I'd gone to college in Santa Cruz. I knew what those words meant, and even vaguely, what he was talking about. Vaguely. "Tell me what that has to do with me."

"We decided that your approach is not inconsistent with the people's struggle. It might be that I, ah, misjudged the revolutionary moment."

Great. Just what Judge Hilz would want to hear.

"And I'm supposed to care because…?"

"Damn, she *is* a ballbreaker," Charlotte interjected. "You and me could be friends, snake-girl."

With her draping herself all over Cal? "Don't count on it, dead-girl."

"Would you two shut up? We're changing our tactics. I won't say it was a mistake trying to kill you, but that is no longer our strategy. You're off the hook—for now. Come on, Charlotte. We're out of here."

The two waved their capes over themselves and weren't there any more. Since they operated at room temperature, even the girl's heat-sensing vision couldn't detect them. I headed over to the defense table.

Ventoro gave me a short nod.

"I'll do the best I can for you," I promised.

"Don't tell me, tell the judge."

So, how come I was taking all the heat for being the bitch when everyone else seemed to have it as bad as I did?

We all rose when the bailiff announced Judge Hilz's arrival, then Deat did his thing about the serious nature of the crime and the need to send an example to the community. He also made a big deal about Ventoro's unwillingness to admit his guilt, trying to argue that this showed that my client would go around assaulting more normal women if given half a chance.

When my turn came, I reminded the judge that this was Ventoro's first offense, that the conditions of the assault were unclear despite the jury's verdict, and that Ventoro had spent a number of weeks in jail already—more than many first-time offenders receive as their sentence.

For a miracle, Hilz smiled at me and announced his verdict from the bench. Ventoro was released for time served. He'd be on parole for the next year.

Judge Hilz gaveled the trial to an end, told me that I was officially on the job as a court-appointed attorney and that he expected to see me in his chambers the following Monday so we could go over the upcoming caseload. After that, he had the bailiffs remove Ventoro's handcuffs.

"I can go?" Vic 'the Vampire' Ventoro seemed hopelessly confused by the idea that he was no longer a prisoner.

"You'll have to see a parole officer, and I suggest that you confine your romance to private spots from now on."

"Everyone said they'd throw the book at me."

I didn't want to rain on his parade, but I had to tell him the truth. "They threw it as hard as they dared. Neither Hilz nor Deat wants an appeal. And they got a conviction, which plays to the fearful voters back home."

"I feel like I'm going to get arrested as soon as I walk out of here." He looked at the bailiff, who glared back at him. "I can't do it. I can't make myself move."

"Tell you what, Vic. We'll grab a taxi. I'll take you back to your place and we can make sure it's habitable before you move back in."

"Why?"

I raised an eyebrow. "Why what?"

"Everyone knows you're the bitch-queen. Compared to you, even that other one, Hapsburg, was a sweetheart. So, why are you being nice to me?"

I decided I had nothing to lose by telling the truth. "Because I just learned that everyone calls me a bitch-queen. I don't mind being snake-girl, but I'd think a werewolf would want the 'b' title."

"Heh-heh." His laugh could get annoying, but I was happy to hear any laughter. Just one day earlier, he'd been at the point of throwing his life away. Even a nerdy laugh was progress.

"I brought you a pair of jeans and a windbreaker." I figured you'd rather not go home in prison clothes and they cut up the clothes you were wearing when they arrested you."

"You shopped for me?"

"I'm only a horrible person on Tuesdays, Thursdays and weekends. You lucked out by hitting me on a Friday. Now, go change in the washroom. All we need is for you to get arrested for indecent exposure."

"I feel more secure now that you're sounding like yourself again." He reached into the bag and pulled out a leather motorcycle jacket. "Hey, cool. When you buy windbreakers, you go all-out."

I shook my head. "I can't claim credit for that. Must have been Justin."

"Who?"

Right. Vic had been in jail ever since the transformation. "A vampire motorcycle gang leader. Be careful of him. He leaps to conclusions."

Vic nodded, changed quickly, and joined me in front of the courthouse.

The taxi was waiting, as were Cal in his Mustang, and my mother, Becky, and Lisa on the courtroom steps.

I wanted, so much, to shove a couple of twenties at the taxi driver and have him take Vic wherever he wanted to go, but I'd promised.

"Give me a second," I told Vic.

"Check out that babe." He pointed at Becky. "You think you could get me her number?"

"If she's interested, she'll call you," I said. "Do *not* go after her."

"Oh, yeah. People are paranoid."

I walked over to Cal's car feeling a little silly swaying on my four-inch heels. "I'm not a bitch."

"I'm cool with that. 'Course, sometimes being a bitch is a good thing."

"Meaning?"

"Come for a ride with me and I'll show you."

Okay, let's see. Take a ride in a smelly taxi with a prisoner just out of jail who thinks he's god's gift to women, or ride with a hunk who'd helped me through the trial and who sent my hormones revving into high gear. The choice was obvious, but it wasn't easy.

"I promised Vic I'd take him home."

"Bummer. Want me to come with you?"

More temptation. "Not a good idea. He needs to decompress, try to adjust back to the world of the mundane. Stories about magic and myth isn't what he needs right now."

"Got it."

I barely summoned the energy to put a little extra hitch in my walk for Cal as I headed back to the taxi. Life would have been so much easier if I was better at being the bitch.

* * * *

Dropping Vic off took more doing than I'd anticipated. His ex-girlfriend had changed the locks on his apartment, which meant he had been a two-timing slimebag, even if he wasn't a rapist. It also meant we had another taxi trip to where his cousin lived. I tested my credit card's limits by buying him another couple of shirts, a few packages of underwear, and some frozen pizza so he wouldn't starve over the next couple of days, then caught the bus back to town.

The party at the Beachside Inn had moved outside to the pool area to celebrate one of Santa Cruz's beautiful December days and Jade was probably violating eighteen separate city ordinances by manning (womaning?) her blender in the public area.

Lisa ignored the cold, swimming laps so fast her wake made the motet pool look like a Jacuzzi while Fernando looked on. The man's puppy-dog expression hit me like a punch to the gut. I was happy for Lisa, of course, but I wished someone felt for me what Fernando obviously felt for Lisa.

Amelia and Kay had dragged Julian Hale over from the law office and he was dancing with Becky. I didn't see worship in his eyes, but hot desire wasn't a horrible substitute.

Jade silently handed me a drink, watched me chug-a-lug it down, then tugged me back to the motel room we'd all shared.

"So?"

"I can read the girls' minds a bit," I said, "but I can't read yours at all."

"So, what are you going to do with your hunk?"

"If you mean Cal, he's never been interested."

She shook her head firmly. "He's a guy isn't he? And he's straight. Why wouldn't he be interested?"

"Because I'm the bitch-queen."

"Some guys get off on that."

I glared at her. "Would it have killed you to try a little denial? I mean, I am your sister, after all."

"Of course you're not a bitch. It's just that you, well…" she sucked her cheeks in and out while she searched for a non-'b' word. "… well, you just like to win."

"You make a better bartender than a picker-upper."

"Want my advice?"

"Does it involve hooking Cal with a blow-job? Because that was Mother's advice and it didn't work."

"You gave him a blow-job and he didn't like it? You know how to keep your lips over your teeth so it—"

"Jade, come on. This is way too much information. I went to college. Of course I know how to do it. And he turned down my offer."

"You probably tried to make it sound like a negotiation, right? You put out in return for free rent or something. Right?"

"Nothing like that," I lied.

"Wear the dress Lisa picked out for you. And go over to his place now."

"What if he tosses me out again?"

"Then you'll know he really isn't interested and you can get on with your life. That Julian Hale is sort of good looking in an older-guy sort of way."

"Eeew. Besides, he likes Becky." Why it was okay for Becky to hook up with him and totally gross for me to was something I wasn't prepared to consider.

Jade ignored my protests, made sure I put on my dress, admired the silly thong I was wearing, and then bundled me to her car.

"Mom, watch Franky while I drop Erin off, will you?"

"No problem. And Erin, remember what I said about you-know-what." She made the shape with her lips so everyone at the party would know-what too.

"You guys are ridiculous."

I hadn't driven with Jade in a couple of years. Considering that she hit eighty on the windy mountain road leading to Cal's house, it hadn't been nearly long enough.

She parked at the end of Cal's driveway. "Get out."

"But what if—"

"Do it, Erin. What's the worst thing that could happen?"

I came up with some real doozies but I'd gotten out of the car before I could lay them on her. And she whipped a rubber-burning 'u' turn once I was out, not even waiting for me to close my door.

I'd left my bag back at the motel, which meant I didn't even have bus fare.

Persuading myself I had no choice, I knocked on Cal's door.

"Hey." He looked delightfully rumpled in a pair of jeans, bare feet, and a sweatshirt with the sleeves ripped off that displayed his hard-muscled arms.

Sharon leaned forward and put her tongue in his ear.

"Stop it, Sharon," I hissed.

Then I started laughing. With all those esses, I sounded more like a snake than the girls did.

Cal had to think I was going crazy, but he invited me in.

"Congratulations on your trial, Erin. I'm proud of you."

"Thanks. I owe you a lot."

"And so you're here to pay your debts?" He ran one of his long fingers down my bare arm.

"Want to make something of it?" I knew I was making a mistake, but that confrontational lawyer business dies hard.

"Actually—"

I interrupted him before he could say anything that would set me off.

"Back up and forget I said that, Cal. Sometimes my mouth gets ahead of my brains. Here's the deal. I like you. You're smart, fun, you've got a great body, and I've really enjoyed spending time with you. Now, if you're not interested, I'd understand. Sometimes the chemistry just isn't right. And lots of guys think the vegetarianism is weird and unnatural. So, if that's it, don't worry about it. And hey, then there are the girls. They're part of the package. You want me, you get snakes along with me. Sort of like fortune cookies at a Chinese restaurant, except most people like fortune cookies, or at least don't mind them. And I can be a bitch. Did I mention confrontational? And my venom is poisonous. It doesn't give you a sexual high like Charlotte's bite."

I was babbling. And I hadn't even started on growing up in a Tibetan/Irish household with a mix of Catholic and Buddhist beliefs, an interfering mother, or the fact that my career choice was so unsavory that even politicians run against it whenever they had the chance.

In fact, now that I thought about it, I had a lot of nerve throwing myself at Cal like this. How many times did he have to tell me he wasn't interested before I got the message?

"I bet you're thinking you need a court order to get rid of me," I said. "Tell me to get lost and I won't bug you again."

"You are totally mixed up." He shook his head sadly.

"Okay, that's close enough." I swiped away the traitor tear and turned to go.

"Come on, babe. What kind of guy would take advantage of a woman who's lost her home and thinks she needs to put out if she wants a place to stay? Of course I couldn't return your, um, ardor at that point."

"What about the bitch thing?"

"There is that. Are you going to be a bitch *all* the time?"

"I can keep it under control once in a while."

"And you're not just looking for a quick lay? Because—"

"Maybe a quick one first, but I'm not in a hurry after that."

"I think I can live with that." He reached for my face and brushed Jennifer back.

"What—"

"Sometimes you talk too much."

He made sure I wasn't talking for a long time, stopping my words with his lips, his tongue, his whole body.

* * * *

Having a bad hair day can be tough, but I figured I'd survived the worse of it. Maybe things would work out with Cal and me, I sure hoped so. But whether they did or not, the girls had helped me find something I wanted to do, and had opened my eyes to the ways some people saw my flaws.

All in all, the transformation was a gift, for me at least.

When Jennifer wrapped herself around Cal's right arm and Sharon did the same around his left, I wondered if Cal thought the same.

www.ingramcontent.com/pod-product-compliance
Lightning Source LLC
Chambersburg PA
CBHW070007260626
47159CB00005B/1705